Faithful

Faithful

*Family Tangles: A New Spin
On Some Ancient Tales*

Jennifer Johnson

Print ISBN: 978-1-946608-01-7
Print Release: January 2017

Editor, Karen Block
Cover Design by Calliope-Designs.com
Stock art by iStock

DEDICATION

To my own dear sister Stephanie who legend has it took my whuppin's for me, and to all the other sisters in my life, including Sister Ginny, Barb, and Leona.

Strong Women. May we know them. May we raise them. May we be them.

FAITHFUL

Family Means Everything

Nila Miller has always taken care of her twin sister, Lil, even giving up the boy she'd been in love with years ago.

Now that boy, Noel Dearing, is Lil's husband and Nila's best friend. They have a great relationship until Lil decides a baby will complete their family. Because of a medical issue, Lil can't have children of her own so she asks Nila to be a surrogate mother, and Nila has never been able to say no to her sister.

"...and he loved Rachel more than Leah."
Genesis 30: 30

Chapter One

"What do you think about having Noel's baby?"

Nila stared at her twin waiting for the punch line, examining the face so much like her own for a hint of mirth. Nothing.

"I think it would be weird since he's your husband." Noel also happened to be Nila's best guy friend and her brother-in-law.

"I need you to get over the weirdness, Nila. Dr. Garber has scheduled me for a hysterectomy next month."

"Lil! Why didn't you tell me?"

Lil had never been on birth control in the seven years she and Noel had been married. In the last year, they had been trying in earnest to conceive with no success. When Lil began having severe abdominal pain, she had gone to see her OB/GYN.

"I am telling you."

"Is it...?" Nila couldn't make herself say the word.

Lil gazed out the window, tears filling her eyes.

"Lil!"

"No."

"Lil, please. It's not...?" Nila begged.

"It's just a uterine tumor."

"Just a uterine tumor? *Just* a uterine tumor? Does Noel know?"

"Not yet."

"Geez, Lil!"

"It would be a good idea for you to get checked out though. As soon as you can, just in case."

Lil stood up and walked over to the counter pulling a tissue out of its decorative box and touching it to the corner of each eye. She sniffed and glanced up at the ceiling. Nila studied the woman.

"Are you sure it isn't cancer?" Finally, Nila pushed that word past her lips, the disease that had killed their mother after she had suffered round after round of chemotherapy. "I mean, a tumor usually means cancer. Right?"

"They're going to run a few tests, but the doctor says the shape of the tumor indicates it is fibroid and non-cancerous. The surgery will take care of it." She squared her shoulders and sniffed again. "But not the problem of Junior." Sitting back down across from her sister, she grasped her hands. "I can't have him now, so I need you to do it for me."

"You guys are on the adoption list, Lil. You should give it time."

Lil snorted. "Three years on the off chance we'll be approved?"

"Well, it's not the end of the world if you can't have kids. Lots of people don't have kids, and they do fine."

"But we want kids. We really want them. Noel..." Lil gave a watery laugh. "Noel opened a college account. Did I tell you? He's determined the baby's going to UK."

The back door opened, and Noel walked in. When he saw the two women, he stopped. Looking from one to the other, his expression turned to stone. Nila sat back as the charged air shot back and forth between husband and wife.

"Oh, Noel!" Lil sobbed. He was across the room within a second, and she launched herself into his arms.

Noel held her head to his chest and buried his face in

her hair. Anguish ripped at Nila's heart. She shoved her chair back, picked up her purse, and walked out of the house not wanting to impose on this private moment between Lil and Noel.

By the time she got to her car, Nila's breaths were coming in short gasps. She sat in her car working to unclench her teeth. She beat on the steering wheel a few times.

It should have been me. My uterus with the damn tumor in it!

What did she need her uterus for anyway? It's not like any man would ever want to have a baby with her.

****

The purple sky indicated the impending appearance of the sun. Nila sat on the ground at the park with legs outstretched warming up for her morning run. She expected Noel to join her any minute because they had a standing running date three days a week. The triangulated relationship among the three of them had been ironed out years ago when Nila moved back to Cedarton a few years after Lil and Noel married. Nila and Lil kept their sisterly bond when Noel was absent. Nila and Noel hung out without Lil. And Nila always made herself scarce when Noel and Lil were together. There was nothing more pathetic than being the third wheel.

Heavy footsteps approached, their staccato beat announcing Noel's arrival. He and Lil lived less than a mile from here, so he ran instead of driving.

"Come on, slow poke, or I'll leave you in the dust."

"We'll see about that, Dearing." Nila shot from the ground and took off in a sprint.

In seconds, he caught up with her, and she slowed as they matched their rhythm and speed. One lap around with no words.

"You okay?"

"Sure."

"Really okay with all of this?"

"She's got to have the surgery. Of course, I'm okay with it. We'll try to adopt. If we can't…" He didn't finish.

"If you can't?"

"We won't have kids."

"Lil is talking about artificial insemination."

"No extraordinary measures, and besides, it's not fair to you."

"Who says I'll be the surrogate?"

Noel grinned at her. "Yours will be the only available uterus, Sister. What? You think we'd just open up the yellow pages under *Surrogate Mothers*?"

How ridiculous would that be? Nila knew in ancient times women had babies for other women, but it wasn't so common now. What did they call those women? Handmaids, maybe. She wiped the sweat off her brow with her forearm. "How far we going today?"

"Eight miles?"

Nila suppressed her grimace and nodded instead.

"I was thinking of getting her a dog. Maybe it'll get her mind off obsessing about a kid."

Nila cast him a disparaging glance. "Right. Kids. Dogs. Same difference."

****

Yours will be the only available uterus.

Nila sliced through the cardboard with a box cutter and lifted the lid revealing soccer shoeboxes. Could she really carry Noel and Lil's baby for them then give it up?

She sorted the boxes by shoe size before placing them neatly on the storage shelf. As owner of *Play It! Sports*, Cedarton's only dedicated sporting goods store, Nila could unpack inventory flawlessly while working through a problem. She had bought the store from the previous owner using some of the insurance money from her mom's death. The success of the store demonstrated her passion for sports and her good business sense in the three years of her ownership.

She had thought about having her own family from time to time instead of horning in on Noel and Lil. She had been out with a few men here and there, but nothing had ever come from any of it. Lil had been the one to have boyfriends; Nila had been the one to be a friend to boys.

As twin sisters, they had always been close. A long ago

memory surfaced in Nila's mind. They had been five years old when the wreck happened. Lil lay in the hospital bed in the pediatric intensive care unit, breathing with the benefit of a ventilator. Nila sat on her mom's lap.

Nila cast a troubled gaze at her twin. "Mama? Is Lila going to be okay?"

"I hope so, sweetie. She inhaled a lot of smoke in the accident, and the doctor says it hurt her lungs."

Nila began to cry. "I'm scared."

Her mother wiped the tears from the little girl's cheeks. "You've got to be strong for your sissy, Nila. She's depending on us now to make sure she's okay."

"What if she dies like Daddy?"

Mom held Nila's hands in her own. The sadness and determination in them struck Nila even to this day. "Nila, darling. Lila is so very fragile right now. I don't know what's going to happen, but it's in God's hands. The best we can do is love her and take care of her. Okay?"

"I do love her, and I promise I will always take care of her, Mama. I'll take care of my sissy no matter what."

Nila had taken that promise to heart throughout the years. She had often put Lil's needs ahead of her own and done what she could to keep Lil from getting anxious because it often triggered her asthma.

But Lil was asking a lot.

Could Nila give up a baby she carried even if she was giving it to her own sister, knowing she would always be a fixture in the child's life? Not as Mommy, but as Aunt Nila?

Could she?

Nila sat back on her heels and imagined Noel's baby. His chocolate eyes. The endearing curly-blond hair. She didn't know much about genetics, but she hoped their baby would have his dad's good looks.

Their baby. Not her baby.

Nila shook her head. No. Lil was going to have to figure something else out. Noel had said no artificial insemination. His insistence they take no extraordinary measures would get her off the hook.

****

"Cool!" Benny Fitzgerald yelled when a six-foot geyser shot forth from a two-liter soda bottle.

Nila grinned at her eight-year-old neighbor. "Should we go for six candies?"

Nila slid the white mint nugget through a homemade funnel into the opening of the bottle then jumped back to avoid being spewed. The hard coating, reacting to the carbonation, created an impressive soda fountain and made a heck of a mess on her back deck.

"Wow!" Lil called as she boarded the stairs.

"Hey, Sis." Nila stood back with hands on hips surveying proudly the soda covered wood and half-empty bottles before noticing her sister's hands cuddled a small blanket to her chest. "What 'cha got?"

"My new baby. Come inside and let me show you."

Nila hid her surprise. Had Lil flipped? "I'll see you, Benny."

"Sure thing, Miss Nila. Can I come back tomorrow?"

"Yeah, dude, but you bring the pop. We went through all my bottles in less than eight minutes." She high-fived the boy before the women walked into the house, their childhood home and where Nila still lived.

Once inside, Lil uncovered the cutest kitten Nila had ever seen.

"Aww! Let me hold it."

"Isn't she precious? Lil handed the tabby over, and Nila cradled her close to her chest.

"You cute little thing," she crooned.

"Noel brought her home last night. Hey, listen. Have you made an appointment with Dr. Garber? He really wants to make sure you're okay since we're twins."

"No, I haven't gotten around to it."

"You need to. I'm not trying to be bossy, but—"

"But you are."

"Promise me. As soon as you can. Okay?"

"Okay, okay." They sat on the couch while Nila stroked the kitten's soft fur. "Have you named her?"

"I was thinking *Daisy*. What do you think?"

"Daisy's good. Daisy is a fine name for my little niece."

Lil gave her best *sister* gaze to Nila.

Uh oh.

"You know, Nila, I wouldn't mind if you made love to Noel, because if the result would be a real niece or nephew for you, that would be awesome."

Uneasiness filled Nila at the sincere expression on Lil's face. She did not want to disappoint her, but this was crazy.

It couldn't happen. It just couldn't.

Noel was Lil's best friend, and sex with him—even for the benefit of a baby for Lil—was creepy.

Okay. Not creepy.

And that was the problem.

Nila had loved Noel for a decade, but he was her sister's husband. And no one else knew that horrible secret. Not Lil. And certainly not Noel. There absolutely could not be anything physical between Nila and Noel, no matter what. Nila's heart couldn't take it.

She'd nursed that crush and suppressed it when Lil married him. Nila had gotten the next best thing—his friendship. And that was enough. It worked well for all of them. Sleeping with him would mess with the delineated boundaries of their relationship.

So, no way.

But Nila would have to be careful so not to upset Lil.

Nila cleared her throat. She refused to even acknowledge making love to Noel. "The thing is, Lil, Noel won't consider artificial insemination." She might be willing to give up nine months to house her niece or nephew, but she was not willing to go down the path of making love to Noel to do it.

"I know that. We're going to have to do it the old-fashioned way."

Nila shook her head in disbelief.

"Yes. Having sex." Lil raised her voice in defense.

"With Noel?" Nila cocked her head and stared hard into the face of her sister to make sure she had the facts straight.

Lil couldn't really expect Nila to have sex with Noel or him to agree to it.

"Of course with Noel."

"Lil, the old-fashioned way would be to give up."

"Please."

"No!" Heat suffused through Nila. *Please don't tell me Noel is in on this. Was he actually contemplating…?*

"I will do anything."

"I am not sleeping with Noel." There had been a time long ago when she had been working up to it, having a relationship with Noel that was more than just a friendship. But then she had brought him home one Thanksgiving and caught him and Lil making out less than twenty-four hours later. Within six months, they were married with Nila as the maid of honor. Shortly thereafter, she transferred to the University of Tennessee and lived there after graduating until their mom became sick.

"It's the only way."

"It isn't the only way."

"He won't agree to artificial insemination."

"Because of me, Lil. I'm the problem." Noel might have said asking her to be a surrogate wouldn't be fair to her, but Nila knew the truth. He wanted Lil's baby, not Nila's.

"No, I'm the problem. You're the solution."

"Look. If Noel and I…have sex, I might…you know…start liking him. It could mess everything up. I don't want to be the other woman."

"I'd be honored for you to be the other woman."

"I can't have sex with him."

Lil heaved a sigh and stood. "I better go." She reached her hands out for Daisy.

Nila relinquished the kitten. "Don't leave mad."

"I'm not mad. I know I'm asking a lot, but it's the only way I can think of that won't take forever."

"A couple of years on the adoption list isn't forever."

Lil flinched as if Nila had hit her. "A couple of years is too long." She walked to the back door and opened it.

Nila followed her to the back porch. "You've been

trying for seven. What's two more years?"

Lil didn't answer. She began to descend the wooden stairs but stopped short. "What's that?"

Nila looked beyond her sister to a stream of smoke from down the block. "It's probably just a barbecue or something."

"Somebody's…house…is on…fire."

Oh, boy. Lil is having an asthma attack. She'd had asthma since she'd been in a car fire that had claimed their father's life. She hated open fire of any kind—even going so far as replacing the gas stove with an electric range when she and Noel bought the house they lived in. She hadn't had an asthma attack brought on by seeing fire in years. Not since just before their Mom had died.

Lil gasped for breath. She staggered down the stairs and stood grasping the rail. Her labored breathing worsened.

"Just calm down. Calm down, Lil." Picking up her sister's purse, Nila wrenched it open and looked for her atomizer.

Where is it?

Nila turned the purse over and dumped it on the ground. Why'd she keep so much crap in her purse? Nila spotted the inhaler and picked it up, shaking it as she did so. She pulled off the cap and held it to Lil's mouth pressing down on the atomizer to deliver the medicine. Nila rubbed her back and peered into her face, making sure her twin was getting some relief.

"Okay?"

Lil nodded.

Nila then turned her attention to the smoke from down the block. "That smoke appears to be coming from the Jones' backyard. It's probably just the Jones boys playing with their dad's fire pit. Not worth getting upset over."

"They…shouldn't play…with fire."

Nila knelt down and gathered up the scattered contents on the ground and began putting them back in Lil's purse. "They're kids. That's what kids do. You better get used to it if you really want a baby. One day you'll come home and

Junior's going to have a box of used matches and a guilty smile on his face." She stood and handed the purse and key ring to her sister. "You can't freak out on him like this."

Lil took the purse and walked around the corner of the house to the driveway where she'd parked her SUV. Lil pressed her key remote and the car chirped, its doors unlocking automatically. "Does this mean you're...going to do it?"

Nila sighed. "Has Noel actually agreed to this?"

"He will. He will...come around. He's always wanted...kids. He'll get used to the idea... He'll be so grateful to...hold his son, to have his son. You'll...see."

Nila reached forward to the bundle Lil still cradled to her chest. Scratching the kitten's ears, Nila refused to meet her twin's appealing gaze.

Noel won't agree. Oh, please, God, don't let him agree to do this.

Nila had to convince Noel to agree to the insemination. Otherwise....

Nila gulped. Oh, no. There absolutely could not be an otherwise.

****

They met on the court. Nila dribbled and threw a hook shot. Noel blocked, but he was too slow.

"Why won't you agree to artificial insemination?"

"I'm not talking with you any more about this." He caught the ball and threw it right back to the basket.

Nila jumped and blocked it, dribbling and pivoting out of his reach "Dearing, don't be such a jerk. You know how bad she wants a kid."

"It wasn't meant to be." He stole the ball and blocked her retrieval with his arm.

"I don't accept that."

"Well, you're both going to have to." He ran across the court, jumped, and shot. The ball arced through the air and scored without even touching the rim.

The ball bounced, and Nila palmed it. "You want kids." She dribbled, and Noel attempted a steal.

"But Lil can't have them."

"I can, and I'm willing." Nila blocked, faked a left, turned, and shot the ball. It ricocheted off the rim, and Noel caught it before it hit the ground.

"No."

She watched him pounding down the court, sweat making his shirt stick to his muscular back. She took off after him, reaching him before he could shoot. "Our genes are the same."

"No."

Nila raised her arms to block Noel's throw. "Are you afraid your kid will turn out like me instead of her?" For a second she took her eyes off the ball and focused on his face. She didn't want it to be, but his answer was important.

"There's nothing wrong with you." He didn't make eye contact, but used her brief distraction to shoot, and nailed the basket.

Except you chose her. The thought popped into her head, surprising her with the intensity of the feeling accompanying it.

Nila gave up the basketball game, resting her hands on her hips and attempting to sound convincing even though her lungs were burning from exertion. "Dearing, there's only one alternative, if you won't agree to doing it in a cup."

"That's bullshit!" Noel rested the ball under his arm and nailed her with a harsh look. "The only alternative is no kids." His response left no doubt in Nila's mind Lil had mentioned the sleeping with her to reproduce plan. Oh, but it hurt. To think sleeping with her repulsed him that much. It raised her hackles.

"She is about to lose a part of herself that makes her a woman. What if you had to have your testicles cut off? You think it wouldn't bother you?"

"Oh, spare me, Nila! This is none of your business, and you can butt the hell out of my marriage." He slammed the ball against the wall and stalked out of the gym.

Nila watched him leave. *No way. No how.*

He'd rather be childless than to suffer through sex with her.

Chapter Two

Lil took hold of the idea of Nila and Noel sleeping together like a dog to a tasty bone. She wouldn't accept Nila's insistent rejection of Lil's suggestion. Was Lil doing the same to Noel? Putting the pressure on him? Nila couldn't bring up the subject to him. It was too painful.

Nila shook her head at her sister as they sat across from each other in Nila's office. "I don't understand why having children is so all-consuming to you."

Lil leaned forward in the chair. "I need this to happen."

"Why?"

"Because I just need to know that Noel is going to be…" Lil sighed. "Nila, there's a chance of us—all of us—to be a family, no matter what. I think a baby is what it's going to take."

Nila hit the end of a pen rapidly on her desk top and studied her sister. "Are you and Noel having problems?"

"No. Not ever. He's always been the best husband I could have hoped for. But, maybe I…should have…maybe things should have been different. I love him enough to give him whatever it takes."

"It's not your fault you all don't have children. It's just one of those things. Noel doesn't blame you. Of course, he doesn't. He's okay with being childless. He told me so."

"But I'm not okay with it. Please. You can't imagine how bad I'd like us to have a baby. Especially now."

Nila threw the pen across the desk and sighed.

"Oh, by the way. I made an appointment for you with Dr. Garber for next week."

"I'm fine. Geez, between you wanting me to sleep with your husband and bugging me about going to the doctor, I'm about ready to move back to Tennessee."

"Stop being such a grouch. I just want to make sure your uterus is in good shape so you can carry the baby."

"There may never be a baby. Even if Noel agrees to this, it's a long shot. You've been trying for seven years. What makes you think it will be any different for me?"

"We have to try."

Nila shook her head in denial. "You've got to let this go."

Her sister stood, her back straight as she glared down at her. "You promised. You promised you'd always take care of me no matter what."

Nila froze at Lil's icy tone. Resentment bubbled up inside her. Yes, Nila had always felt she needed to take care of Lil. But this wasn't a drive to the ER or going to the pharmacy to pick up her medicine. This was much bigger. Too big. "That's not fair. You've always pulled that since we were kids to get your own way."

"But you've always taken care of things when I needed you to. You're good at it."

"I'm not putting my life on the backburner for this. Did you ever think maybe I want to have a baby for myself? Or a family of my own, dammit."

Lil pulled in a raspy breath then reached to put her purse over her shoulder, grabbing her inhaler as she did so. She sucked in a dose. Obviously, Nila's resistance and the idea of not having a baby had upset Lil and triggered the asthma.

"I'm sorry."

Nila also stood placing her hands on the desk top. "No, I'm sorry, but it's too much. He's your husband, Lil. I can't do that to you...or him. He's my best friend. You and Noel—you're all the family I have."

Lil's expression melted and became appealing. "We don't have to be. You could bring our baby into our family. Don't you see?"

"No, I don't. We're taking a chance on something that—"

Lil's face blanched stopping Nila's words. Nila hurried around the desk as Lil fell back on the chair.

"Lil? Lil! Are you okay?" Nila placed her hand on Lil's head, feeling her clammy skin.

Lil pushed her away. "I'm okay. It's fine. Just a side effect of the…" She blew out a puff of air.

"The what?"

"The tumor. It hurts sometimes."

"How long has this been going on?" Nila reached for her cell phone. "I'm calling Noel."

"No, you're not." Lil grabbed her arm. "Don't say anything to him. You want to help me? Sleep with him. You can give him the one thing I can't—a child. You say he's your best friend. Be a friend to him and give him what he's wanted from me since the day I married him. Be my sister. I need you, your uterus. Please, Nila."

Nila leaned against the edge of her desk and gripped her phone as she stared at Lil.

"I can't do it now," Lil said. "You're going to have to do it for us."

****

Nila's menstrual cycle had always been regular as clockwork, and according to all of Lil's *Get Pregnant* literature, tonight was the night. Or tomorrow night. Maybe she could just do it tomorrow night. *Please, not tonight.*

At midnight, her cell rang.

"You're not chickening out, are you?"

"Yes."

"You get over here right now. He's asleep."

Dread weighed down Nila's limbs. In resignation, she picked up her keys from the table near the door and headed into the night. She drove over to her twin's house, her twin's bed.

"This is a bad idea," she greeted Lil, when Lil let her in the house twenty minutes later.

"I take full responsibility."

"I'm afraid I'm going to lose my sister and my friend."

"I wish you would trust me."

Nila sighed.

"Come on."

"This is wrong."

"For the greater good. Think of the greater good."

"He'll know. He'll know I'm not you."

"Oh, please. It'll be dark. He won't know."

"Lila, he can tell us apart."

"You bathed with my soap. You have on my lotion. I've worn my hair like yours for months now. Just don't speak, and he won't know. Your problem is you talk to him like an equal. Let him take the lead. For this one time, let a man take the power."

That was it. That had been how Lil had taken every boyfriend she'd ever thought about being interested in until she fell in love with Noel. Lil had let them think they had the power. Fools. Every one of them. Especially the one sleeping upstairs.

Lil took Nila's hand and led her up the stairs. Outside the closed bedroom door, her stare pierced her twin's. Without a word, she pulled her gown over her head and stood there naked. Nodding her head in command, she held the shimmery silk in front of her. Nila stripped, leaving her clothes in a pile. She began to speak, but Lil shook her head. She gestured for Nila to take the gown. A moment passed as Nila judged the determined gleam apparent in Lil's eyes even in the dim hallway.

This is wrong. So wrong.

Lil grabbed Nila's arm and marched into the bathroom shutting the door softly behind them.

"The greater good," she declared in low tones.

"It's wrong to deceive him."

"The greater good. Noel is an only child, and so are we. If you don't do this, there won't be any more Millers or Dearings."

Nila sighed. "I...I probably should use some lubricant."

"It's Noel. Do you really need any?" Lil arched an eyebrow. "Let's be honest, Nila. For this one night, would you just be honest with me. With yourself. Then tomorrow we'll go back to pretending he's just your best friend, and that's it."

Nila's heart thumped in her chest. *She knows. She knows I'm in love with Noel.*

She had never, never even hinted. "My God, Lil. I would never have—"

"I know. I know that. It's okay. Really."

"But how long—"

"It doesn't matter. You've been so faithful to me and so has Noel. I love you for letting me have him when you knew him first. When you loved him first. Tonight, I'm giving you my permission, and my blessing, to let him love you, to love him again. I'll be insulted if you don't orgasm. I want even the first second of Junior's life to be bliss." Lil stepped forward and held her gown up and over Nila's head. "The greater good, sister."

"You're going to destroy this family," Nila said as the cloth flowed down over her.

Lil smiled mischievously. "Oh, no. I'm taking every possible step to cement this family into its future." She pulled a robe off its hook next to the door. "Make me proud." She wrapped it around herself, turned off the light, and opening the door, she slipped through it without a sound.

****

Nila stood next to the bed allowing her eyes to adjust to the dark. Putting her hand out, she touched the mattress. Her heart banged in her chest. How could Noel not hear it? She felt for the comforter and sheet and edged her way under the bed linen without shaking the bed. Inching up to the pillow by degrees, finally Nila settled herself.

And there lay Noel. Nila could only make out his large form on the other side of the bed, his head turned away from her on the pillow. So still. Nila inhaled attempting to slow down her heart, to detach herself from the burden of her sister's wishes to betray and conceive.

What should she do? Wait for him to pounce on her? Maybe she should have gotten some more direction from Lil other than let him take the lead. How could he when he was obviously asleep? Nila propped on her elbow and stared at the back of Noel's head. She waited, willing him to wake up and turn to his wife and make love to her.

Come on, Noel. Do your duty.

Nila reached her finger over and poked him. *Oh.* Poking was not letting him lead.

Wake up!

How could she wake him up so he could lead himself into her? Nila was contemplating the problem when Noel turned on his back simultaneously kicking the covers off himself. It was dark in the room, but not so dark that Nila couldn't see he wasn't wearing any pajamas. Of course he slept naked. Of course.

She gazed at him, the part of him which would play a necessary role in cementing the future of the Millers and Dearings. The quickest way to do this was go to the source. She stealthily crawled out of the covers and knelt over Noel, taking him in her mouth. He awoke in an instant, tensing then relaxing. His hands moved over her, found the hem of her gown and lifted it. Nila broke contact briefly while he wrenched it from her body. He pulled her up toward him, and for a second Nila resisted not wanting to get too close to his face, to give it away, to kiss her friend, to lose her buddy.

But Lil's words rang in her ears. *Let him take the lead. Let a man take the power.* She acquiesced; she went pliant. He pulled her tightly to him, wrapping his arms around her, delving sweetly in her mouth, loving Lil or who he thought was Lil. Nila's eyes stung, and she squeezed them closed, shutting out the yearning for her sister's husband then inviting it back in. Noel ran one hand over her back, around her ribs, and cupped her breast. Nila gasped as pleasure exploded and engulfed her body.

Just from his fingers on her nipple? She couldn't survive extended foreplay with Noel. This wasn't for fun. His erection pressed at her thighs. She extricated herself from his arms and kissed his chest, pressing him on his back with her hands. *Quickly.* She had to do this quickly and get out of there before it became more than making a baby. Noel could never be anything but her buddy.

Not ever.

Down lower, she slid her leg over him, positioned her

body over his, and with her hand guided him inside of her, filling her.

For a second, she paused then began a rhythm guided by instinct and her own need. No, Lil's.

Remember. This was for Lil.

Noel's arms reached for her pulling her down to him, his mouth seeking hers, molding itself to her, his body meetings hers in sync. Her body thrummed with pleasure, gripping her, overcoming her, making her forget. This was about a—*oh, Noel.*

Oh, hurry. Nila's back arched. She broke the kiss and panted, driving this man inside her, feeling her climax coming, so close, so close.

Dearing. What you're doing to me.

Noel tensed immediately.

Had Nila spoken?

Forcefully, Noel lifted her and pushed her away from him. He grasped her left hand and felt her fingers for the engagement and wedding rings which were not there. And his hand was gone.

He knew.

Noel jumped out of the bed and stood, his chest heaving, his breathing matching her labored ones. Seconds ticked. Tension pressed Nila on all sides.

"Tell your twin she wins. I'll impregnate you, but I won't cheat on my wife. Not even with you."

"I'm sorry, Noel."

"Get out. Now."

Nila scrambled off the bed toward the door. She knew it! Of course, they couldn't fool him. She hurried through the door a second before it slammed behind her, the lock clicking into place. With shaking hands, she pulled on her clothes. The door to one of the guest bedrooms opened, and Lil appeared.

"What happened?"

"He knew. I told you we couldn't fool him."

"What did you do?"

"I may have said his name."

"You said his name?" Lil asked in disbelief.

"I don't know! He kissed me. I...I mounted him. I got carried away—"

"Well, there's your problem. What do you mean riding him like a horse? I told you to let him take the lead."

"His lead was asleep along with the rest of him. I was trying to hurry up."

Lil marched over to the door and attempted to open it. "Noel, honey. It's Lil." She knocked. "Why is this door locked?"

"Because I'm sleeping alone. I have had enough of the Miller sisters tonight," Noel roared through the door.

With wide eyes, Lil turned to Nila.

Nila reached to her sister and pulled her to the stairs. "Let him alone. I think he agreed to let me be artificially inseminated."

"Really?"

Nila repeated Noel's words as they hit the bottom stair, and Lil jumped up and down in excitement hugging her sister. "That's wonderful!"

"Lil, Noel is really ticked. I think we're both in the doghouse."

"He'll get over it. Noel is too impatient to mope for very long."

****

Noel hadn't shown up to run for over two weeks. Nila continued her exercise routine without him. She'd lost him. She'd lost her buddy because of Lil's stupid scheme to have a baby, no matter the cost. She didn't put the blame on her sister. Nila had been the one to go in that bedroom. She could have said no, but she'd given in to Lil. Now they were in the midst of a SNAFU that would never be sorted out.

When Lil texted her and asked her to stop by after work, Nila wondered whether Lil was going to brainstorm with her to somehow work out a solution to this muddled mess. Noel had yet to make up with Lil either. He hadn't been coming home until late and sleeping in the guest bedroom, refusing to even speak to her.

Noel's car was in the driveway while Lil had parked on the street.

Nope. This was not going to be brainstorming; this was going to be forcing the issue.

Ignoring the urge to run in the other direction, Nila trudged toward the house, feeling the hood of Noel's car on the way. Still warm. Continuing on, Nila let herself in the front door, and marched on to face him, her sister's husband, to undergo the soul-ripping episode she was sure her sister had in mind to put everything right.

As if it ever could be.

Nila entered the den to find Noel sitting on the recliner and Lil on the edge of the couch.

"Hi, sis." She patted the space next to her. "Sit down, please."

Nila dared a glance at Noel who stared at the wall in front of him, with tight jaw, his hands gripping the arms of the chair.

"I know what y'all are thinking, and that's not why I wanted us all here together tonight. Not exactly. The thing is…."

Lil sniffed. Nila turned her attention to her sister and watched her square her shoulders and lift her chin.

"Dr. Garber had me meet with an oncologist today, and the news is bad. Really bad."

"Why didn't you—" Nila began.

"I could have—" Noel said at the same time.

"Stop!" Lil commanded. "I went by myself because I didn't want to worry either of you if it was nothing. But it is something, and the doctor is talking about months here."

"Months of chemo?"

"No." Lil blinked rapidly, but a tear escaped and trailed down her cheek.

Nila's hands flew to her mouth. *No! No!*

"Obviously, there will be no hysterectomy. Ironically, the tumor there is non-malignant, not even related to this other. But the tests Dr. Garber ran during the exam showed elevated CA 125 levels. So elevated that he didn't think it could be accurate. He ran another test and sent me over for a CT scan. He has scheduled a consultation with Dr. Wynn on the chance that the tests came back showing cancer, which they did."

"But, why did he wait so long for this, Lil! You had your exam with him weeks ago!" Noel demanded.

"They left a couple of messages." Lil shook her head squeezing her eyes shut briefly. "I thought they were just wanting to confirm the details of the surgery. They sent a registered letter, and as soon as I called today, they had me come in."

"We'll fight it!" Nila determined.

"Of course we'll fight it," Noel agreed.

Lil closed her eyes. Her chest expanded with her inhalation of breath. She opened her mouth and expelled the air slowly as Nila had seen her do in Yoga. "No. We're not fighting it."

"Lil!" Noel's eyes widened.

"Noel, I don't want to spend my last weeks on earth sick as a dog from chemo. I saw what Mom went through, and Nila and I swore…"—Lil turned to Nila though she still spoke—"we swore we didn't want to go through that."

"But, Lil, Mom was twenty years older than you are. And that was three years ago. I'm sure they can do so much more now. Honey, you've got to fight this."

"I've made up my mind."

"Well, you're going to change it." Noel stood up and paced the room.

In typical Lil fashion, she didn't argue, but Nila knew she also had not acquiesced.

"I'm discussing options with Dr. Wynn. No matter what happens, Nila, I want you to move in with us. Noel, I will not have you blame Nila for the other night. I made her go in our bedroom and pretend to be me. You said you'd agree to artificial insemination, so I've made an appointment for you and Nila for the next time she's—"

"How can you even think about a baby right now?" Noel shouted.

"This family needs a baby."

"Then do the chemo. Do radiation. Do whatever it takes, but you're not giving up!"

Lil sighed. "All right, Noel." She stood up and walked to the kitchen. "I'm fixing myself a drink. A strong one. Who's with me?"

****

Because of Lil's diagnosis, Nila underwent a gynecological examination though it was months yet until she was supposed to have her yearly check-up.

Dr. Garber smiled kindly at Nila. "I don't know which news to give you first."

"Start with the worst and work your way from there."

"Well, I can tell you the worst news. Because your identical twin has ovarian cancer, you will also get ovarian cancer. It is a definite. One hundred percent risk. To save your life, I am advising you to have a prophylactic hysterectomy. That's the bad news."

Nila's heart skipped a few beats.

A hysterectomy to save her life!

Oh, no! She'd never have children—either her own or her sister's. Since the night of Lil's news, nothing else had been said about artificial insemination. Though Nila had moved in as Lil requested, she and Noel had avoided each other by some unspoken mutual consent. How was this bad news going to affect the already somber mood of the Dearing household?

This was it. The end of the Millers and the Dearings. No little babies with Noel's dark eyes.

Nila took a shuddering breath.

"The good news is you do not have cancer right now, and my big hope is with close monitoring we can put off having the surgery for a little while."

"That would be good. I need to be able to take care of Lil without worrying about having surgery."

"I think you should schedule the surgery as soon as you deliver, no matter what."

"As soon as I deliver? Deliver what?"

31

"That's the best news. You're pregnant."

Nila's jaw dropped. "I am not."

"Oh, yes. You definitely are."

"I couldn't be!"

Dr. Garber arched his eyebrows. "You aren't sexually active?"

"No. Well, I mean only one time, and he withdrew before he...."

Dr. Garber shook his head. "You know what I call people who practice the withdrawal method as birth control?"

Nila stared at him with wide eyes, not yet able to form a coherent word.

"Parents." He crossed his arms and studied her. "I want to congratulate you. This is the best news, or at least good news, isn't it?"

Nila nodded. She supposed her head wobbling back and forth was a nod. How could she possibly be pregnant? Noel hadn't even...they hadn't even...

Oh, sister!

Chapter Three

Ten minutes later she unlocked the back door and walked to where her sister was settled on the corner of the couch with Daisy on her lap.

"Do you still want to be a mama?" She handed the pregnancy test she had taken at the doctor's office to her sister.

Lil grinned up at her. "You're not tricking me just to make me happy, are you?"

Nila shook her head sitting on the cushion next to her sister.

"I thought you said he pushed you off before anything happened."

Nila shrugged and laughed even with the tears spilling down her cheeks. "He wasn't quick enough, I guess."

"Oh, yes, he was, and praise the Lord for it."

Daisy purred loudly as the sisters embraced each other laughing and crying at the same time.

Nila went back to her house before Noel arrived home from work. She used the excuse of checking the mail and watering the plants to let Lil tell Noel he was going to be a dad. She couldn't possibly imagine Noel's reaction to her pregnancy, and with the way Lil was beaming, there was no way she would be able to keep it from him.

****

Two days later Nila rose before dawn and dressed to run. In the silent house, she crept down the stairs in her socks with her shoes in hand. When she let herself out on the porch, she saw Noel in T-shirt, shorts, and running shoes leaning against the porch post waiting on her.

She had been avoiding him since Lil told him, alternately dreading and anticipating the moment. Hating to see the regret she knew would be there on his face. Hating that the wrong sister was pregnant. Hating that the wrong sister was dying.

For a moment they stood in the dark facing each other. Noel pushed off the pole, approached Nila, put his arms around her, and pulled her to him.

"What are we going to do?" Nila asked against the front of his shirt.

"We're going to have a baby."

"But Lil," Nila's voice broke. "Lil won't be here to enjoy it."

"Nila." Noel kissed the top of her head. "She's enjoying it already, so stop making yourself scarce. Let her suck up every moment of the baby while she's still here. Okay?"

A thousand questions had rampaged through Nila's head since she found out she was pregnant. Would Noel want the baby? Would he want to share custody? How could they possibly work out making a life for Lil's baby?

"It should have been me." The bitterness filled Nila's tone as she grated out the remark.

"If it should have been you, it would have been you." Noel stepped back but caught her hand and pulled her to the stairs. "Hurry up and get your shoes on. Let's see how Junior does with us running a couple of miles and getting back before Lil wakes up."

****

Weeks passed, and the pain which had motivated Lil to go to the doctor in the first place increased. She agreed to discuss aggressive treatment with the oncologist, but by then the cancer had already metastasized. The first round of chemo did little to shrink the cancer, though it weakened Lil considerably. When she learned the treatment had done little to cure her, she reverted to her original stance.

All the talking and begging and threatening from Nila and Noel did not persuade her. She was through fighting the cancer.

Nila decided to take out her frustrations on some baseballs, so she went to one of the batting cages, an addition she had set up last year adjacent to the store. She picked up a bat, entered one of the cages, and shut the gate behind her.

Turning on the machine, she positioned herself.

How? How could Lil give up when she had given the chemo only the one chance to work?

The ball shot out.

Whack!

How could she have talked Nila into having this baby and now just abandon all of them because she was too much of a wimp to put up with the side effects?

Whack!

So what if she was weak and might lose her hair? Those were temporary. Death was permanent.

Whack!

What the heck was she supposed to do now with Junior? Would Noel even want a baby he involuntarily created?

Whack!

And would she be willing to give him up since he was going to be the only baby she'd ever have? Why did life have to suck so bad?

Whack!

Nila swung the bat so hard she lost her balance and fell against the fence. As she regained her footing, a ball struck her on the shoulder.

"Oooph!"

Already the baby was affecting her body, making her clumsy, weepy, stupid, and fat. Nila lifted the bat high over her shoulder and charged the divider, pounding the metal bar a few times before she kicked it over to get a good whack of the machine, but another ball shot out and pelted her stomach knocking the breath out of her. Nila dropped the bat, doubled over, and clutched her middle.

The baby!

"Nila!"

Metal scraped against metal, and Noel entered the cage. He pushed the power button on the pitching machine, shutting it off. Nila squeezed her eyes closed attempting to get back the breath the ball had knocked out of her.

"Are you okay?"

No! Of course she wasn't okay. Her sister was dying!

For a moment she couldn't speak. Noel placed his hands on her upper arms and leaning over her, he peered into her face. "I'm taking you to the doctor right now."

Nila shook off his hands. She straightened and worked to steady her breathing. "I'm fine."

It was only the second time he'd touched her since they made Junior.

"You just got whacked in the gut with a baseball."

"What are you doing here?"

"Let's go." Noel stepped to the gate, opened it, and waited for her to precede him.

Nila was fine. She was sure Junior was too, but she hated to take the chance.

Even though Nila didn't have an appointment, they were able to get her back to see Doctor Garber within half an hour. When he and a nurse stepped in the room, he peered first at Nila then Noel over his glasses.

To Noel he said, "I'd like you to step outside for a moment, please."

Noel did without a word, and Dr. Garber closed the door behind him. "What happened?"

"I got hit with a baseball. Two, actually."

"Where?"

"At the batting cages at *Play It! Sports.*"

Dr. Garber arched his eyebrows. "Not where it happened—where it hit you."

"Oh. My stomach and my arm."

"Let me see."

Nila shed her shirt and lay back on the examination table as he instructed. Dr. Garber peered at her skin already bruising from the hits.

"I'm really okay. Noel insisted I come. I think it's nothing."

"Was Noel with you when this happened?"

"Well, I guess he was, but I didn't know it. I was..." Nila took a deep breath. "Lil won't do any more treatments. She's giving up, Doctor. I thought I would hit some balls and work off some steam, but I'm getting so damn fat and clumsy that I fell against the fence. And then I took the bat and started smashing the divider when the machine pelted me in the arm, but I didn't turn it off and so it pelted me again right in the stomach. Noel must have seen the whole stupid thing because he came in the cage then and turned the machine off."

"Hmm."

"What's that mean?"

"It means I want to run a couple of tests, check you out, and have a talk with Noel."

Twenty minutes later, Dr. Garber, Noel, and the nurse entered the room again. Nila grabbed her shirt and stuck her arms and head through it. Geez. She didn't expect Noel to come back in here.

"I apologize. I assumed Noel was the father," Dr. Garber noted as he observed her scrambling into her shirt.

"I am."

"He is."

They spoke at once.

"Yes, but it's not what you think," Nila continued. "He's Lil's husband."

"Hmm."

"It's really not what you think."

"What do I think?"

"That we...well...we did, but it was Lil's idea. She's been wanting a kid, and after you told her she had to have a hysterectomy, she got this idea..." The nurse's mouth dropped open; Dr. Garber's eyebrows went even further north. In desperation, she looked at Noel who was biting his lip trying not to laugh. "Wipe that smirk off your face, Dearing, and help me out here."

"Nila impersonated her twin sister and came onto me while I was asleep."

"It got you and Lil a baby, didn't it?" Nila snapped.

"It certainly did and saved us a bunch of hassle with adopting."

"I'm glad it was worth all you had to suffer through."

Noel glared at her. "What's that supposed to mean?"

"All right. All right. That's enough." Dr. Garber announced. He snapped a folder down on the counter, opened it, and studied its contents. "I've got some concerns about your AFP test from the blood we took. It can indicate birth defects, so I want to do an ultrasound to see what we can see."

The air whooshed out of Nila's lungs. The baby had been the only ray of hope in this whole horrible episode, and now there might be something wrong with him? Her glance flew to Noel and the haunted look he cast at the doctor.

Dr. Garber held her hand and guided her back on the table and asked her to lift her shirt so her no-longer-quite-flat stomach was exposed. He placed gel on the skin, and with the sonogram camera, he rolled it around on her body. Nila stared at the monitor as if her life depended on it.

Oh, please, please, God, let the baby be okay.

"Hmmm."

"What?" Nila studied the curves and shadows on the screen not able to make anything out. "Please. He's okay, isn't he?"

And then a completely clear image which Dr. Garber zeroed in and froze on.

Nila and Noel gasped in unison in their recognition of it.

Two fetuses.

Twins.

"Multiple fetuses explain the elevated AFP. They look fine, and it explains why you're measuring bigger than normal." Dr. Garber pressed a button, and a picture of the image began printing out. "You're saying *he*. One appears to be a boy, and since they're sharing a sac, that means they're identical and, therefore, the same sex. I'm sure you knew that already." He tore off the paper and handed it to Nila, while the nurse wiped the gel from her skin.

"Because of the health issues we've already discussed, Nila, and now with twins, I want you coming in every other week. Also, any more accidents, falls, or injuries, I want you in here the day of." Dr. Garber shot Noel a dark look. "The day of."

In shock, they left the doctor's office. Twins. Two babies. It shouldn't be such a surprise since she and Lil were identical. Twins tended to run in families. But with Lil getting sicker, how was Nila going to handle not one, but two newborns?

****

Noel stared at Lil and the untouched applesauce on the plate in front of her. "Lil sweetheart, you really need to eat."

She gave him a little grin as if she knew a secret she wasn't sharing. "I ate a little."

"Eat a little more." He shifted in the office chair he'd brought into the nursery so he could eat lunch with her.

Dutifully, she dipped the spoon in the bowl and brought it to her lips. He noticed, though, when she took it out of her mouth, the spoon was still full.

God, help me. She isn't even trying.

Setting the spoon down, she fixed him with an affection gaze. "You know I love you."

"I love you too. That's why I want you to eat."

She reached forward and took his hand holding it in hers. "Do you remember the day we bought our wedding bands? It was at *Pollucks*. Remember that sweet lady who helped us pick them out? She said the rings were a paired set." She placed her hand over his so their rings clinked together. "When I die, I want—"

Noel reeled back as if she'd slapped him, but she held his hand in a surprisingly strong grip.

"Noel, listen to me, please. I want you to put your ring on my finger, so the set can stay together."

No! He shook his head, his eyes and throat burning as he watched her damned determined expression.

"Will you give me your ring when the time comes?"

"How can you—"

"Because I'm not afraid of where I'm going, but I want a little piece of you to take with me. Only that piece."

Noel gripped her hands. He was losing her. He was going to lose her.

She struggled to sit forward and the TV tray fell sideways. When Noel moved to pick it up, Lil said, "Just leave it for now. Promise me. It's okay. Promise me, Noel."

He bent over her and gathered her to him. "Okay," he whispered.

"And you'll take care of Nila. She's taken care of me most of my life, given up a lot for me. A lot."

Noel picked her up and held her. He sat on the chair with her on his lap letting her surround him, her scent and skin. He rubbed his tears off his face into her hair. "Dammit. You could have fought this," he croaked.

Lil sat back and gazed in his face. She kissed his cheek and wiped the tear trail. "You've…known her longer than you've known me. I want you to make things right between you and her. It's okay with me."

"We're right with each other. I've forgiven you both for tricking me that night. I mean, my God, you're finally getting the baby you wanted. Two of them."

She smiled, but shook her head. "Of course, I'm happy about the babies, and they're going to need as much love as we can possibly give them. You and Nila make it work, okay? In case I'm n—"

"Stop it. Stop talking like this."

"All right." She laid her head on his shoulder. "Thank you for making me so happy. I love you."

Noel sniffed and smoothed her hair. He turned and kissed her lightly. "Loving you makes me happy. It makes me sad too."

"I know." She wound her arm around him and squeezed. "I'm kind of tired, honey. And Nila will be here in a little while. You can go on back to work. I'll just rest until she gets here." She leaned away from him and patted him in dismissal.

He carefully held her as he stood then settled her back in the chair. "I'm not leaving you alone. I can wait until she gets here."

"Don't be silly. She'll be along any minute. I enjoy being in the nursery. I imagine the boys are sleeping in the cribs, and we're all taking a noonday nap. Let us be so we can rest. We'll be fine, really."

Noel felt his blood pressure rise. He straightened. "I'm not leaving you."

She snuggled down in her chair, her lips turning up in contentment. "You and Nila hover too much. Honestly, what do you think I'm going to do? Run away?"

No. I think you're going to die.

She sighed as she gazed up in his face as if she could read his thoughts. "You worry too much."

****

Nila looked up from the box she had just opened. "Lil! This is ridiculous! Six hundred dollars for cloth diapers?"

"They're not just any cloth diapers. They have Velcro fasteners and a comfortable leak proof, yet breathable, outer shell. I bought eight of each size." Lil had bought from every Internet baby site she could find.

"Well, if you kick the bucket before the juniors make their appearance, you can forget me using these things. I'm not washing poopy diapers in the washing machine. That's disgusting."

"Do you know how many years it takes a disposable diaper to break down in a landfill?"

"No, and neither do I care."

"Try to pretend for the babies' sake that you *do* care about the earth." Lil grimaced.

"Are you hurting?" Nila checked her watch. "The hospice nurse should be here by four."

"Stop fussing over me. I'm just tired."

Lil had insisted on having her recliner in the nursery. She had supervised the design of two of everything in University of Kentucky blue, of course.

"Want to put your feet up?"

"You know what I'd love? You to stop babying me and a chocolate milkshake from the Tasty Freeze."

"Really?" Lil had lost thirty pounds in the four months since her diagnosis. Nila worried when she didn't eat. "The nurse will be here in about half an hour. I'll go then."

Lil squinted her eyes. "Do you hear that?"

"Hear what?"

"A voice is saying, *Lil! Lil! Hurry and eat me! I taste so good. Please go get the poor chocolate shake. It needs me.*"

Nila wrinkled her nose at her sister's silliness. "Okay. I'll indulge you since the milkshake is calling you." She bent over and kissed her sister's cheek. "Want to get in the bed?"

Lil shook her head and closed her eyes with a satisfied grin on her pale lips. "Did you spill some of that baby powder? It smells like a new baby in here."

"It's probably those six hundred dollar diapers. They better be scented for that much money." Nila walked the door and glanced back one more time at Lil. "Don't try to get up while I'm gone."

"I'll be right here."

In ten minutes she was back with shake in hand. "Lil, here you go, Sweetie."

Lil didn't rouse.

"Lil?"

Nila knelt beside her twin. "Babe, I got your…" Putting her fingers on Lil's cold arm, Nila gasped. "Lil!" She shook her arm. "Please, Lila!" Nila fell over the body of her sister, hugging her, holding her, weeping, "Oh, no. My sister. My sister. Lil, what am I going to do now?"

Chapter Four

Nila placed her hand on her stomach and shifted on the folding chair set on the artificial turf next to the grave site of her twin. The awning provided protection from the December rain which misted from the low, gray sky. Nila had forgone the requisite black for a cream-colored cotton, A-lined dress with a matching, lined jacket. Her pantyhose rubbed the skin where they touched, reminding Nila she'd pulled them out of her dead sister's dresser drawer. Not yours. Not yours, each itch indicated. At the time, and without any pantyhose with her, Nila hadn't thought twice about it. They'd borrowed clothes from each other whenever the occasion arose. But now…now it felt inappropriate, as if she were wearing stolen property. Beside her, Noel, her brother-in-law, sat rigid in suit and tie.

How did he stand it?

Nila stared at the casket.

Reverend Michael Summers officiated the service. He was a close friend of Noel's. It was strange to see him in his black church robe since Nila was used to seeing him on the ball field where he coached Little League every summer.

"I will not leave you as orphans," Michael said. "This was a promise Jesus made to his disciples."

But Nila felt like an orphan.

Her parents were dead, and now she had lost her sister, her only sibling. She had extended family, but no one really close except Noel and the twins she carried. With Lil dead, Noel wasn't really her family. Not anymore.

The babies were all she had.

She rubbed her belly as if she were caressing their little heads.

I'm sorry, guys. Sorry you got stuck with me.

The minister said his benediction and walked over and shook her hand. She smiled in gratitude at him. He had been so kind throughout Lil's illness. He hadn't judged them in any of this. After Reverend Summers moved down to Aunt Verdie and Uncle Walt, Noel turned his face to her.

"You okay?" He glanced at her hand still rubbing her middle. "You're not hurting, are you?"

Nila sighed and removed her hand. She stared morosely at Lil's casket poised over the rectangular hole in the ground. Nila knew the funeral people would wait until the mourners left before lowering her sister into her grave.

Nila sniffed and blinked back the tears threatening to spill. "I'm okay."

They sat there while everyone else stood and walked to the line of cars on the road.

Nila finally spoke. "I don't want to leave her."

"Me neither," Noel replied. "But she's not there. Not really. Not according to Michael."

Michael knew the babies Nila carried were Noel's. Nila was pretty sure Noel had confided in him when Noel had found out Lil was determined to have a baby come hell or high water.

Bracing her feet on the green mat covering the ground, Nila stood. She stepped toward the casket and pulled four white roses from the arrangement resting on top. One for Lil. One for Nila. One for Baby One; One for Baby Two.

With one last gaze at the casket, Nila turned and stepped carefully around the headstones of her parents to the waiting limousine.

The mourners gathered at the Dearing house after the funeral. A few of Lil's former students had attended the service. Nila was pretty sure the glances they cast her way stemmed from how much she looked like their teacher. A conversation with a third grader confirmed it.

The little girl's red-rimmed eyes widened as she spotted Nila.

"Mrs. Dearing?"

"No. sweetie. I'm Nila Miller. Mrs. Dearing is my twin sister. Was. She was my twin sister."

Tears spilled down the little girl's cheeks making Nila's

own eyes fill up. She dropped on her knees and opened her arms.

"Come here."

Sobbing, the girl stepped into her arms and Nila hugged her tightly. "You're one of Mrs. Dearing's students, aren't you? She loved all of you so much. You guys were an awesome class. She'd tell me how much fun it was to be your teacher." Nila pulled back. With her thumbs, she wiped the child's face. "Now, let me see. I think you must be Hannah Grace. Mrs. Dearing told me about your pretty blue eyes and that you have short hair to show off your pierced ears."

"Are you sure you're not Mrs. Dearing?"

Grief sliced through Nila, but she focused instead on little Hannah Grace. What would Lil say in this situation?

"I'm sure. I knew Mrs. Dearing my whole life. I miss her so much. You miss her too, don't you?"

****

The day after the funeral Nila walked through the back door into her brother-in-law's house with short blond hair. Noel greeted her with raised eyebrows. His gaze encompassed her no longer chestnut hair, traveled to her swollen stomach, as it had done for the last several months, before settling on her face.

"You okay?"

What kind of question was that? The unsuitability of her still being in Lil's house after her death washed over Nila like a cold, stinging, ocean wave.

"I can't stay here."

"What?"

"Lil's gone. There's no reason for me to stay anymore. It doesn't look right me being here."

"It doesn't look...?" Noel grimaced and clenched his eyes, pain evident in his stance.

Nila's chest burned at the site of him. She couldn't stand it. She had to get out of here. Now. Heading out of the room and toward the stairs, she went to pack. When she came back down later, Noel was gone.

Monday dawned bright and Nila dragged her fat self out

of bed and stumbled into the bathroom. She managed to get ready for work and make it to the store before it opened. At lunch she started to dial Lil to see if she was hungry, but as she punched in the third digit Nila realized there would be no more lunches. Sighing deeply, she stuck her phone back in her purse and went back to work.

Several times in the weeks that followed, Noel called her, but she'd let her voicemail pick up. One day he showed up at the store in his suit and tie looking so handsome. She was used to seeing him in sweats and tees, so when he had on his *geek gear*, as he called it, Nila's breath caught. Resolutely, she turned her gaze toward the hooks she had been wrestling with.

"Want to go to lunch?" He stared up at her on the ladder as she took down a display poster from the wall. "Should you be doing that?"

"Lay off, Dearing. I'm not an invalid."

"I know you're not an invalid, but surely someone else can climb a ladder here since you're pregnant."

Nila let the poster fall to the floor next to him and descended the ladder in careful steps. Ricky appeared next to Noel. She really didn't want her employee to hear Noel's griping. Ricky had been hovering too much as it was. She appreciated his concern as her assistant manager, but it was misplaced.

With both feet on the ground, Nila dusted her hands on her pants. "Ricky, will you take that poster to the back, please?"

"Sure." The young man picked it up along with the ladder and left them.

Nila glared at Noel. "Don't mother me in front of my employees. It undermines my authority."

Noel rolled his eyes. "Why haven't you been showing up to run?"

"Because I don't feel like it." Nila had been so fatigued lately. When they closed the store at nine, she went home to bed until the next morning when it was time to open again.

"Let's grab a bite."

"I can't. I've got a distributor coming in today. I've been waiting for him to show up."

"Let Ricky fool with him."

"No. I need to take care of this."

"You need to eat."

"I am eating. I eat. I sleep. I work. The exciting life of Nila Miller."

"Let me bring something back then. We'll eat in your office."

"Fine." Nila rubbed her eyes with her fingers.

No. It wasn't really fine, but it was easier to give in than to stand here and argue with him. It was hard enough not thinking about Lil without Noel's grief-stricken expression staring Nila in the face.

****

She continued on in her routine of work and sleep until one Friday night she went to bed and didn't get up the next morning or the next evening. Sunday came and went. Then Monday.

"Nila. Nila!"

Warm fingers touched her neck. She opened groggy eyes to peer at Noel who grimly stared back at her.

"Are you sick?"

Nila turned her back to him and closed her eyes. "Would you leave me alone? I'm tired."

"Blech. You reek. When's the last time you took a shower?"

Nila didn't respond.

He snapped the covers back.

"Hey!" she protested attempting to hide the parts of her that the too small T-shirt and boxers didn't cover.

"Come on. You're getting in the tub."

"No, I'm not. Just get out of here. Please!" She reached down to cover herself up, but Noel grabbed the sheet and comforter, bunched them in his arms, and threw them off the bed.

Fine. If he wanted to be a jerk, she'd just ignore him. The bed gave under Noel's weight. Arms came around her and picked her up.

"Put me down!" Nila pushed against him, but his arms were like steel bands. She was afraid to do too much because if he dropped her, it might hurt the babies. "Dearing, can't you just leave me alone?"

Taking her into the bathroom, he deposited her in the bathtub and before she could get up, he turned on the faucet. Nila gasped as cold water hit her legs and bottom. Within seconds, it warmed and Noel poured a generous amount of body wash under the rushing water.

"You want to take your clothes off?" He was sitting on the edge of the tub crowding her.

She brought her knees up close to her body and glared at him. "What do you think?"

"I think you need to get rid of the stinky clothes. How long have you been wearing that shirt?"

"What day is it? Wait." Nila squeezed her eyes. "I can't have the water too hot. It's not good for the babies."

When she opened them, she noted Noel had his hand in the water testing its temperature. He was too close. "It's not too hot. Let's get you washed up, so you can get out."

"Fine. Leave. I'll wash myself up." Nila noted how her shirt was sticking to her stomach and breasts. She might as well be naked for all the covering it was at the moment. She crossed her arms over her knees. Why couldn't he leave already?

Noel stood up, reached to the shelf, and took a folded washcloth in his hand. He sat back down on the edge of the tub, pushed his sleeve up, and with the cloth, dipped his hand in the water again. Sliding off the enamel surface, he knelt on the floor beside the tub. Nila risked a quick glance at his face—stubble showing he hadn't shaved for days. His dark eyes were bloodshot. He wasn't sleeping well like the widower he was. Did he miss Lil as much as she did?

He moved the cloth over her short hair. With his other hand, he wiped the drops of water falling over her face.

"I don't know what you were thinking by butchering your hair and bleaching it that ungodly color," he murmured.

"Lil's students kept mistaking me for her. I'm not Lil."

Noel's eyes darkened. In pain, perhaps, because she had mentioned Lil.

Nila stretched out her legs in front of her. Her hand left the water to reach up and move the strands of hair that had fallen across his forehead, but she stopped herself. Instead she turned her face and studied the faucet and the pouring water. Out of her peripheral vision, she noted Noel poured soap on the bath cloth, setting the bottle aside, and rubbed it over her scalp.

"I know you're not Lil."

Are you sorry that I'm not?

Nila lips could not form the question. She already knew the answer. Of course, he was sorry she wasn't. Who wouldn't have wanted his wife spared, pregnant with his children?

God, she was pathetic. *Why? Why couldn't it have been me?*

With a gentle hand, he bathed her face and neck. In spite of herself, her muscles relaxed under his ministrations. He shut off the water and gripped the edge of the tub, peering at her face. The cloth moved over her shoulders and back first over the shirt then underneath it. Nila's head dropped forward. She felt like purring her appreciation.

"Lie back. If you're going to insist on keeping the shirt on, at least, we can get it clean, too." His smooth voice reverberated over Nila.

She lay back dipping her hair below the water then pushed up to lean back against the tub.

Noel reached into the water, placed his hand over her calf and pulled her leg toward him, moving the cloth over her ankle and foot, then the other leg. His hand moved up her leg, but stopped at her knee. He patted her thigh. Then his hand was gone.

"If you'll tell me where the sheets are, I'll change your bed."

Nila sighed in comfort. She hadn't felt this good in weeks. With eyes closed, she worked to reply. "Not necessary."

"Where?"

"Hmmm." Oh, yes. This was nice.

"Nila. The sheets." Noel's voice penetrated her relaxed fog.

"Hall closet. But don't fool with it."

"Here." Noel reached into the water and took her hand placing her fingers around the bath cloth. "You wash up your other parts. If you don't, I will."

"Sure you will." Sarcasm laced her tone.

Noel stood up. He grinned down at her. "I'm not bluffing. Don't make me prove it to you. I'll give you five minutes, then you're getting some clean clothes on, and we'll go for a run."

"Yeah. I hear they're going to make whale running an Olympic sport."

"You aren't that big. You're barely showing. A baby bump. Isn't that what they call it?"

"More like a mountain."

"Nah. A hill at the most. You can still run, and if it's too much for you, we'll power walk." Noel strode out of the room.

Nila finished bathing listening to the sounds of Noel pulling out clean sheets from the closet, his tennis shoes squeaking across the floor in her bedroom. Down the hall he went and the washing machine turned on. His footsteps approached, and he entered the room with purposeful strides, pulled a folded towel off the shelf, shook it out, and held it up in front of him.

Nila shook her head at him. "I'm capable of getting out of the tub and drying myself off." At least with the bubbles in the tub she was somewhat camouflaged. No way was she standing up with the shirt and a pair of boxers clinging to her like a second skin.

He waved the towel slightly. "Humor me."

"I'm not humoring you. I'm nearly naked here, and it feels uncomfortable."

"You've been naked with me before."

"Yeah, in the dark about fifteen pounds ago, kowtowing

to Lil's demands."

"All right." Noel dropped the towel on the floor. "I'll be in the living room waiting."

Chapter Five

Two miles. Not bad considering the weight she had gained and that she hadn't run in a couple of weeks. Nila thought she could go further, but Noel slowed, and so did she.

"Tell me you feel better."

"I do." Her breathing was a little heavy, but it was a good heavy.

"I don't want to nag you, Nila, but lying in the bed is the last thing you need to be doing."

"I miss her. Noel, I miss her so bad."

"I know. I miss her, too. Sometimes I think I hear her walking up the stairs or I catch a scent of her perfume."

"If I could have died in her place, I would have. She had everything. All I've got is the store."

Noel stopped, and Nila turned to face him. Noel stood tense, his hands on his hips. "You've got more than the store. Now stop talking like that."

"You don't know what it's like. She wasn't just my sister; she was my best friend. The other half of me."

"And she was my wife, my better half. I feel like…" Noel began walking again looking determinedly at the ground in front of him. Nila matched his pace. "Like part of my body's been hacked off."

"Your heart?"

"No. My heart's still here because it hurts so damn much."

They approached a bench and both sat down on it. Nila's gaze fell on a black walnut tree growing on the other side of the path. A squirrel scampered across one of its branches. "If she was the other half of me, and the better half of you, that makes an odd equation."

Noel didn't answer right away. When the silence stretched, Nila looked at him. He sat with his hands clasped between his spread knees, staring at the tree.

"Did you ever stop and think maybe she knew she was dying when she convinced you to have a baby for us?" Noel said it so matter-of-fact, like he was discussing the weather.

"Of course she didn't know!"

He turned to her. "I think she was trying to make a new equation because she knew she was dying."

"Why do you think so?"

"She said something to me one time about making things right between you and me."

"What do you mean making things right between us?"

Noel sighed. "The way things were before Lil and I met."

Nila shrugged. "We've always been friends, Noel. You and Lil getting together didn't change that."

"I know." He straightened and stared at the tree. "Best buds."

Nila studied his face at the bitter tone in his voice. "Don't get all weird on me, Dearing. You have a problem, just spit it out."

"No problem." His normal tone of voice was back. He stood and reaching for her hand, he pulled her to her feet. "When's your next doctor's appointment? I want to be there."

****

"Why do they have to take blood every time? I don't get it."

Nila watched Noel prowl the examination room like a caged animal. She shrugged. "They're making sure my ovaries are okay."

Noel turned his stormy gaze to her.

"I'm going to have ovarian cancer. One hundred percent chance since Lil had it, so they run a test to make sure I don't have the cancer yet."

Noel's eyes widened at the news. "Why didn't you tell Dr. Garber to cut your ovaries out already!"

"Because I was pregnant by the time I found out. They can't take out my ovaries with me pregnant. They have to

53

wait until after."

"Why are you just now telling me this?" He growled.

"I don't know, Noel. What does it matter?" Nila settled back further on the examining table glad on this visit, at least, she got to keep her clothes on. She didn't want him in here, but Noel insisted. "I'll have a hysterectomy, and I won't be able to have any more kids, but that will be okay because I'll have the boys."

He crossed his arms over his chest. "You'll have the boys?"

"Well…yeah."

"But you don't want children. You've never wanted kids. You told me that years ago."

A vine of unease branched around her heart. She put her hands to her stomach, feeling as if she needed to shield them from the anger emanating from Noel.

She focused on the ceiling. "They're mine."

"No. They are *my* kids." He jabbed a finger in the air at her. "You're the surrogate."

"Be serious, Noel. If it was up to you, I wouldn't even be pregnant. We had to trick you to—"

"Just because Lil is dead does not mean I don't want my sons! How could you think that?"

"How could you think I wouldn't want them?" She risked a glance at him and found him watching her.

"You were willing to give them up to Lil."

"That was different. She's my sister. I'd always be in her life. You and I have no ties."

Noel's eyes narrowed. His nostrils flared. His jaw clenched. "We sure as hell do. You're carrying them."

"You know what I mean."

"They are living with me. The agreement you had with your sister was that you would be pregnant for us, and you have to honor it."

"I can't give them up. Not now." Maybe not ever. Even if Lil had lived, Nila wasn't sure anymore if she would have been able to give up the babies.

"Those kids are mine. You want to be a part of their

lives—fine. Move in."

"Don't you tell me what to do! I'm not like Lil who would let you have your way about every single thing."

"Tell me you knew your sister better than that."

Nila flinched.

"I thought so."

"I can't move in with you."

Noel scrubbed his face with his hands. "Okay. I'll move in with you then."

Nila laughed at his absurd comment. "No."

Noel leaned back against the counter. Dr. Garber came in with the chart in his hand. "How are we doing?"

Neither of them answered.

He looked from one to the other of them. "Sit down, Noel," he said as he moved the only chair in the room next to the examining table where Nila was perched. When Noel did so, Dr. Garber studied them both.

"What's going on?"

"Noel wants custody of the kids."

"Nila was supposed to be a surrogate. Lil dying does not change anything."

"It changes everything. I am not giving them up!"

"There are two babies. Why don't each of you take one?"

Nila gasped. "What a horrible thing to say! We would never split them up." She looked at Noel for confirmation. "Can you believe he'd suggest such a thing?"

Noel grimaced. "Separating them really isn't an option."

"What other option is there if you both want them?"

Noel ran a finger back and forth along the seam of the counter. "That's what we were discussing when you came in,"

"Noel, I understand your position, I think, but Nila doesn't need any more stress right now. Already her blood pressure is elevated. I don't like that. Work it out amiably. Understand? Otherwise, she's going to end up in the hospital."

Noel sighed deeply. "I'm moving into her house."

"No, you're not."

"That's actually a good idea. Nila, unless you go into labor early, we'll schedule a caesarean section and go ahead with the hysterectomy." Dr. Garber wrote something on the chart in front of him. "You'll need someone at home anyway. There is no way you can take care of two newborns by yourself after having a surgical procedure."

"When did I lose control of my life?"

"When you climbed into bed with me."

"Oh, shut up. That was a rhetorical question!"

The doctor gave Noel a stern look. "Noel, less stress. Less."

Noel threw up his hands. "This might be a good time for you to tell the doctor you're depressed."

"Shut it, Dearing. I'm not."

"Sleeping for three solid days?" Noel snapped.

"Nila, is that true?" Dr. Garber asked.

"Look. I was just tired. I went to bed Friday, and Noel threw me in the tub Monday. It wasn't quite three days."

"Hmmm."

Nila glared at the doctor. "I'm fine."

"She probably would still be in bed except I went over there and made her go for a run with me."

"Running?" Dr. Garber shook his head. "Nila, you shouldn't be—"

"Argh!" Nila turned her wrath to Noel. "See what you did? I am not giving up running until I have to. I am sick of everybody telling me what to do. Dearing, would you just butt out of my life! Just because I'm pregnant does not mean—"

"Oh, hell, yes it does! Get used to it!"

"Noel. Out in the hall, please." Dr. Garber stood up and went to the door. To the nurse, he said, "I want a complete work up."

Dr. Garber motioned for Noel to follow him down the hall into his office. Noel had been here before. The first time Dr. Garber had all but accused him of hitting Nila when he had been the one to turn the pitching machine off.

"Sit."

Noel complied.

"You've got to keep yourself in check. She's got enough going on without you putting more stress on her."

"She's being unreasonable."

"She's pregnant. It's hormones. You've got to be more understanding. More loving."

"Hah! More loving? She hates me. She doesn't want me anywhere near her."

"Come on, Noel. Yes, she does. But even if she doesn't, you have got to give her every consideration. She's carrying your children, man. Her health is your top priority." Dr. Garber pinned Noel with his stare. "Isn't it?"

"Yes."

"Then take care of her."

"She doesn't *want* me to."

"She's carrying your children. If you'll quit pushing so hard, she'd probably be glad for someone to take care of her. She *is* tired. She *is* grieving. She needs you. You know that, don't you?"

No one spoke as Noel drove them back to the sporting goods store where he had picked Nila up to take her to the doctor. In the parking lot, Noel eased the car into a space near the door. Before he could turn off the engine, Nila was out of the car stalking to the entrance. Noel waited until she had gone inside before he sighed and gave up the thought of going after her.

How could his life be any more screwed? He had lost Lil and he was losing Nila. If he lost Nila, he'd lose his kids before he'd even met them. What had Lil been thinking when she convinced Nila to sleep with him? How could she possibly have thought it wouldn't screw up the tenuous relationships they'd worked out when Nila moved back home to take care of their mother? Oh, Lil had never minded the time he and Nila had together. She had known he and Nila had made a connection before he even met Lil. She'd also known his and Nila's connection had never progressed past their friendship. Lil knew he'd never cheat on her, especially with her own sister. Was she counting on that to still be the case after her death? They had never talked about it, but maybe they should have. Hadn't Lil considered Nila would want to keep the boys if Lil wasn't around to raise them?

Dammit.

What the hell had Lil been thinking?

Chapter Six

Nila had been home from work ten minutes when the doorbell rang. It could only be Noel this late.

She scraped the chair back from the table and grabbed her plate with the filet of cod—leftover from lunch—she'd heated up in the microwave. Walking across the house, she opened the front door. There stood Dearing still in his business duds. He held a canvas bag, and a pet carrier sat on the porch next to him.

From inside the carrier, a cat meowed plaintively.

"Is that Daisy?"

"Yeah. Can we come in?"

Nila stood back opening the door wider. Noel picked up the carrier and entered. She followed him into the living room where he set the carrier down. Crouching, he opened the gate and the tabby shot out.

"What's the deal? You going on a trip or something?"

Noel straightened and gestured for them to sit down. *Uh-oh*. It was one of those kinds of talks. When Nila had settled on her recliner and Noel the couch, he leaned toward her.

"I think Daisy ought to live here."

Nila sighed. "I'm not really a cat person."

"Since when?"

Nila shrugged.

"She's lonely at my house."

"My life is not conducive to taking care of an animal."

Noel's gaze dropped to her stomach, then he met her gaze and arched an eyebrow.

She didn't like his silent implication. So what if she didn't want the cat? She'd make room in her life for her babies. "You're the idiot who got her a cat. You take care of it."

"I'm not home very often anymore. I think it'd be good

if Daisy stayed here."

He was going to insist. He obviously didn't know pregnant women weren't supposed to be exposed to cat poop.

"It's not a good idea, Dearing." She shook her head and speared a piece of fish with her fork and ate it. Daisy jumped on the arm of the chair and began to purr. She made for the plate, and Nila fed her the last morsel of fish.

"Don't you think you need to start making some changes in your life? Here it is half past ten and you're just now eating supper. How are you going to take care of two kids with your schedule like it is? Maybe if you had Daisy here, it would—"

Nila stood up causing Daisy to jump on the floor. "Have you ever heard of toxoplasmosis?" she yelled. "I can't change her litter box because some cats carry it in their feces. If I get it, it can cause birth defects or make me miscarry." She stalked into the kitchen. "The cat can't stay. I can't take care of it." She took the plate to the sink and ran water on it.

Noel followed her in the room. She didn't look up from scrubbing the plate.

"Is it the cat which could infect you or the litter box?"

Nila didn't answer. She rinsed the soap from the plate and placed it in the drying rack.

"I can change the litter box every day. Would that work?"

"I guess so except it'd mean you'd be over here bugging me every day," she groused.

"I'll come over while you're at work."

"Great," she said sarcastically and turned to face him crossing her arms. "A new phase in our relationship—you getting a key to my house."

"You've always had a key to my house."

"I had a key to my sister's house."

"You still have it, don't you?"

He was making a point. Lil was gone. It really was only his now. "Yes."

"She's a sweet kitty." Noel placed his hands in his

pockets and watched her.

"I know." Her throat closed up, and she tried to clear it. "Why does this have to be so hard?"

He approached her and cupped her shoulders. "Because she's gone, and we still love her. We still miss her."

Lil.

"Please take the damn cat. I swear I'll clean out the litter box every day."

Nila looked down at his chest, the pinstriped shirt with white buttons. "Fine. She stays. If you don't hold up your end of the bargain, I'm opening up the door and throwing her outside."

****

"You feeling okay?" Noel asked at the one-and-a-third-mile point. When Nila didn't answer, Noel slowed his pace. "Let's walk."

"No." The air stung her lungs as she sucked it in.

"Tell me how much of a jerk I am."

Nila ignored him. He was trying to get her to talk to decide how out of breath she was. She knew she wouldn't be able to pass the test, so she kept silent.

"Nila, come on. This is good enough."

He was a jerk. He could recite the Gettysburg Address right now with no pulmonary effort whatsoever. Nila's whole body ached, but she wanted to make two miles. She had to. She gripped her stomach and the pregnancy support she'd bought hoping it would give her more time until she had to give up running. She glared at the path in front of her and concentrated on the sound of her foot falls. *Keep going, Miller. You can do this.* She didn't look, but she knew Noel was with her—could hear his feet too. They were a fraction of a second behind her own pounding rhythm.

"Let's turn around. That way if you get tired, we'll have less distance to the car."

Nila ignored him. If she didn't have to stop to do it, she'd kick him. If she did stop, she knew she'd never pick back up again. She knew she needed to breathe through her nose, but she couldn't get enough oxygen that way.

I am going to make it to two miles. Or die. Two miles would be past the baseball diamond. She could do it.

Ahead the fence shielding the dugout loomed.

She was closer.

Her foot caught, and she stumbled. Before she could hit the ground, Noel grabbed her, pulling her backward and against him, but the force of the move was too much for his balance. They landed on the grass at least, hard on their butts. She slid off his leg hoping she hadn't broken it.

"That was fun," Noel quipped.

If Nila could have gotten enough force behind it, she would have spit on him. He got to his feet and grasping her middle, he hauled her to hers before she could do the flailing-fat-woman-stuck-on-the-ground routine.

"Don't ask me if I'm okay. I'm really sick of that question." Nila brushed off her sweats and trudged toward the baseball diamond.

Noel followed catching up to her within seconds. "How about 'Are you well?' Or 'Will you make it?' Will either of those work?"

"No."

"When are you going to give me a break? How's that for a question?"

"No one asked you to come get me and harass me into running with you, so I could knock you flat when I pulled my daily klutz routine."

"Fine. We'll start walking from now on."

"Don't humor me." Nila knew she was being a bitch. She couldn't help it. Every molecule of Noel ticked her off, though she didn't know why. He was trying; she knew it. She considered the practice of the praying mantis that decapitated her mate after copulation. Oh, yes. Kill him before he irritated and angered her in her hormone-crazed, pregnant state. Her lips opened in a grin, but whether it was because of the absurdity of praying mantis sex or the dark glee of killing Noel, Nila wasn't sure.

They walked in silence toward Noel's car. When they arrived, he had the door open before she could reach the handle. She sat inside and wiped the sweat from her forehead. When Noel sat down beside her on the driver's side, he watched her. "You want to get some breakfast? I saw the pancake house has stuffed French toast."

Nila's mouth watered. She had seen that commercial. Oh, my gosh, the food had looked so delectable. So, this was his plan. Feed the beast French toast so she would not bite his head off and chomp it into little pieces.

"Okay."

Perhaps she would let him live long enough to pay the check.

****

Nila stood naked in front of the full length mirror in her bedroom and surveyed her image. She ran her fingers over her body's slope—skimming her fuller breasts, then caressed the firm flesh of her stomach.

The mound at her middle testified her pregnancy to the world. Even frumpy clothes didn't hide it anymore. And she'd had to give up running. It wasn't the constant imbalance that had finally convinced her to give it up, it was the extra weight. She used to feel good when she ran, but now... Nila shook her head. Now, it hurt her back and hips. She struggled to get a good breath, and this gut was just too big for fast motion.

Man, she hated giving up running. She'd been an avid runner since junior high, usually running three times a week in the mornings and three times a week after work on alternate days. Now what? She'd be pregnant three more months, and it'd take her at least that long to work back up to where she had been before she'd crawled into bed with Noel.

Her cell phone rang, and she walked through the house to retrieve it.

Teeny, a woman who used to work at the store greeted her. "Hi, Nila. Ricky said you left early."

"Yeah. We've got a delivery tomorrow, and he barely can make it by nine so I asked him to close. What's up?" As she talked, Nila rummaged through the clean clothes basket looking for one of the two pairs of maternity shorts she'd bought. Snagging a pair of panties and a bra, she headed to the bathroom for a shower.

"My sister's got two kids, you know, and I borrowed her pregnancy work-out DVDs and thought I'd bring them to you. Interested?"

Nila placed her garments on the bathroom counter as she caught her reflection in the mirror there. "Yes. I was just thinking about how much I miss running and how big I'm getting."

A smudge on her stomach caught her gaze, and Nila peered closer at the mirror.

"You're pregnant. You're supposed to get big."

"Oh, crap. I think I just found a stretch mark." Nila touched her stomach at the offending spot. "Oh, it is. It is!"

"I'll stop at the pharmacy on my way over and pick up some cocoa butter cream. It's supposed to help with that."

Nila snorted. "Nothing helps with it except not getting fat."

"Repeat after me. 'I'm not fat. I'm pregnant.'"

Nila grinned and began putting on her clothes. "You're pregnant?"

"No, you are. Say it. 'I'm not fat. I'm pregnant.'"

"I'm not fat. I'm pregnant. Happy? Come on by with those DVDs. I feel the need to work out with other non-fat, pregnant women."

Chapter Seven

The store phone rang, and Nila answered it. "*Play It! Sports.* May I help you?"

"Hello, *Play It! Sports.*"

Nila's hand gripped the phone at the sound of Noel's voice. "Hi."

"I was thinking a double bacon cheeseburger from Eddie's Grill."

Nila grinned. She had been craving cheeseburgers for weeks. It was ironic because she had been a vegetarian since college. She surmised pregnancy took more protein than she was getting in her normal diet even with the vitamins the doctor had prescribed.

"Are you game?"

Nila glanced at the clock. It was only four-thirty, but she was starving. Tonight was her night to close the store. "Yeah. If we can go now. I need to be back by the time Ricky leaves."

"Okay. Meet me out front. I'm about two minutes away."

Nila grabbed her purse. By the time she found her assistant manager and told him she was leaving on her dinner break, Noel was waiting for her on the front curb. He stood next to the open passenger door. She wrinkled her nose at him as she sat down inside the car. "What? I can't open my own door now?" she asked before he shut the door and walked around the car and slid into the driver's side.

He didn't rise to the bait. "Do you want two cheeseburgers?"

Yes, actually. "I'm thinking to ask if they'll just fry the whole damn cow and dip it in a vat of melted cheese."

Nila worked to get the seat belt across her body. Clicking it shut was becoming more and more difficult. She slid the buckle further along the belt and was able to fasten it.

"Hmm. You *are* hungry."

"I was about to order a pizza when you called." She was sure she could have eaten the whole thing.

"So what time will you be home tonight?" Though he asked the question in a casual tone, Nila prickled. She'd heard his lectures before about her working too many hours, working too late at night.

"I'm the owner of the store. I close up three nights a week," she said defensively.

"So, nine-thirty? Ten?"

Nila felt her ire rising. "Why do you want to know?"

"I'd like to bring some things over to the house tonight."

"What things?"

"My things."

Nila digested those two words for a moment as Noel drove toward the restaurant. Eddie's sign came into view, and Noel steered the car into the parking lot. Without any words, they exited the car, and Nila preceded Noel inside the building.

After they sat at a table and a waitress took their orders, Nila spoke. "I don't want you living with me. This is awkward enough without us complicating things by sharing space."

Noel's gaze burned into hers until Nila looked away. For years, Lil had been their buffer. Even when she hadn't been with them, their mutual connection with her had delineated clear boundaries. With her death, those boundaries didn't seem so clear anymore.

"Dr. Garber said—"

"I know what he said. I'm thinking about asking Teeny if she'd like to move in with me. She was working at the store, but she's taking classes at the community college now. She's looking for a place to live."

Nila watched Noel for his reaction to her words. His tense jaw and flashing gaze told her he didn't like what he'd heard. Finally, he spoke. "I love my children. Already."

Jennifer Johnson

Tears gathered in her eyes at his words and at the intensity in which he said them.

"Please don't deny me my right to be around them," he said.

Nila pushed up from the table and stood. "I'm going to the bathroom," she mumbled before hurrying away as fast as her unwieldy body would take her. Once there, she shut and locked the door. Leaning against it, she pushed the heels of her hands against her eyes.

This wasn't fair!

Her whole life she had watched Lil be the best at everything except athletics. She had been the golden girl—cheerleader and homecoming queen. She had married Noel and graduated with honors. Even dead she was still calling the shots, and Nila was expected to put aside her own desires and wants to make the very best life for the children Lil convinced her to have.

Well, she was going to give these babies the very best life, but not as a substitute for Lil.

These are my babies. Mine.

She knew Noel loved them, too. But she was more than a surrogate. She was their mother. Not Lil.

Nila sucked in a deep breath. She opened the door and marched to the front of the restaurant. The waitress who had waited on them stood behind the counter.

"I'd like my food to go, please."

"But what about your husband?"

Nila shot daggers at the woman who glanced down at Nila's stomach and back to her face. "Boyfriend?"

"Forget it." Nila marched out the door into the late afternoon and started back to work. She'd just order a pizza when she got there. Maybe two.

Hard footsteps beat the pavement toward her. She recognized his rhythm but kept walking. Noel ran ahead and turned to face her blocking her path.

"Sorry. I'm sorry." He didn't look sorry. He looked—and sounded—angry.

Nila stopped. "I am more than a baby machine. I am the

mother. I am *the only* mother of these children."

Noel raised his hands in a gesture of surrender. "Okay. You're the mother. The *only mother*, but I'm the father. *The only* father."

"Well, I don't want to play house with you. I might want to get married someday. I deserve to go out on dates and have a love life, and I don't want you around glaring at my boyfriends."

Noel's expression changed. He laughed. Nila balled her fist and punched him in the gut.

"Ooof!"

She walked around him and crossed the street. Ten more blocks to the store.

"Oh, come on, Nila. Get you a boyfriend if you want one," he called and caught up with her again. Walking next to her, he tried again. "I won't glare at anybody, and you'll need a babysitter anyway."

She didn't respond.

"I'm the dad so I won't even charge you. Can't we make this work?"

Nila slowed her steps. "I don't know."

"Let's go back to Eddie's and eat. We don't have to decide anything right now."

Nila sighed and allowed Noel to guide her in an about-face. "I'm always giving in to you."

"That's because I'm always enticing you with food."

"I'm through with giving in. To Lil or you."

They crossed the street and entered the parking lot. "No one is giving in. We're just eating supper."

"You're not moving in."

"I'm not moving in," Noel agreed.

Nila was pretty sure he was lying. She didn't care. She just wanted something to eat. She didn't want to think about the implications of Noel moving his stuff into her house or even of her having his children. Just the cheeseburgers. That's all she wanted to think about right now.

****

Noel was a pest.

And he wasn't fooling anyone.

Nila's lips pressed together when she saw his car pull into her driveway. This was the fourth day in a row Noel had shown up with food in hand and two of something for the babies. Yesterday he had brought diaper bags. The day before it was two bibs. What would it be today?

Nila let the curtain drop and leaned back in the recliner raising her feet higher on the foot rest. Daisy purred from her perch on the chair arm. When the knock sounded on the door, Nila didn't move. Past experience told her he'd let himself in if she didn't answer after about a minute.

Oh, her feet hurt.

The door opened. "Nila, it's Noel," he called.

As if she didn't know.

He walked into the room. With him the aroma of cheeseburgers and the take-out bag confirmed it. He'd brought dinner. The other bag had the purple pineapple logo on it. The purple pineapple was a baby boutique across the street from Noel's office building. Outrageously expensive.

"Hey."

He knew better than to ask how she was.

"Hi."

"Want me to bring you a tray?"

He knew better than to ask if she was hungry because she was always hungry. Even at ten thirty at night.

"Sure."

He went to the kitchen and brought the tray back. He set it next to the chair, reached in the bag, and pulled out a wrapped burger and a bottle of water, condensation down its side attested to its cold temperature. He picked up Daisy, who mewed in protest, and set her on the floor.

"Did you eat dinner?"

Nila reached for the sandwich. "I ate some yogurt at five. Baseball season is starting up, so it was pretty crazy. And Danny didn't show up again."

She bit into the burger and chewed in appreciation.

"What are you going to do?"

"If he does it again, I'll have to fire him. He misses as

often as he shows up. It'd be one thing if he'd call, but he doesn't. I need somebody I can count on, you know?"

"Yeah." Noel settled back on the couch. He still wore his suit though the knot on his tie was loose and the top two buttons on his shirt were undone.

"Did you come straight from work?"

"Yep. Baseball season for you is tax season for me."

"You look tired."

"I am."

"What time'd you go in this morning?"

"Five-thirty." He yawned as if punctuating his statement.

"You need to go home. You must be beat."

"I'm fine." He reached up and unknotted his tie.

Nila noted his action but didn't comment. She didn't want him to get too comfortable. She didn't mind him here too much, but she was ready to hit the sack as soon as she ate his food offerings and could heave herself out of this chair. Or maybe she'd just sleep here.

She finished off the burger and drank some of the water.

"What'd you bring from the Purple Pineapple?"

He reached into the bag and pulled out two silver rattles. Daisy, who had settled on the chair again, laid her ears back at the noisy objects. "What do you think? Cute, huh? They can engrave them with names as soon as we decide on them."

Nila wrinkled her nose but said nothing.

"Have you thought about names?"

"Have you?"

"Nothing that rhymes."

"Agreed. Mom and Dad named us Nila and Lila. Lil hated it so much that when we started kindergarten, she insisted everyone call her Lil. I guess that was her way of setting herself apart."

"Did it bother you?"

"No. You know what I would be if I took the *a* off my name? *Nil*. Nothing."

Noel sighed and shook his head. "Nila, you could never

be—"

"Don't." Nila set the bottle down and leaned forward as she pushed in the footrest. "I wasn't fishing for compliments."

"I know that. You set yourself apart too. You excelled athletically. Lil could never have accomplished what you have, not only with sports but also with running a business."

Nila digested that bit of information. It had been a lot easier playing softball, soccer, and track when Lil had been nowhere on the field. It was as if they had chosen different hobbies so they could distinguish themselves from each other.

"You were always the more organized one."

Oh, no. Now he was making comparisons. If he continued on, Nila would come up short next to her beautiful and intelligent sister. She decided to change the subject before that happened.

"So, have you thought of specific names?"

Noel shrugged.

"You have. Just tell me."

"I had a name picked out for one. Two?" He shook his head.

"What's the name?"

"Benjamin Daniel Dearing."

"Sounds good."

"You mean, you'll let them have my last name?"

Nila huffed. "Look. I haven't forgotten Lil wanted this so there would be another generation of Dearings."

"What about the other baby?"

"We could call the other baby Daniel and let both babies have Miller as their middle name. That way we'd both have our names on both of them."

"Okay."

"Really?"

"Sure."

Nila yawned glad that the names, at least, were settled. "Thanks for the late dinner." She stood up and stretched. "I think I'll head off to bed. You can let yourself out, right?"

Noel stared, his gaze burning up at her. She looked away from his intensity, but yearning unfurled in her chest. She wanted to go to him, to sit down and cuddle up next to him.

"Kiss me, Dearing," she'd say.

And he'd smile down at her, settle his mouth on hers and....

Time to leave.

"Goodnight, Noel." She willed her feet to move and breathed a sigh of relief when she entered the darkened hallway.

Was this what life was going to be like from now on? How could she stand it? How was she going to get a handle on her horny hormones especially when he was giving her the bedroom gaze? Why did he look at her like that? Was it because she was carrying his children? Was he remembering those moments they had shared in bed before he realized she wasn't his wife? Nila wanted to march back into the room and ask him, but she was too afraid of what he would say, of hearing his regret that his wife was dead and she was not.

Before dawn the next morning Nila awoke at the sound of Noel's car in her driveway.

What?

She slid off the bed and walked to the window. Pushing aside the curtain, she watched his car back out of the driveway and pull onto the street.

What was he doing?

Had he spent the night here last night?

Nila turned and went into the hall. Entering the bathroom, she noted the residue of water in the sink and shower, the faint scent of a male soap, probably Dial or Irish Spring. She walked across the hall into the guest bedroom. The bed was neatly made but not quite how she had made it. The pillows were too high up on the bed. Walking to the closet, she opened the door and shook her head.

Men clothes—suits on one side, pressed button downs on the other. One pair of running shoes on the floor next to an overnight bag.

His more casual clothes, underwear, and socks filled

three of the dresser drawers.

Well, this explained why he was so insistent she take Daisy. Nila laughed at his cunning. The sneak! When had he moved in?

Chapter Eight

Noel sat across the conference table from Dr. Wynn, Lil's oncologist. Noel had requested the meeting after receiving billing from the doctor's office for a visit nearly six months before she told him she'd seen the doctor.

"So you're telling me she knew she had cancer in February of last year?"

"Yes."

Noel shook his head. "I don't understand. She didn't say anything to me. Not until Dr. Garber sent her a registered letter because her blood levels were off."

"I'm sorry, Mr. Dearing." The other man shook his head in sympathy and peered down at an open folder in front of him. "Dr. Garber and I had a consultation with your wife February sixth. Dr. Garber strongly encouraged your wife to have you there as well, but she refused."

Bile rose in his throat. "Why?"

"She wanted to know what she was facing, I suppose, before she told you."

"Why didn't you tell me?"

"Legally, we cannot disclose any medical information without the patient's expressed permission. She specifically asked for new disclosure forms to restrict access to anyone except your insurance company." Dr. Wynn pulled out two forms and slid them across the table toward Noel.

He recognized Lil's signature and noted the date. "But she was my wife. How could she do this?" What had she been thinking? Why hadn't she trusted him with the truth?

Adjusting his glasses, Dr. Wynn picked up another paper and read it. "I met with her again in early April and noted she had an identical twin. I advised her to get her twin, Nila Miller, tested as soon as possible. Even though Lil had refused any treatment initially, she did express her opinion that her twin would want treatment but had concerns because Ms. Miller was trying to get pregnant."

"When did you say that was?"

"April second."

"Lil knew, then, she would never have children?"

"She knew after our initial meeting February sixth. We also told her at that time about the ovarian cancer and how critical it was for her to get treatment as soon as possible."

Son of a bitch. Lil had known even before Nila had gotten pregnant. She had known she would die without treatment, and she had still convinced Nila to sleep with him.

Why?

Why would she want them to have a baby for her when she knew she wouldn't be around to raise it?

And how long had Nila known? He had assumed she found out the day the letter had come. The same time he had found out.

But now? Now he wasn't sure of anything.

****

Nila had waited for Noel to show back up at her house for four days now. But he hadn't. No food. No gifts for Benjamin and Daniel. Not even a phone call.

Oh, sure, Nila had called him and left messages on his voice mail. She'd texted him and talked to his secretary at work but so far nothing.

What had happened?

Nila drove by the house but saw no lights on, so she went by his office and found his car in his executive space.

The glass building was open though it was nearly eleven at night. The lobby was vacant except for a man mopping the floor. When Nila couldn't get Noel to the door at his office, she took the elevator back down to the lobby and approached the custodian.

"Hey," she greeted him. "I need to get in to see someone in Stuart and Dearing upstairs. Can you let me in?"

He stuck the mop in the bucket and peered at her. "They're closed."

"I know, but my brother-in-law is working, and I can't get him to answer the phone."

"Who's your brother-in-law?"

"Noel. Noel Dearing."

"All right."

They rode the elevator to the fourth floor and he unlocked the glass door for Nila. She stepped in the outer office, lit only by a desk lamp on the secretary's desk. Nila's footsteps echoed in the silence as she walked down the hallway to where she knew Noel's office was. The door was closed, but a shaft of light shone under the door.

Nila knocked, waited a few seconds, and tried the handle which moved under her hand. She pushed it down and opened the door.

Noel sat behind his desk staring at his computer screen. One hand moved the mouse while another punched buttons on an impressive adding machine.

"Dearing?"

He looked up. "I thought you were Jeff coming to empty the trash." He stretched but kept his seat. "Is everything okay?"

"I don't know. I haven't seen you for a few days."

"It's tax season." His face, void of emotion, matched his monotone.

Nila looked around his office and took a seat on the leather couch across the room from his desk. "Take a break, Dearing." She patted the cushion next to her. "Come here and tell me why you're giving me the cold shoulder after moving all your stuff into my guest bedroom."

He pushed his chair back, walked to the chair across from her, and sat on its edge. With his arms resting on his knees, his gaze pierced hers.

"I want you to tell me when you found out Lil had cancer."

Huh? "The night she texted me and asked me to come over, after you and I...when you weren't talking to either one of us because..." Nila couldn't even voice the betrayal of what she and Lil had done. She went on to answer his question. "She told both of us the night she invited me over."

"She never said anything to you before that day? Any

hint? Any comment that made you think something more could be wrong?"

"Noel, what is this—"

"*Did she?*" The intensity in his question and expression shocked Nila. She searched her mind trying to remember.

"Well, she kept bugging me about getting a checkup. She made an appointment for me with Dr. Garber and hit the roof when I canceled it. I'd never seen her so mad. But she said it was because…well…." Nila rubbed her stomach.

Noel's gaze dropped to her hand. He sat back and sighed. "You'd tell me the truth about this, even if she told you not to. Now you would, right?"

"I wouldn't lie to you, Noel. What is this about?"

"Lil knew she had cancer back in February. She kept it from me, from us, for almost six months."

Nila shook her head in disbelief. "No. She knew about the tumor in September, and that she couldn't have kids. But she didn't find out about the cancer until later."

"She met with Dr. Wynn in February. She knew." When Nila didn't respond, Noel continued. "She planned on dying the whole time she was trying to convince both of us to have a baby."

"I can't believe it."

"I couldn't either, but I met with Dr. Wynn. I saw Lil's signature on the HIPAA papers. She didn't want me to know."

"Why?"

"I wish to hell I knew." Noel stood up, gripping his hair in an agonizing pose. "When I think of all that time she could have been having the treatments." He stalked over to his desk, picked up a framed picture of the two of them, and threw it at the wall. "She might have lived, but she didn't even try, didn't give me the chance to make her try!" The glass on the frame broke punctuating his statement. "I hate her for that!" With a guttural cry, he picked up the edge of his desk and shoved it toward the wall, knocking the monitor askew and sending papers flying everywhere. The adding machine cracked as it fell to the floor.

Nila watched her friend come apart, her heart breaking for the pain evident in his actions.

Oh, Lil, how could you do this to him?

Breathing hard, he paced the office.

"Dearing, where's your gym bag? Go get your workout clothes on and run a few laps around the park. When you've calmed down, come back up, and we'll talk about it."

Without a word, he stalked to a door, opened a closet, pulled out a duffel bag, and started to strip in jerky movements. Nila watched him in surprise. His jacket, tie, and shirt thrown to the floor, shoes and socks kicked off, then pants. Next his undershirt, and he stood wearing only a pair of briefs.

Oh, man.

Bending down, he unzipped his bag, pulled out a Tee and some shorts, and dressed quickly. Picking up the bag, he fished out his running shoes and socks, stalked over to the chair across from her he had vacated earlier, sat down, and put them on.

Still without a word, he left.

Nila released the breath she had been holding. She had tried to ignore the warm tingling in her body that had begun when Noel had taken off his shirt and had morphed into a white hot wave of lust when he had shed his pants.

It was wrong. She was horrible for drinking in the sight of him, his toned body, his flesh, when his grief was so raw, when he was so emotionally vulnerable.

Images of them together ricocheted in her head, his lips touching hers, the feel of him inside of her, his warmth, his body the night they had....

Nila shook her head. No. Noel was her friend. He needed her tonight as his friend.

She pulled herself off the couch and began cleaning up the torn apart office.

****

When Noel entered almost two hours later drenched in sweat, Nila had fallen asleep on his couch. The only hint of his tantrum were the shards of glass protecting the picture of

Lil and Noel on their wedding day at the bottom of the wastepaper basket. The frame itself was unharmed, and Nila had carefully placed the picture back inside it and set it in its original place on Noel's desk.

"I'm sorry," Noel said as he stood over her, waking her with his apology.

Nila sat up and rubbed her eyes. "Don't be. Come on. Let's go home. I'll drive us, and we'll talk on the way."

"Okay."

In the car a few minutes later, Nila began. "You have a right to be angry. She should have told us."

"I just don't understand why she didn't. I don't think she ever would have if I hadn't been home when she got the registered letter."

"Maybe not."

"I had the right to know."

Nila didn't meet his eyes even though they were stopped at an intersection. The red of the traffic light shone in the car coloring her breasts with a dark arc from the steering wheel. The shadow made an incomplete arrow that pointed to her abdomen. "Yes, you did. But she knew when we found out that we'd push her to get treatment."

"Right."

"She was afraid of dying like Mom did."

"It wasn't the chemo which made your mom suffer, it was the cancer," Noel stated. He'd said the same thing to Lil several times in trying to convince her to get treatment.

"But the chemo prolonged her life, and the last few months weren't so good."

Noel huffed. "I know that."

The light turned green, and Nila eased through the intersection and turned onto Rossway Belt. She was taking the scenic route, it seemed.

"But I don't think you know how much it bothered Lil. She tried to help me when Mom got so bad, but she just couldn't take seeing Mom like that. You know she didn't come over the last three weeks. Not even once."

Noel blinked. *What?* He shook his head in disbelief.

Nila reached across the darkened interior and took his hand in hers. She squeezed. "It's true."

"Oh. I didn't...I didn't know. She always had an excuse when I'd come by here."

"I know, Noel. But I never blamed her, because, you know, she was with Dad when he died, and so I figured it was my time to be with Mom."

They rode the rest of the way in silence. At Nila's house, she got ready for bed while Noel took a shower. It was past two in the morning, and they both were exhausted. When Nila lay down, the twins began their nightly wrestling match. She grinned in the darkness. When she heard Noel exit the bathroom, she called to him.

He stood at the door with the towel draped around his waist.

"Come here," she invited as she lay against her bevy of pillows.

He hesitated. "I should—"

"The babies are moving. Come feel them. It'll lift your spirits." She threw back the covers and pushed up her T-shirt as Noel climbed on the bed and placed his hand on her extended stomach. In a second, a fetus moved inside Nila. She took Noel's hand and guided it to the spot. Another movement and another.

Noel laughed. "What are they doing in there?"

The room was lit with only the light from the hallway—probably a good thing since it hid the marks on her belly...and Noel with only his towel.

"Probably fighting for room."

He moved and put his head on her belly with his ear next to her skin. "I can't wait to see them. Hold them."

"Yeah."

He cupped his hands around her stomach and kissed the skin there twice.

Oh, help me, God. He's my best friend. He can't be anything but that.

Nila dug her fingers in the sheet so she wouldn't pull him to her and beg him to love her, to make love to her. Noel rested his head on one arm with its elbow against the mattress while he nuzzled her stomach and cradled the other side of the mound with his hand. With his cheek against her skin, the near day's growth of whiskers pumiced her stretched flesh, scratched the itch of taut skin and made her tingle deep in her body. Though his face was shadowed, Nila knew he could see her expression from the hall light.

Please don't let him see how much I want to jump him. What a joke. If I jumped him, I'd probably crush him to death.

"Can I just lie like this a few minutes?"

Nila worked to sound nonchalant. "You can lie there for what's left of the night. I'll have to get up and pee in about four hours though."

"I'm still pissed at her for not telling me and not fighting the cancer, but I am glad she connived us into this pregnancy."

"Really?"

"Yes. What about you?"

"She forced the issue and probably gave me my only chance to have children. And with the only person I would have considered having them with, my best friend. I think she gave us something very precious."

For a moment, Noel didn't speak, then, "Your best friend, huh?"

"Yeah. BFF. But don't let it go to your head."

****

Sometime after Nila fell asleep with Noel's hand cradling her belly, he eased himself away from her warm body and went into the guest bedroom. Though he lay down, he couldn't sleep. Instead, he stared at the darkened ceiling and wrestled with all of the demons that threatened to shred his soul to pieces.

He was in love with his wife's sister. It was sick. He shouldn't want her, but how could he not? She was pregnant with his children. She was his workout partner. She was his football-watching buddy. He'd known her longer than he'd even known Lil. Hell, he'd gone home with Nila for Thanksgiving in college, and she had come onto him. It wasn't until later he realized it was Lil he had been kissing. Not his BFF. Not until the night she crawled into bed with him wearing Lil's gown, smelling like the lotion he had bought Lil for her birthday had he ever kissed Nila, had…yeah.

Had he known it wasn't Lil? Had some part of him realized before she whispered to him in the dark?

Dearing. What you're doing to me.

He'd orgasmed in the same instant. Had he ejaculated because she'd spoken, and he'd realized he was making love to Nila? The possibility haunted him. Because he'd never considered cheating on Lil.

Noel loved Lil. He did.

But when Nila had spoken in that moment, his world had broken apart.

She almost always called him by his last name. Ever since that night, when she said it, he'd think about her on top of him, about being inside her, not realizing his part in creating the lives growing in her right now, changing their future.

Being with her had been different.

Better?

He couldn't say.

He hadn't made love to Lil in so long because she told him it was painful. For the year before she was diagnosed, she endured it only when she deemed herself fertile. Not that he'd ever forced her to have sex. Guys at the gym bitched about their wives never putting out. He figured Lil was just more honest about why she didn't want to.

On the nights she initiated sex, she'd cuddle up to him and kiss him. And wait for him to do everything else.

But the night Nila had gotten in bed with him, she'd gone down on him even before he had woken up good. She'd climbed right on top of him like some beautiful wanton goddess with her skin shimmering in the moonlight.

She'd shocked the hell out of him.

Of course she hadn't been Lil. Lil wouldn't have done that in a million years.

He had known on some level, hadn't he?

He knew Lil had wanted a baby. He just never figured either one of them would be willing to have Nila screw him for one. He should have realized though.

Had he known?

The possibility tortured him because he had sworn before God and every person who mattered to him in this world—including Nila—he would be faithful to Lil until death.

Until death do us part.

Lil had only been dead three months. What kind of man would even think about making love to his dead wife's sister after only three months?

And, oh, he had wanted to. Lying there stark naked with Nila in her shirt and boxer shorts pulled aside so he could touch her stomach, run his fingers across her soft skin, inhale her sweetness, he had wanted to so bad. After the kids had settled down, she had turned on her side murmuring she was more comfortable that way. Thank God she had turned to him and not away. He would have spooned her, his erection pressing into her with nothing stopping him from loving her but those thin cotton boxers she must sleep in.

She had been wearing a similar pair the day he'd found her and put her in the tub. She'd been so drawn and pale, for a second he'd sworn she was dead. He'd thought he couldn't lose them both—not Lil and Nila too.

When she insisted she could finish bathing herself, he'd walked to the living room, shaking so bad he staggered like a drunk. She hadn't realized it, but he'd slept in her house every night for the next week just to be sure she was okay.

He sighed, rolled to his side, and bunched the pillow under his head. He had an eight o'clock meeting in the morning. Geez, he hoped he made some sense when he met with his client in a few hours.

Chapter Nine

Nila followed the last customer to the door and was about to lock it when she saw Noel walking up to the pavement. She opened the door for him. "Hey, Dearing. What's up? Need a UK sweatshirt? They're half off."

He was in shorts, T-shirt, and running shoes. It looked like he'd been sweating already.

"Maybe. You got my size?"

"Would I have told you about it if I didn't? I am trying to make a sale after all."

He walked in, and she shut the door behind him and locked it. Turning around, he placed his hands on his hips. A bead of sweat rolled down the side of his face.

"Did you run here?"

"No. I parked here, then ran to the river and back." He lifted his shirt and mopped his face. Nila looked at his exposed stomach and the hair which started at his naval and disappeared into his waistband. Desire fluttered in her chest, but she ignored it. Walking around him, she headed to the back of the store where her office was located.

Somebody kicked her ribs from inside, and she rubbed her belly near the spot. Noel's shoes squeaked on the floor as he followed her. Entering her office, she snagged her purse and walked back to clear out the register.

She knew if she sat down even for a minute, she'd fall asleep. And if she went ahead and closed out the register, she could take the money by the bank and put it in the drop box.

Noel followed her again. "You want to get something to eat?"

"Where?"

"My house."

The answer surprised her since he'd been staying with her for the last couple of weeks.

"I'm pretty sweaty right now so I thought I could grab

a shower and we could talk."

At the counter now, Nila opened the drawer and began placing money in the bank bag. "About what?"

He leaned his elbows on the counter. "Where we're going to live."

"Oh." Nila zipped up the bag and locked it. She didn't want to have this conversation yet, but time was running out. They were now in weeks to the due date instead of months. "I'm really tired. I just want to go home and go to bed."

"Have you eaten supper yet?"

"Yes. A couple of times. I'm keeping food here in the office so it's a lot easier to eat something even when we get busy." She tucked the bag under her arm and walked around the counter.

"You can stay at my house."

Nila sighed. "I don't want to go there. It reminds me too much of Lil."

"That's where the nursery is, Nila. You have nothing at your house that even hints you're going to bring two babies home in less than a month. It makes sense to go where—"

Nila turned off the light and stood next to the door. "She died in that room. I don't want to...I'm sorry, Noel. I should be stronger than this, but I just...I don't know. It feels wrong not to use the nursery. I mean, geez, we wouldn't even be pregnant if it weren't for her, and I know she worked so hard on it...having everything just so. But I can't get that image out of my head with her in that chair, so still." She shivered. "I don't want to feel this way. I want them to be in the room she decorated just for them. Every little piece of it she enjoyed so much, but I...I'm just not ready for it to be anything but where I lost her."

"Let me drive you to the house. You don't have to go in the nursery. I think you need to do this. You haven't been back since right after the funeral."

"I can't leave Daisy alone all night."

"I checked on her before I came here. She's a cat. She'll be okay until tomorrow."

"I'm too tired to deal with this." They walked outside,

and she locked the door.

"I'll have you in a bed in half an hour. I'll even fix you French toast as a late night snack."

Here he was again dangling food in front of her face like a carrot to a stubborn donkey. They walked to his car, and he opened the passenger side door.

He continued. "I found this recipe for stuffed French toast. It uses cream cheese. And I picked up some blueberry syrup too."

Her mouth began salivating. "That's not fair." She eased into the seat and pulled her legs inside. He walked around the front of the car and joined her.

When he'd closed himself inside the vehicle with her, he started the engine but didn't move out of the parking space. "I've already picked up some clothes for you. I'll bring you to work in the morning as early as you want to come."

"Where will I sleep?"

"You can sleep in the guest bedroom or you can sleep with me." His expression was serious, his gaze sincere. What was he suggesting? It's not like they hadn't shared a bed before. He lay down with her the night he'd felt the twins moving, and he'd been practically naked.

As big as she already was, it wasn't as if sex were really an option. Well, maybe it would be if she were sharing this pregnancy with her husband of so many years. The time she was in the bathtub in her underwear had been the closest Noel had seen her naked. He was offering the intimacy of a shared bed as a friend, as the platonic partner and father to her children. That was it.

"That was your and Lil's bed."

"You've been in it with me too." His gaze dropped to her protruding stomach and he put the car into drive and headed toward the bank building. "We'll try it. If you are too uncomfortable, you move to the guest room. Okay?"

"What about the nursery?"

"We could move the furniture to your house. That way it would still have Lil's loving care, but the space wouldn't hold the bad memories."

"You're going to move in with me officially?"

"I'm going to be a full-time father to my children. If moving in with you is my only option to be with them, that's what I'll do."

"You could sue for custody."

"I'm going to pretend you didn't say that. You're my best friend. These kids are not going to drive us apart. That's the last thing Lil would have wanted. I know that much."

After dropping off the money, Noel drove them to the house. Though she knew he hadn't been staying here for a while, it didn't smell closed up. It smelled— Nila inhaled. It still smelled like Lil and Noel's house. She waited for the wave of grief to knock her down, but it didn't. Instead, the familiarity of the house comforted her. Noel carried the bag he'd packed for her up the stairs. At the landing he waited for her, his eyes questioning.

She headed for the guest room, and he placed her bag on the floor inside the door.

"You want your French toast now?"

She shook her head. "You do understand, don't you? I mean you slept with her every night in that room, that bed. It feels like we're crossing a line."

"Because I offered to sleep with you or because I offered to sleep with you in the bed I shared with your sister?"

"Define sleep."

Noel shook his head and walked out of the room.

"I think it's a reasonable question," she called after him. "My hormones are out of whack, and your wife is no longer alive to make you unavailable. If we end up in your bed, I don't want you cuddling up to me and dreaming about Lil."

He came back to the door and scowled at her. "I've been able to tell you two apart for a very long time."

"Yeah? Except for the night I got pregnant."

His eyes glittered in anger. He was silent for a moment. "Despite your efforts to misrepresent yourself, it didn't take me long to figure it out. I've only made that mistake twice, and I won't be making it a third time."

"Twice?"

"Yeah. Twice."

"What was the other time?"

"I don't want to talk about it." He left the room again, his footsteps stomping through the hall.

"Then why'd you bring it up?" she called.

"Because I'm an idiot." His bedroom door closed.

Nila sighed. She thought back through all the times she, Lil, and Noel had been together. When had he ever gotten confused? He'd always been able to tell them apart as long as he'd known them.

Nila picked up her bag and walked toward the bathroom. The nursery door stood ajar, and her footsteps faltered. The hall light shone through the doorway creating a slanted shape on the floor and illuminating the room with soft light. The UK wallpaper border Noel had hung around the upper perimeter of the room caught her eye.

Nila shook her head and smiled. What the heck did babies care about the University of Kentucky? Lil hadn't asked her opinion though.

I was only going to be the surrogate, the aunt.

The chair where Lil had died was gone. In its place was a nursing rocker with cushions in the dark UK blue which matched the bumper pads in the cribs. Nila stepped into the room and waited for the sensation of Lil's presence or the ache of loss for her twin.

Do you hear that? A voice is saying, 'Lil! Lil! Hurry and eat me! I taste so good.' Please go get the poor chocolate shake. It needs me.

The hospice nurse had suggested Lil sent Nila on the errand because she knew she was dying and it was too hard to leave this earth with her twin clinging to her.

Setting her bag on the rocker, Nila approached one of the cribs and picked up a stuffed UK wildcat.

It was silly really. Lil had never been into sports. That had been Noel and Nila's shared passion. Lil would go out shopping rather than have to listen to the spirited yells and ball chatter. Yet, she had decorated the room with a basketball theme.

Nila brought the stuffed animal to her face and inhaled attempting to detect Lil's scent. She'd been the last one to handle it, Nila felt sure. But there was nothing.

"I miss you, Lil," she whispered. "It should have been you carrying these babies."

I can't do it now. You're going to have to do it for us.

Lil's words again from one of the times she'd tried to convince Nila to sleep with Noel. When Lil had been in the car wreck which had killed their father, she'd almost died. Nila vividly remembered sitting in her mom's lap while Lil labored to breathe in the hospital bed next to them.

Nila had promised then to always take care of Lil no matter what.

And that promise had become a law directing Nila's life.

From then on, Nila had taken care of Lil any time she needed her. Nila had always been the protector, the fixer. If Lil's asthma sent her to the emergency room, Nila had been the one to drive her. If she had an anxiety attack, it was Nila she called to calm her down. She'd always taken care of Lil until Lil and Noel married.

Placing the toy back in the crib, she ran her hand over her stomach as if caressing the boys. "Your mom had a twin, and she decorated this room for you," she murmured. "She loved you guys even though she'd never get to meet you."

Nila left the nursery and went to the hall bathroom to get ready for bed. Opening the bag, she inventoried its contents. Dearing had done pretty good—even to packing her grande T-shirt and big boxers to sleep in. She brushed her teeth, washed her face, and changed clothes. Walking back into the hall, her gaze strayed to Noel's door.

He misses being here. His own bed and room. His house. I've been too hard on him, thinking of myself.

Low voices reached her ears from the other side of his door. She raised her hand and knocked.

She heard his footsteps across the wooden floor, and then he pulled the door, letting it swing open all the way. In long shorts which rested below his hips, Noel stood before her shirtless. "Change your mind about the French toast?"

Skin. Chest. Pectoral muscles. Hair. Man nipples. Shoulders. Triceps. Biceps. Tight abdominals.

Oh, boy.

Finally, she looked at Noel's face, his eyebrows raised, waiting for her answer. Behind him some drama played.

"When did you put a TV in here?"

Noel glanced over his shoulder and stepped back. A flat screen was mounted on the wall. Nila recognized the sitcom rerun.

"A while back."

Lil had never wanted a TV where she slept. She'd said it was a bad habit to watch TV while in bed. Nila walked into the room. Somebody kicked her from inside, and she moved her hand to the spot.

"What's wrong?" Noel spoke in an anxious tone.

"Nothing." She rubbed her stomach when she was kicked again. "They do this every night. It takes about an hour for them to settle down again." He pulled back covers on the bed inviting her to sit so she did. She yawned. "I'm so tired by this time of night, but do they let me sleep? No. They're ready to play football."

"Want to watch TV with me?"

"Okay." He'd switched sides since Lil died. She'd always had the side closest to the door.

It was one of her quirks left over from the car fire which had killed their dad. She was more comfortable close to an exit.

Nila slid off the mattress and walked around the bed to the far side. She pulled the comforter and sheet down and propped the pillow against the headboard.

Glancing up at Noel, his stance snagged her attention. He stood frozen except for his eyes which bore into her.

"What? That's your side of the bed, right?"

His eyes fell to the bed and back to her.

"Dearing, work with me here. That is your side of the bed, isn't it?"

"Yeah." He breathed the word.

"Is this too awkward?" One of the twins kicked her, and

she moved her hand again over her stomach absently.

Noel shook his head as if to clear it. "No. No. It's okay."

Was he thinking of Lil?

"It is too awkward." She pulled the comforter back up. Why had she come in here anyway? Not to watch TV. That had been his idea.

"It's awkward, yes, but we're in new territory here." He crawled across the bed and pulled back the comforter again. Taking her hand, he tugged it gently. "If we remember that we're friends first, we'll be okay."

Nila followed the tug and sat on the mattress.

Friends first, and what second?

Noel held up the covers, and Nila worked to get her legs up on the bed. This sure had been easier forty pounds ago. The domestic coziness of this set-up gnawed at her.

"Are we just watching TV or are we sleeping together?"

Noel, recovered now from whatever had haunted him earlier, grinned. "Define sleeping."

"Unconscious rest." Nila searched his face. "That's what you meant, right?" She'd loved him for so long, but they'd had so many changes to deal with since Lil had died. Sex would complicate what was already a convoluted situation. And anyway… "The last thing I'm sure you'd want to do is get intimate with a whale. Talk about awkward."

"Nila—"

She grasped his hand and placed it underneath her shirt on her stomach. "Let's drop it. Here. You can feel the game in progress."

Noel reached over with his other hand and pulled at her shirt, but Nila stopped him. "Don't."

"Why not? I've already seen you."

"I wasn't as big then, and the room was dark."

Noel reached behind him and turned off the bedside lamp. Now the only light in the room was the flickering picture from the TV screen. Still too much light in her opinion.

She shook her head. "It's gross. I'm huge."

"You're supposed to be huge. You're pregnant." He

linked his fingers through hers and lifted the cotton material revealing her stomach.

Nila sighed morosely as she examined her body, the dark line caused by the hormones, the veins showing through the thin skin, and the stretch marks.

"Geez, you're right. Your stomach is massive. Sure you didn't swallow a watermelon?" He splayed his hands over the mound trying to capture any movement of the twins.

"Pretty sure."

Somebody kicked where his hand was, and he gave a startled laugh. "Doesn't that hurt?"

"Not exactly."

He cupped her body with his palms waiting. Nila stared at his hands on her, his long fingers, the wedding ring no longer there. He'd buried it with Lil.

He turned and scooted across the bed. Standing up, he walked out of the room. "Wait here. I'll be right back." When he returned, he had the cocoa butter cream she'd seen in her bag earlier. Smearing some on his hand, he knelt on the bed and smoothed some on her skin working it around the mound and down the sides.

"Does that feel good?"

Nila nodded.

His arm grazed her breast, and Nila bit her lip as a wave of lust crashed over her.

I don't care if I'm a whale. Make love to me.

He dipped his finger in the jar again. "If you'll sit up and turn around, I'll rub your back."

Desire and unease played tug of war in her head. "I...I thought this was supposed to be watching TV."

"You don't want your back rubbed? Seems like as much weight as you're carrying in the front, it'd make your back muscles tired."

Nila took a sustaining breath. She repositioned herself to give him access to her back. He pulled down her shorts and tucked the bottom of her shirt into her neckline.

I'm exposed. He can see most of my back, my fat belly....

He must have seen her stiffen. "Nila? You can trust me.

I'm your buddy," he murmured. "You know that. Right?"

She took a deep breath. *Right. Friends. Buddies.*

She closed her eyes and went into Yoga mode. *Relax. Relax.*

She felt the bed shift, and one of his legs cradled her hip and thigh.

Friends. Relax.

One of his hands held her shoulder while the other one firmly traced a path alongside her spine and up the other side.

Oh, it felt good.

With the palms of his hands, he arced out from her spine across her back. His movements were sure as if he'd done this to her a hundred times in this bed.

In this bed, his hands had roamed over her, confident and familiar. He'd pulled her to him fastening his mouth to hers.

Friends

With his knuckles, he twisted into her flesh stimulating the muscles and flattened his hands rubbing her skin in wide circles.

He'd kneaded her breast and held her tightly to him while he'd kissed her. She broken the contact then knelt over him guiding him inside of her.

Buddies.

His fingers curled over her hips, the cream creating a slick friction. She dropped her head and watched his large hands exploring the surface of her extended stomach before moving to her hips cupping them, pressing inward and testing the firmness of her body.

He'd filled her, and she'd quickly found a good rhythm. He'd reached forward and brought her mouth to his kissing her as he matched her motion.

Just friends.

Nila bit back a moan of pleasure, but whether it was from her memories or the magic his hands were presently working, she wasn't sure.

He's my buddy. I've got to stop this.

His breath tickled the skin at her neck. He was that close. His fingers now moved below her hips to her lower back. Much lower, below her panty line.

Oh, Dearing, please love me.

Nila turned her head over her shoulder, licking her lips, anticipating...

Noel's hands disappeared and the bed shook with his weight sliding backward. By the time Nila turned around, he was at the door.

"I'm going downstairs to grab a bottle or water. Sure you don't want me to bring you a snack?"

Disappointment and self-recrimination rose up inside Nila. She reached behind her and tugged her shirt from where he'd tucked it. "You don't have any yogurt, do you?"

"Cheeseburger flavored?" he teased.

"Ha ha," she said sarcastically. "Fix me the French toast then. And hurry up. As soon as the twins settle down, I'll be ready to...get some unconscious rest."

"What to drink? Milk? I've got almond and soy."

"Since when?" She eyed him suspiciously as he'd spent many a year making fun of her vegan eating habits.

"Since I've been staying at your house, I've developed a taste for that healthy crap."

"Almond." She anchored her body on her hands and scooted down under the covers fixing the pillow under her head.

He didn't respond, and when she looked at the door, he was gone. She watched the images play on the TV screen while the last few minutes ran through her mind. Had he been coming onto her?

No. Not Dearing.

They were friends. Buddies. It was just new territory. He'd said so himself. They just had to figure out how to forge it.

****

Noel paused outside of the bedroom door with the breakfast tray of food in his hands. He closed his eyes and blew out a breath.

This is Nila. I am not going to get turned on again. I'm not going to get a hard on. I'm going to think about being a dad and the twins in the bed with us.

He'd been an idiot to touch her, to move his hands over her skin, to rub that cream all over her while visions of them together taunted him. As big as she was, he'd have to be creative about making love to her. He'd thought of three different positions while he massaged her back.

Stupid jerk.

He'd been about to kiss her neck when he'd heard her sigh and she'd turned her head just so, her tongue darting across her lips. He knew if she noticed his erection, all pretense would be gone. All of his reassurances of trust and platonic agreement would be exposed as the lies he knew them to be. So he'd jumped off the bed and hidden on the other side of the door using the first excuse that jumped into his head.

I will not make love to her tonight. If I touch her, it will only be her stomach to feel the boys. That is it.

That is absolutely it.

One last deep breath and an appeal to his rod to behave, he pushed the door open.

Nila lay curled on her side, her head and arm resting on the pillow and her other hand resting on her swollen belly. The sweet maternal image shot to his heart making it ache.

She lifted her head, fatigue prevalent on her face.

"Uh-oh. Somebody's fading fast. I can tell."

She yawned and stretched. "Another two minutes and you would have been too late, Dearing."

He placed the tray on the middle of the bed careful not to spill anything as he sat down.

"Oh, my gosh, that smells good. If I open my mouth, can you just throw it in?"

He chuckled. "Yeah, sure. I'm game."

"How messy is it?"

"Not too much without the syrup."

"Okay. Try to have better aim than when we play basketball."

"Are you serious?"

She started to sit up. "I should have known," she said

with a twinkle in her eye. "I mention your sucky aim, and you back pedal on me."

"Lie back down," he challenged. "As big as your mouth is, I'll have no problem."

She settled back on the pillow with a sexy smile. "Twenty bucks says you'll miss."

"Open up, big mouth." He cut a piece of the French toast.

She did so, and he reached over with the fork and popped it in her mouth.

"Hey," she chewed. "Oh, that's good," she commented. "You're supposed to throw it in my mouth."

"That was a hook shot."

Her eyes glinted at him. "Well, you can forget the twenty bucks. You've always cheated at basketball because you know that's the only way you can beat me."

"One more chance," he countered.

She finished chewing and swallowing then opened her mouth.

Noel separated a morsel of the delicacy and balanced it on the tines of the fork. He judged his aim and flicked the fork causing the food to fly far north of its target.

"Loser." She sat up and picked up the plate. "That's catapulting, and I ought to make you pay me twenty more bucks for wasting food."

She settled back on the pillow and placed the plate on her stomach. Gesturing for him to give her the fork, she speared another piece of toast when he surrendered it. She brought it to her mouth and closed her eyes in pleasure when her lips closed over the utensil. "Thank God you can cook better than you can play."

Noel tore his attention away from her lips and snagged his water bottle off the tray. "Enough with the insults, or I'll bring you veal next time."

Digging into the food, she shook her head. "Please don't. I'll probably love it, but I wouldn't be able to sleep at night."

She reached for the glass on the tray and took a long

drink. Holding it next to her, she made eye contact with him briefly before gazing across the room. "I went into the nursery."

"Did you do okay?"

"Yeah. Not as bad as I thought it would be. It's like I felt her in there. I didn't expect it."

He had that sensation of Lil's presence throughout the house at different times since her death. Was it wishful thinking or something more? He'd been meaning to ask Mike about it.

Motion from the plate snagged his attention.

What? Holy cow, the kids were knocking Nila's plate around on her stomach. He studied her face. She hadn't even noticed it. He eyed the dish as it shifted and tilted.

Man, that was weird. He stopped himself from grabbing the plate, whipping up her shirt again, and looking for evidence of their activity.

But, no. He didn't want to distract her from the subject at hand. Nila had given him the opening he'd been looking for. "So, do you still want to move the nursery to your house?"

Leaving half the food on the plate, she placed it back on the tray. "I don't know. Do we have to decide tonight?"

"Nila, I hate to push the issue, but when you have these kids, we're going to have to live where all the baby stuff is."

"I bought car seats last week, and they're already in my car. Plus I've set up a playpen in my office at the store, so it's not like I haven't done anything."

Noel wanted to roll his eyes. "A playpen at the store?"

"Yeah. That's all they'll need at first."

His temper rose a bit, but he kept it in check. *Fine.* She didn't want to deal with it? He would. She wouldn't be able to drive home from the hospital. He'd just bring her here.

Finishing off the milk, she wiped her mouth with the napkin he'd folded next to the plate. "Thanks."

She laid her head back and sighed. Sitting up, she pushed the covers away and allowed her feet to slide to the floor.

"Where are you going?"

"Bathroom." She loped around the bed.

He still couldn't believe she'd chosen the side nearest the wall. Lil had always been so stubborn about where she liked to sleep. He figured Nila would be the same way.

Nila continued her commentary as she walked to the door and into the hallway. "I'm going to brush my teeth. Again. I'm going to pee. Again. Then I'm going back to bed. Again. This time to rest unconsciously."

I guess it really was the end of the discussion.

No problem.

Noel had a plan. He'd stick with it. When the babies arrived, he'd bring them home from the hospital.

His home.

In a few minutes, she was back in the bed, and he hit the power button on the TV. He listened to her breathe in the darkness and felt himself get stiff.

"This is weird," she announced. He shifted to his side to face her but kept his distance. "Do you think it is?"

"Different, yes. Not weird."

"Why are we sleeping together?"

"Selfish reasons," Noel admitted. "I want to be close to my boys, and I thought it might be hard on you being back in the house."

"*Your* boys?"

"*Our* boys."

She grunted and sat up.

"What's wrong?"

"I'm going to get another pillow to put between my knees."

Noel reached under his head and pulled one of his pillows out. He stuffed it under the covers and pushed it to her.

"You don't have to give up your pillow."

"That's okay." He smiled in the darkness as she maneuvered it pulling the covers askew. "I'll fold this one in half. I don't mind."

Nope. I don't mind at all.

Hours later he awoke when she got up to go to the bathroom, and another time when she returned to the bed from a second trip and scooted close to him. The sky had lightened outside the window when her stomach made contact with his. Tentatively he moved his fingers forward and encountered her warm tight flesh. Her shirt must have ridden up, and he splayed his hand across the mound.

Nila sighed at the contact. Was she still awake? Noel peered at her face visible in the dim predawn light. Her eyes were closed, her face relaxed.

Her skin bumped under his hand, and he smiled at the contact.

Hi there, son.

He gazed at Nila.

Thank you for making me a dad.

He felt a swift kick under his hand, and Nila grunted softly. She turned and faced the other way, pressing her back to his chest and positioning her butt at his crotch.

Uh-oh.

He moved a few inches away, and she followed. His body responded immediately at the contact.

Was she awake?

"Nila," he murmured.

No response.

He breathed deeply and thought of being a dad, changing diapers, auditing people…. Her leg shifted slightly, and her foot rubbed against him before tucking it under his calf.

Not helping.

He was fully erect now. Experimentally, he moved against her.

Stop. I should…. He touched her hip then ran his hand along her skin to her stomach.

She's pregnant. We don't need to….

Nila shifted again, pushing back against him. How could he not do this?

Because it's wrong. I have to stop. God, help me, I'm going to make love to her….

****

Nila dreamed she sat on a beach with a basket full of watermelons in her lap. When she shifted, the basket stayed put. Still, she wasn't about to let a heavy basket keep her out of the water. Hefting the load with her, she stood and walked toward the clear water, sparkling in the bright sun. She waded into the waves, and the sand dropped off so that the water was lapping at her thighs.

Oh, my. That felt nice.

Bending over, she dropped her hands in the warm ocean and sat down shimmying her butt against the hard-packed sand. She'd hoped the basket would be lighter in the water, but it didn't seem to make a difference. Nevertheless, the water was wonderful. Its motion caressed her body, and she sighed in pleasure.

Reaching down, she untied her top and flung it behind her.

What the heck was she sitting on? A rock? She shifted and so did the rock.

Now, *that* was interesting.

Nila began to reach behind her to investigate what exactly was taking liberties with her bottom, but when she shifted...oops. Some pent-up gas escaped, and the bubbles reached the surface.

Oh, great. I have this great tropical dream, and this watermelon basket makes me bubble in the water.

A rumble erupted from behind her. Not her this time. And not any bodily function. It was more like...a guy laughing.

A guy like Noel.

Nila awoke with a start. She was flush against Noel who lay on his back chuckling.

What the...?

She raised up and blinked. "Dearing?"

"Yeah?" A fresh burst of laughter.

"What's wrong with you? What's so funny?"

"Nothing. I'm sorry." He wasn't chuckling any more, but she could still hear amusement in his voice.

Then it hit her. She closed her eyes in embarrassment. "Oh, geez. I farted, didn't I? I'm sorry. It's the pregnancy."

"No. It's..." Another wave of laughter erupted. "It's okay. Just unexpected, but very timely."

"A timely fart? Well, that's a new one. I'm so glad my flatulence amuses you. Can you shut up so I can go back to sleep for another half hour?"

Chapter Ten

"You're about three centimeters dilated. The babies are a good size, and you're close enough to your date that we could go ahead and send you over to the hospital later today," Dr. Garber informed her as he removed his examination gloves and threw them away. "A cesarean section is really the way to go. I'm going to have to cut you open anyway. It will be easier on the twins."

Nila sat up on her elbows. "Today? Are you serious?"

Dr. Garber nodded as he helped her sit up all the way. "I can have the nurse call and check on bed availability. If they have a five o'clock opening, I'll meet you over there, and I can be home in time for dinner."

"Wow."

Dr. Garber smiled at her. "I'll be relieved to get those ovaries out. We're on borrowed time, you know."

"Yes. Let me call Noel."

"All right." He stepped to the door. "I'll come back in after a few minutes and give you a chance to get dressed and call him. You can let me know what you all decide."

Nila quickly shed the paper gown and put on her clothes before reaching for her cell phone. Noel picked up on the first ring.

"Hey. Want to be a Dad by dinner time?"

"Are you in labor?"

"Not yet, but I've started to dilate. Dr. Garber says he can schedule a caesarian for later today."

"Well, if you're ready, then let's do it."

"Okay."

"Listen. My mom and dad are chomping at the bit to be here. I know we haven't really talked about it, but I think they could be a big help when you get out of the hospital."

Noel's parents had been overjoyed when Lil and Noel had told them they were going to be grandparents. They hadn't batted an eye with the unusual circumstances of the pregnancy. In fact, she and Noel's mother had had a conversation after the funeral.

The older woman had been washing dishes in the kitchen when Nila had come in looking for some respite from all of the mourners.

"Oh, hi, Nila. I was just washing up a few dishes." She smiled over her shoulder, her eyes kind.

"You don't have to do that, Madelaine."

"Of course I don't. But I want to." She picked up a dish towel and dried her hands as she turned to face Nila. "You're starting to show."

Nila took a deep breath and smoothed her hand over her stomach. "Yes."

"I can't tell you how much what you're doing means to Bernie and me." She shook her head. "To think out of so much sadness, a miracle happened. Two miracles."

Nila nodded.

"I'm so sorry that Lil didn't get to see the children born."

"Me too."

"I want you to know that Bernie and I will do what we can to help you. We're so grateful to you for giving us these grandchildren."

"Please. I know you are, but I can't…" Nila couldn't finish her sentence. She shook her head.

"Oh, dear." Madelaine hurried over to her and grasped her hands peering into her face. "I'm sorry. I didn't mean to make it worse. I just wanted you to know you are part of our family too, even if you weren't carrying my grandbabies. But since you are, well, you've got us as family."

Her words had meant so much, especially after Nila's dark thoughts at Lil's graveside.

Nila was thankful for such caring people. Of course, she wanted them to be here for the births. "Call them and tell them to hit the road. If they leave by noon, they ought to be here in time."

****

Surreal.

The word pretty much summed up the whole situation.

She'd gone to work and tied up a few loose ends with Ricky and gone home thinking she'd shower before going on to the hospital. Under the warm spray, she soaped up her stomach moving her hands around the firm flesh.

"Well, guys, ready to meet me?"

Her voice echoed off the tiled walls.

The bar of soap slipped out of her hand and hit the enamel tub. Nila eyed it critically. It was near impossible to retrieve anything from ground level these days. She left the bar near its resting place next to the drain and washed her hair. When she finished showering, she dressed in matching sweats and blow dried her hair.

Who knew when she'd have time to blow dry her hair or even take a shower after they arrived?

She shook her head in amusement. After they arrived. As if company was coming.

When she switched off the dryer, a light tap sounded on the door.

Noel.

He'd found her. Since the night he'd taken her to spend the night with him, they'd been house swapping, though they hadn't shared a bed again. Nila figured it was because she'd farted on him. Lil had always been so proper about things like that. She'd probably never passed gas in the bed with Noel.

He'd never mentioned her indiscretion though. The next night before she'd closed the store, he'd called and asked where she was going home.

"Mine, I guess."

"I'll come over then."

"Is this how it's going to be?"

"Yeah, until I can talk you into staying with me again."

"Noel." Nila sighed in frustration. "What is this about?"

"You're getting close to your due date. I think we need to stay close for now."

"For now?"

"Jim's has a special on their hotdogs. Two dogs with the works and a bag of chips for four bucks."

Nila held the phone away from her ear and glared at it. "Stop trying to distract me with food."

"I'll make a batch of brownies with homemade whipped cream."

A few days here. A few days there. Daisy was getting used to going back and forth in her carrier.

He looked at her with a matter-of-fact expression on his face. "What time are they expecting us?"

The hospital, he meant.

"About half an hour from now. I've already done all the pre-op paperwork."

We're going to have a baby. Correction: two babies.

Nila searched Noel's face for any sign of anxiety or excitement. Nothing.

"Anything you want to do before we go?"

Ugh, this was weird. "Change my mind?"

Noel grinned and patted her belly. "Too late for that, little mama."

Nila wrinkled her nose. "There's nothing little about me."

Noel removed his hand and rested it on the counter edge. He watched her for a moment. "Lil would have been so happy to have seen the boys. Just to hold them one time."

"One time wouldn't have been enough. Babies are like that, you know. All cute so you can't help but love them and you can't give them up."

"We won't have to. They're ours." His gaze softened, and his hand grasped hers.

"You're getting all pansy on me, Dearing. Stop it." Nila stepped forward and pushed him with her massive stomach, though she didn't pull away from his hand-holding. It felt good to connect with him, but when he didn't step away, her guts fluttered. She was pretty sure it wasn't the boys moving either.

"Move."

He didn't.

"They are ours," he stated.

She watched the front of his shirt. His stomach was warm against hers. "This was Lil's idea."

"Yes. The idea was her gift to us. But Benjamin and Daniel are ours. Yours and mine."

Move. Move. Please move.

Nila glanced up at his face and the warmth she saw there caught her attention. His gaze was steady on hers. Not challenging—seeking...but seeking what? Acceptance?

He lifted his hand still holding hers. Touching his chest, then hers, he spoke. "Daddy. Mommy."

"If you'll move, we can go to the hospital and start the mommy-daddy thing. Okay?"

This impending parenthood was making Noel all sappy, and if he didn't stop, he was going to get her all sappy too.

She was going to be a mommy today.

She pulled her hand out of his and shoved him back. "Get out of the way. If you want to stay here and get all sentimental, fine. But I'm leaving, *Daddy*."

****

"What's taking so long? Geez. The reason to be here is so we could do it on a schedule," Nila griped as she told her brain to move her foot then watched her foot do nothing. Here she lay helpless in the hospital bed because of the spinal, and Doctor Garber was late.

"He's delivering a baby next door," Noel supplied.

"Well, I was here first, and mine was scheduled."

Noel didn't even look away from the TV as he flipped through the channels for at least the fiftieth time. "The nurse said the other woman's been here since three this morning."

"Well, so what? He said he'd have time to do this now."

He didn't reply, just went through another rotation. If Nila could have moved her leg, she would have kicked him in the face. It was his fault she was even here. "How about some comfort here, Dearing, you jerk."

Noel rested the remote on his knee and turned his face to her, arching his eyebrow and giving her *the* look.

"Don't give me that look."

"What do you want me to do, Nila? I'm waiting, too. I'm just as anxious as you are to get on with this."

"Yeah? Well, a little sympathy wouldn't kill you, would it? I'm the one about to get my stomach cut open." Her voice caught at *stomach*, and she cleared her throat hoping to cover it. "I can't even move here. What if there's a fire or something? What am I...?" Nila's voice trailed off as Noel dropped the remote and vaulted from the chair.

He stalked over to her and sat on the edge of the bed, his gaze steady and sure as he kept eye contact. "I won't leave you. I won't. If there's a fire, I'll unlock the brakes and push the bed out."

"Out the window? We're on the fourth floor."

"I'm sure the elevator still works even in a fire."

"Right." Sarcasm filled her tone. "Like I get top priority. You know they're going to get the sickest people out first."

Noel shook his head and sighed.

"Go ahead and tell me I'm being an idiot about this. You hate being here. You didn't ask for any of this. You didn't even want to..." Noel turned toward her as he stood. Leaning down he, scooped her up. "Noel! What the hell are you doing?" She grabbed his shoulders. "You're going to break your back!"

"If there's a fire, I'll carry you out. Okay?"

"You couldn't carry..." Nila stopped as his lips thinned in determination. He'd carry her down the stairs just to show her he could and kill them both. "Okay. Fine. Put me down before you really do hurt yourself."

"You're not as heavy as you think you are."

"I'm up to one fifty-five."

"Yeah. And all the extra weight is right where the twins are. From the back, I can't even tell you're pregnant."

Had he been looking at her from the back? "Put me down."

"Tell me I can do it."

The sheet fell from her legs, and her gown had bunched up to her stomach. *Eeep.* Though she couldn't feel a draft against her bare skin, she knew she was exposed. "I'm not wearing any panties."

He blinked but kept his gaze on her face. "I'm aware of that. Tell me."

"Fine. You're a big strong ass who can carry me down three flights of stairs."

The door opened, and Noel's mom walked in followed by his dad. In a quick movement, Noel set her down on the bed and picked up the sheet to cover her. Nila wondered if Madelaine's shocked expression was at Nila's bare butt or that Noel was holding her in his arms. In a second, she'd recovered and smiled at them serenely.

"Hello. I was afraid we weren't going to make it in time," Madelaine commented as she set her purse on the chair and walked around the bed to hug her son. To Nila's surprise, the older woman hugged her as well and kissed the top of her head. "How are you feeling?"

Nila glanced at Noel before answering. "Impatient." She straightened the sheet and studied his dad, whose eyebrows had nearly elevated to his hairline.

Dr. Garber strode into the room dressed in scrubs. A nurse accompanied him. "Sorry to keep you waiting. Ready to get this show on the road?"

A lump formed in Nila's throat. Terror and excitement wrestled for dibs in her chest.

"Any questions before we go to the delivery room?"

Nila shook her head, unable to form a word.

"Can you give her something to calm her down? She's a little anxious," Noel asked.

"I don't need anything," she snapped.

Noel gave her another look before turning his attention to the doctor.

Dr. Garber nodded. "We most certainly can give you something to relax you a bit."

"I really don't need anything."

"Just take it. You're in a foul mood. This is supposed to be a happy time."

Nila glared at Noel. Yeah, happy for him. He wasn't numb from the chest down. He wasn't about to have his guts taken out along with two babies.

"Why don't you let me order you something?" This from Doctor Garber as he watched the monitor which showed Nila's vital signs and the fetal heartbeats. "Your blood pressure is a little elevated. The medicine will help you relax."

"I don't need it."

He nodded then turned to them. "Okay. If you change your mind, let one of us know. I'm going to go ahead and approve it just in case. See you in a few minutes." He exited with the same determined stride with which he'd entered. The nurse unplugged the cord from the monitor and looped it. She began to pull up the rails, and two orderlies came into the room to assist. In seconds, they were pushing the bed toward the door.

Nila's eyes sought Noel's. He wasn't going to stay here, was he?

"Dearing," she called.

No answer. She was in the hallway now.

"Noel!"

"What?"

"You're coming, aren't you?"

"I'm right behind you. Mom's with me too. We've got a parade going down the hall."

In the delivery room a few minutes later, Nila glanced up at Noel.

Was he as freaked out about this as she was? They were about to be parents.

The anesthesiologist who she'd met earlier attached monitors to her body. An attending nurse began strapping down her arms.

"Are you serious? Why are you tying down my arms?"

"To keep them immobile. It's okay. Everyone has their arms restrained." She fixed a partition below Nila's neck.

"What's this for?"

"I'm preparing you for the procedure."

"If you put that there, I won't be able to see."

"Right."

"Well, I want to be able to see my kids being born. Move that thing."

"The second Dr. Garber pulls them out, we'll let you see them. I promise."

Nila huffed.

"I'm sure it's standard, Nila."

"Nothing is standard for me. I've never done this before."

A man walked in the room in scrubs, mask, and a plastic visor. When he looked at Nila, she realized it was Dr. Garber. He stood aside while the anesthesiologist positioned himself at her feet. "Feel that?" he asked.

What had he done? "No."

"How about that?"

"No."

"How about this? He'd moved to the side of the bed at her middle. "Any pain or sensation."

"What are you doing? Poking me?"

"Do you feel it?"

"No."

"We're in good shape then." He nodded to Dr. Garber who picked up something from a nearby tray, then his arms were hidden behind the divider.

Nila watched his visor and the reflection there of his hands.

Oh, my gosh. He's doing it. He's cutting my skin.

She looked at Noel to see if he was watching. He was. She turned to watch Dr. Garber, but the nurse adjusted the paper wall below her neck, and she couldn't see anything now except Noel and the ceiling.

Pressure or…something moved against her. The gurney rocked a bit. What the heck were they doing down there? *Geez.* No wonder they needed her strapped to the table. If she wasn't tied down, she'd probably roll right onto the floor.

I'm going to be a mother.

Nila closed her eyes.

Lil, I wish you could be here, you jerk. You talked me into this, and now you're not even here to meet these babies.

She opened her eyes and looked at Noel. His expression was tense, waiting as he returned her gaze.

"What's happening?"

"I can't tell," Noel answered. "Dr. Garber's in the way."

A snippet of their conversation reached her ears.

"Did Dr. Garber just say he'd seen Serena Garner in concert?" she asked Noel.

He grinned down at her. "I think it's his daughter who's a fan."

"Let's hope so."

A piercing sound from one of the monitors filled the room. "What's that?"

"I don't know. It's going to be okay though."

"Is it too late for that relaxing drug? Hey!"

She heard Dr. Garber chuckle. "If you still think you need it in five minutes, we'll give it to you, Nila."

Five minutes?

"Don't worry," a nurse with a surgical mask appeared over the partition. "You're doing okay. We're almost there."

More movement from the people working on her. *Geez.* She had no idea surgery had so much motion to it.

Noel flinched, a sound of shock escaping his mouth.

"What?"

"Umm." He shook his head. "A geyser. Amniotic fluid, I think."

That meant….

"Here's the first one," Doctor Garber announced.

Noel's hand touched her shoulder, squeezed it. "Nila, he's…oh…he's beautiful."

"And there you are," the doctor continued. "The second."

Nila watched Noel's face as he witnessed the first seconds of the babies in the outside world. His eyes teared up, and he crouched down to her smiling. "You did it. You did it." He kissed her cheek, and a tear dropped on her face.

A baby's wail filled the room.

That's my baby crying.

Joy bubbled in her throat, and she laughed.

"Does anybody want to hold a baby?" a woman's voice came from somewhere in the room.

"Noel?" his mother asked.

He looked back at her. "I've never held a baby, Mom. You better do it. And bring him over here so Nila can see him."

Nila laughed again. "You better get used to holding a baby. We've got two n—"

Madelaine walked into her line of vision holding a tiny baby all bundled up so that only his face showed. His eyes were squinched shut, but his skin was pink and smooth. In a second, his lids lifted and he blinked several times.

Nila attempted to move her arms so she could hold him. She grunted and lifted her head. "I want to…." She tried to free her arm.

"Mom?" Noel reached for the baby, but a nurse approached with the other one.

"Here you go, Daddy," she said and handed the bundle to him. This baby was crying, his mouth open with his wails.

Noel gingerly set him on Nila's shoulder and chest and held him there, stroking him. In a moment, the infant quieted. He studied Nila, and his lower lip stuck out then quivered.

"Hi, sweetheart," she crooned.

Madelaine placed the baby she held on the other side of Nila. She looked from one to the either. "Hey, Dearing?"

"Yeah?" He held the baby with one hand and wiped his eyes with the other.

"We make pretty babies, don't we?"

"We certainly do."

"Which one is Benjamin, do you think?"

"This one. The cry baby." Noel rubbed his little body, and he closed his eyes. Then the other baby began to cry.

Nila laughed. "Maybe he wants to be Benjamin."

Noel leaned over. "Hey, little fella. We were thinking Daniel for you. You like that name? Daniel?"

He shivered and nuzzled his head.

"That looked like a nod to me, my Daniel boy," Noel

whispered. He closed the distance between him and his son and kissed his head. Then he kissed Benjamin's.

Nila's heart swelled.

A nurse spoke. "Okay. We need to take them for a few minutes, and we'll bring them to you in recovery. All right?"

"Okay." Nila raised her voice. "Dr. Garber. Hey, Dr. Garber!"

"Yes, Nila? Did you want that medicine to relax you now?"

"No. I want you to tell me those are the best looking kids you ever pulled out of a woman's uterus."

Chuckles filled the room.

****

Noel and his dad sat in the family lounge waiting for Nila to get out of recovery. They had gone to the nursery window hoping to view the boys, but the curtain was closed.

"How's it feel to be a father?" Bernard asked.

Noel grinned at the older man. "Pretty damn good. Can't wait to see the little guys again. Get to know them."

The older man nodded. "What's going to happen with you and Nila? That was an interesting scene your mom and I walked in on. She's giving you custody, right?"

The exhilaration he'd been high on for the last hour faded a bit. He shrugged his shoulders.

"You haven't worked it out?"

"We've sort of worked it out."

"Sort of?" His dad sounded skeptical. "I thought she was the surrogate for you and Lil."

"It's complicated, Dad."

"How complicated? You did make a legal agreement about the kids, didn't you? The legalities of it help make it less complicated."

Noel sighed. "She and I haven't...We didn't pursue it."

Bernard paused before he answered. "Oh. So she's keeping the kids?"

"No. We both are."

"Joint custody?"

"We both...will have...full custody."

His dad's eyebrows rose in surprise. "Are you two living together?"

"We're sort of living together."

"Sort of? Sort of? What are you—sixteen years old? I know you've always been buddies with her, but, come on, Noel, Lil's only been gone five months. And they were sist—"

Noel stood up. "Dad, you're not telling me anything I don't already know or haven't thought about a thousand times."

Madelaine walked in the room at that moment. She looked from her husband to her son. "Is everything okay?"

"Noel just told me he's shacking up with Nila."

"Dad!"

"Bernie, really!"

"Dad, I don't need your permission or your blessing in this. Nila and I both want the kids, and this is the best we can work out. And if you don't like it, well...get over it."

Chapter Eleven

Nila lay on her side and, with the help of a nurse, held Benjamin to her breast. He nuzzled her skin, opened his eyes briefly, then settled back into sleep.

Nila gazed into the perfect little face. "How come he doesn't want to eat?"

The woman sat on a chair next to the bed and held the baby to his mom. "He's tired. He had a big day today. Don't worry about it. When he's hungry, he'll eat."

Nila blew out her frustration. She still couldn't move, and it had been over an hour since the twins had been born. Katie, the nurse, had propped her on her side with about fourteen pillows to her back.

"Maybe I won't be able to nurse."

The other woman patted Benjamin's body, then tickled his foot. "The important thing is you two are together right now. Contact is good for mama and baby."

"What about my other baby. He needs contact, too. Can't I have both with me?"

"Oh, number one will be along, but I can't hold both of them to you. There isn't room, my dear."

Nila glared at the woman before she looked at the little sleepyhead who had no interest in her nipple whatsoever. How humiliating. And on top of that, Nurse Ratched refused to call her babies by their names.

I swear if she calls them number one and number two again, I'm going to ask her to leave.

A short time later, Nila sat on the hospital bed gazing at Benjamin and Daniel who lay on the bed in front of her. They wore matching long-sleeved shirts with the hospital logo emblazoned across the front and little knit hats Madelaine had made for them and bracelets identifying them by name.

They were perfect. Absolutely adorable.

Noel came in the room after walking his parents down to the parking lot. He sat on the foot of the bed, his attention on his sons.

Nila glanced at his love struck expression and recognized it. "Can you believe how beautiful they are?"

"No, I can't. I can't believe they're ours."

Daniel, who wore the green cap, began to squirm. Noel stood and reached down to pick him up. He held him close to his chest and walked back and forth in the room.

When Daniel continued to work up to a cry, Noel leaned over Nila and surrendered the baby. She hugged him to her and watched him shake his little head in discontent.

Uh-oh. Maybe he wanted to nurse. She glanced to Noel. He'd never seen her breasts before. It was stupid to be embarrassed, but….

Noel stepped back. "I'm going to grab a bite to eat. I'll be back in a little while. Want me to bring you anything?"

"If you're going to Mom and Pop's, I'd love a cheeseburger."

"I can do that. See you in about half an hour?"

Relief washed over her. She nodded and heard his footsteps approach the door. Looking down at Daniel, she smiled at him.

"You're not hungry, are you?" she whispered as she pulled aside the nursing gown and placed his face at her breast. He'd nursed once already for a few minutes. She'd been ecstatic he was so quick to latch on, unlike his brother. In a short while, he'd fallen asleep, and Benjamin had started squirming. Nila had called the nurse for help.

How was she going to care for two babies?

A few minutes later, the lactation expert named Susan stood over Nila, who lay reclined on the bed naked from the waist up.

No potential for embarrassment here.

Daniel and Benjamin lay on either side of Nila while Susan instructed her how to nurse both infants at once. The woman placed a small pillow on Nila's stomach.

"Now, you've got to protect your incision, so when you

can, keep this pillow here." Then she grabbed Benjamin and slid him over Nila's ribcage then placed Nila's arm over him. "Hold him in place like this." Nila was about to yell at her about manhandling the newborn, when the woman pinched Nila's nipple until it beaded with moisture then rubbed it against Ben's lips.

Nila tried to hide her mortification at this woman playing with her boob.

"Wake up, little lazy bones," Susan scolded to the baby. She tutted. "Boys are so lazy."

She walked around the bed. "Anyway, you've got him over there." She maneuvered Daniel into the exact position at the other breast and held Nila's flesh to encourage the baby to nurse.

Is this what it had come to? A strange woman fondling her breasts while Noel went out for cheeseburgers.

Oh, please don't let him come back until this is over with.

Susan propped Daniel in place with a pillow, then walked around the bed, and repositioned Benjamin who had slipped and was crying about it.

"You need a doughnut," she declared.

"A doughnut?"

"Yeah. It's a pillow shaped like a big C that fits around your waist. It makes nursing a snap."

"If it's shaped like a C, why do they call it a doughnut?"

Susan shrugged. "Tell your husband you need one. He can get one at the gift shop downstairs. I made them start stocking them because I'm always sending dads out to get one."

Nila let the husband comment slip by. No use in going into the complicated story as to why the dad was not her husband.

"I imagine the gift shop is closed this late."

"Oh, yes. But tell him to get one first thing in the morning and bring it up, so I can show you how handy it is."

Nila pursed her lips and glanced at Susan, who was playing with her boob again trying to encourage Benjamin to eat. The woman had just squirted her nipple with liquid in a little bottle.

"It's sugar water. Sometimes the sweetness clues them in that this is the food source. Come on, little man."

"So, do you get a commission on those doughnut pillows?"

Susan winked. "I should, as many people as I send down there. No. I just got tired of telling people it's a good thing to have, then the daddy would go all over town and couldn't find one. They'd bring back body pillows, throw pillows, pillow pets, pillow beds. So one day I told the gift shop manager if she'd order these doughnut pillows, I could guarantee most of the mothers nursing babies would be interested in having one."

The nurse picked up Benjamin who was wailing at being woken up and having his face pushed onto Nila's breast. She jiggled him around a little bit then set him on the bed and wrapped him tightly in the blanket. "This is swaddling him. You know like baby Jesus and the swaddling clothes? Wrap them up tight. It makes them feel secure."

Nila watched her actions critically. "You're too rough with him. I don't like that."

"Pshaw. Babies are tough." She tucked him in the crook of her arm and held him up. "See? Does he look like I've hurt him? He's content. That's what the swaddling will do. Why don't you roll on your side if you can and let that little one lay next to you and nurse. He's a good eater."

Nila started to move, but it hurt. Susan noticed her discomfort and helped her to move, counseling her the whole time about how to move to lessen the pain and strategies to hold the babies or nurse without damage to her incision.

In a moment, the nurse placed Benjamin next to Nila and carried Daniel to the mobile cradle.

With stricken eyes, Nila appealed to Susan. "Why won't he eat?"

"He isn't hungry yet. He's only a few hours old. Don't worry. You worry about it, it'll prevent your milk from coming down, and he sure won't want to eat then. Just relax and enjoy him being close to you. See how happy he is all snug like a bug in a rug and next to his mama? He's fine."

Susan sprayed sugar water on Benjamin's mouth. He moved his lips a little, then his tiny pink tongue appeared.

"That's it," the woman commented. She pulled Nila's breast until the nipple touched Benjamin's mouth, and *bingo*, he latched on and sucked.

"He did it!"

"Yeah. Stubborn little thing. You may have to work with him a bit more. Some babies take to the breast right away, and some don't. Do talk to your husband about that doughnut, okay? Especially with twins, you really need it."

Husband. Sure.

Noel kept his word, and his knock sounded on the door in exactly thirty minutes with a cheeseburger in a bag for her. The charcoal grilled beef and onion aroma wafted in with him. Nila's mouth watered. She held out her hands.

"Gimme. I need real food."

"Where are Benjamin and Daniel?" Noel asked as he looked around the room.

"They took them back to the nursery. Apparently, all of us need to rest." Nila rolled her eyes. "As if anybody could rest in this place."

Noel sat on the edge of the bed and handed her the bag which she dove into with relish, pulling out the wrapped hamburger. She peeled back the wrapper and took a bite.

She groaned. "Oh, my gosh, I forgot how good these things are."

Noel snickered as he watched her. "I cannot believe how many times I've heard how much you hate for animals to be butchered just so we can satisfy our carnal appetites, then there you sit eating that cow meat as if it's the best thing you've ever eaten."

"I know. I'm sure I'm going to rot in vegan hell for all the animals that have died for my enjoyment since I got pregnant. I hate myself for how weak I am, but it just tastes so good." She ate voraciously, as if she hadn't had a meal in a week.

She nodded her thanks when he opened a bottle of water and offered it to her.

"Don't worry about it," Noel replied. "Your body is probably craving it because you're burning so many calories. You can't sustain two little babies on tofu."

Nila gave a self-deprecatory shrug. She didn't feel like lecturing him about protein from legumes compared to protein from animals. After all, she was the one who had caved.

"You want me to stay with you tonight?"

Nila glanced at the clock on the wall. It was past ten. "You don't have to."

"I know I don't have to. Do you want me to?"

"Do you want to?"

His mouth curled up in a guilty grin. "Yeah."

Warmth spread over her. He was feeling the same gooey excitement she was over those sweet babies in the nursery. She pressed the call button on the bed rail. "I'll see if they can bring a cot in here for you to sleep on."

"No need. The chair folds out into a bed."

"You need to bring anything from home?"

His grin spread over his whole face. He stood and walked over to the tiny closet across the room. Opening the door, he gestured to his red gym bag. "I packed my bag and put it in the car a week ago."

"Clever." She balled up the burger wrapper and stuffed it in the larger bag. Pressing the pillow to her middle, she slid her feet to the floor. "I want to walk to the bathroom. Want to spot me?"

A prick of intense sensation shot through her middle, and she froze.

Noel was at her side in an instant. "Let me get the nurse and get a bedpan." He peered into her face.

"No. I want to get up." She took a couple of deep breaths. Dots appeared before her eyes as pain seared through her gut.

He reached for the nurse call button, and she grasped his hand. "Don't. I'm okay. It's expected because of the incision. They told me…it would hurt when I got up. Help me. I can do it if you help me. Please?" She leaned against his arm and pulled herself up while holding the pillow against her stomach.

She focused on the corded muscles of his arm revealed by the short-sleeved, golf shirt and the lighter colored skin of her hands holding onto him.

Then she was on her feet, and the pain eased.

She exhaled a breath. "It's better. All right. I can do this." She glanced up at Noel. "Can't I do this, Dearing?"

"You can do this. No problem."

He'd always been so good to talk her up when they were working out or running. She wanted to give him a victory body bump or, at least, give him a high five. But as bad as her stomach was hurting, she was afraid to do much more than squeeze his arm affectionately. "That's what I'm talking about, Dearing. Let's go."

****

Oh, Jesus. Oh, Jesus, help me please.

Noel prayed earnestly, as Nila sat on the hospital bed a few days later and bared her breast to Benjamin. At least, he thought it was Benjamin. Mom had knitted different colors for the boys to help tell them apart. Ben's was blue, but he'd lost it. She cooed to the baby as she held him close to her trying to encourage him to eat.

The image was the epitome of motherhood, and Noel was so turned on he couldn't even think straight.

What kind of sick-o was he? Nila was trying to nurse their child, his own son. And all he could think of was how hot she looked.

He'd spent every night on the fold-out chair with a hospital-issued pillow and blanket next to Nila's bed. The boys had spent most of the night before in the room with them. Noel had even taken turns with one of the babies tucked into his side, while Nila held the other one. He'd nodded off a few times but had been too anxious to fall into a deep sleep. In the early morning light, her soft words woke him up. When he'd raised his head, he'd seen her cuddling the baby to her. Instead of opening the front slit made for that purpose, she'd shrugged out of it and it had fallen to the pillow she'd propped Benjamin on. She'd glanced over at Noel then, and her eyes widened.

"Want me to leave?" he asked.

Her eyes dropped to the baby as she settled him against her. "I guess it's okay. After the lactation consultant felt me up in every way imaginable, I'm not as modest as I used to be."

"That's what they're for. Right?"

"I thought they were for selling beer." Her voice changed to a singsong voice as she smiled at little Ben. "Is dat what we thought dey were for? Hmm? No? You knew what dey were for, you sweet thing?"

After Nila had nursed the babies, a woman in scrubs placed both boys in a crib and rolled them back to the nursery, and Doctor Garber had come in to check her incision. While he was there, Noel had brought up a question which had been on his mind.

"Are you going to circumcise the boys?"

Nila turned to him. "We're not having them circumcised."

Noel's ire raised. "*We* haven't talked about it, but I think we should."

Dr. Garber lowered Nila's gown and covered her with the sheet. "You all should talk about it, because if you're going to do it, we need to go ahead and do it today."

"We're not doing it. It's a primitive practice, and I'm not subjecting our sons to it."

The doctor shot Noel a look which he'd seen before. *Be patient* was his message. Easy for the doctor to say. The kids weren't his. "I'll send the pediatrician in to talk to you about it. You can let her know if it's what you want to do," he said before leaving.

As the door closed behind him, Nila crossed her arms over her chest. "No way, Dearing. I'm not agreeing to this. It's a terrible thing to do to a baby."

"I'm circumcised. Don't you think it'd be good for them

to have…"—*Ugh. This wasn't easy*—"to look like their dad?"

"Not necessarily, especially when it means a doctor will cut off the ends of their penises. How can you agree to that?"

Noel stood up. He sat on the foot of her bed. "Nila." He huffed. "I wasn't circumcised as a baby. I wasn't circumcised until I was six years old. I kept having infections. Very painful infections. The doctor thought circumcision would help, and it did. I never had any problems after that. But I was six, and I still remember it."

Nila blinked rapidly. She shook her head briefly.

"It's possible the kids won't have the same problem I did. But it's possible they will. Believe me. It's much better to do it now when they won't remember it, then to wait until they will. I don't want that for them. Please, honey."

She looked at the ceiling, her jaw tight. He waited, but she said nothing.

His dad was right. He had no rights with his own kids because he hadn't pursued any legal action. Right now, he was little more than a sperm donor. She could do whatever the hell she wanted, and he couldn't do a damn thing about it.

He'd left the room and gone home to get cleaned up and check in with his parents who'd accompanied him when he made the trip back to the hospital. When he'd come back an hour later with a big teddy bear tucked under his arm and his mom and dad behind him, she'd been on the bed curled up on her side.

"Nila?"

She didn't respond. He thought she'd been asleep, but when he walked on the other side of the bed, her open blank eyes scared him.

Putting his hand to her shoulder, he touched her. "Nila? What's wrong?"

"I did it," she said woodenly.

Noel glanced at his parents who had come into the room.

"Did what, dear?" Madelaine asked as she approached the bed.

"I signed papers for them to…to be circumcised."

Noel expelled the breath he'd been holding. "Where are they now?" He bent down to peer in her face.

"They're gone. They've already taken them." She cast him a pain-filled gaze.

She'd given in to him about it. He'd thought she'd completely blown him off, but she'd listened to his argument, and she'd changed her mind.

He kissed her cheek. "Nila, they'll be okay. I promise."

"I feel like walking. You think we could go around the block or something?"

"You want to walk around the block?" Madelaine said aghast. "My goodness, Nila. You've just had major surgery. I'm sure they don't even want you out of bed."

Noel shook his head. He agreed with his mother, but the torment on Nila's face tore at his gut.

"Let her walk around the damn block," Bernie declared. "It'll get her mind off of the boys getting their tallywhackers cut on."

Chapter Twelve

Nila stared at Noel's house through the windshield of his car.

"I thought we were going to my house."

"The nursery's here."

"But you said you'd move the furniture to my house."

"I offered to do that, yes, but we never decided anything definite."

No, they hadn't. They'd played musical houses, and she'd put it out of her head as if that would solve the problem.

Noel's parents pulled up in the driveway behind his car. Nila glanced behind her as a car door slammed.

"How long are they staying, do you think?"

Noel grinned. "I can probably kick them out after a few days. Can you handle it?"

"There's only one guest bedroom."

"Afraid you won't be able to blame your flatulence on the pregnancy this time?" He winked when he said it.

Nila studied him, then swallowed some air and burped. Proudly, she smirked at him. "If that's a challenge, I accept."

Noel barked with laughter. "It wasn't. Come on, before Mom snatches one of the kids out of the car seat."

As if on cue, the back door on either side opened and Bernie and Madelaine each began to pull out a car seat. Madelaine was successful, but Bernie had slung out a string of curses in his frustration when Noel took Daniel's car seat for him.

"Dad, you need to curb your language before these little guys learn how to talk. I don't want them picking up any colorful words from you."

Bernie took the carrier from his son. "Well, I got some time, I think." They walked on the walkway toward the front door. "Madelaine? When do babies start talking?"

"Noel didn't speak until he was two, then it was in complete sentences," Madelaine informed her husband. She hefted the carrier with surprising agility up the two stairs to the front porch.

Nila followed behind and gripped the rail as she ascended to join the little party. Even mounting two stairs pulled at her body. Noel studied her progress.

"Want me to pick you up?"

Breathe. Breathe. "I'm doing it."

Noel unlocked the door, and they entered the house.

Can I plead fatigue?

It wasn't a lie. All of the sudden, lying down with the boys seemed like a great idea. Already one of them was beginning to fuss. Daniel, she thought.

Madelaine already had the carrier on the floor unbuckling the baby.

"I think I'm going to go lie down. I can take the boys with me."

"Oh, I think Daniel is okay," the older woman stated as she pushed back the seat belt and picked up Benjamin.

"Mom, I think you've got Benjamin," Noel corrected her.

"Oh, really?" She wrinkled her noise at the infant. "How can you tell?"

"Other than he's still got his bracelet on, he was sitting behind me when you pulled him out of the car. Left to right. Alphabetically left to right. Benjamin was on the left side, Daniel was on the right."

"I'm sorry, my little sweetie. Grandma is going to have to figure out who is who, won't I?"

Daniel's cries were more insistent now. Bernie was trying to free him from the seat, but he wasn't having any luck. Nila resisted the urge to march over there, push the old man out of the way, and take her baby.

"What the hell do they make it so hard to get them out of these damn seats? This kid's locked up tighter than Fort Knox."

Nila pivoted to rescue Daniel when Noel stepped next

to his dad and pulled the carrier toward him. Crouching, he unbuckled the seat and removed the infant with careful hands.

"Bernard," Madelaine warned. "I'm going to start charging you a quarter for every expletive I hear."

Noel straightened with an unhappy Daniel in the crook of his arm. Nila watched him walk toward her.

Oh, good. He's bringing him to me.

She reached her arms out to take the baby.

"Just a minute," Noel said as he came to stand with her. "Mom and Dad? Do you guys want to go upstairs first?"

"What?" Bernie asked, then, "Oh, yeah."

Daniel continued to cry though Noel had him against his shoulder now patting his back. Nila's hands itched to snatch him away, hug him to her, run upstairs, and lock herself inside Noel's room.

Give him to me.

Noel read her expression and nodded as if he understood. Of course, he didn't. He was part of the problem. She didn't want to be here. She wanted to be home. Her home.

"It'll be okay," he said. He looked over his shoulder and watched his parents' approach.

Nila waited while they passed her.

"Dad? Will you take the baby?"

"What? No," Nila said.

Noel gave her an apologetic look. "Let them carry the boys up, and I'll carry you up."

"I can go up myself."

"Really? I'm pretty sure I heard the doctor say no stairs for a while. I shouldn't even have let you walk up to the porch."

Oh, come on. She sighed. "Fine. Let's get it over with." She watched Noel surrender her son to the sailor-mouthed old man. "Be careful with him."

"I've carried babies upstairs before," Bernie chided, marching up the stairs as if he didn't have a newborn's life in his hands.

"Have you done it in the last two decades?" Nila whispered watching his progress.

Noel chuckled. He lifted her with ease. Uneasiness blossomed in Nila's chest. "Don't drop me."

Noel's face was too close. The shade of his eyes darkened. "I won't. Not ever."

The intensity of the moment was too much. Nila looked up the stairs. "Hurry up. I don't want them to get too cozy with our babies up there."

"They want to be there for the surprise."

"What surprise?"

"There's a surprise for you up there."

Nila couldn't quite believe it. "A surprise for me?"

Noel patted her shoulder even as he held her. "Well, for Daniel and Benjamin really, but I don't think they're going to be very impressed."

Noel mounted the staircase without breaking a sweat. Quite impressive, even though Nila wasn't carrying the twins anymore. But neither was she anywhere near the weight she'd been before the pregnancy. At Noel's bedroom door, she noticed an addition to the room—a gleaming, cherry cradle standing on a spindled pedestal.

"Ohhh," Nila sighed.

Noel gently set her to her feet, and she held on to his shoulder to steady herself.

"There's another one like it at the house, but we couldn't fit them both in the car to get them here." Bernie handed the baby who was crying to Noel who held his arms out for him.

"We'll bring it the next time," Madelaine suggested.

"It's so beautiful." Nila touched the basinet, and it rocked gently.

"Dad made it," Noel commented. He shifted the baby who continued to protest. Nila reached over and took him, and Noel hesitated only a moment before he surrendered him. Daniel snuffled, rubbed his face against Nila's shirt, then quieted.

Nila turned her attention to Bernie who smiled jovially.

"I made both cradles a little bigger since I figured they'd be used to being together and so you could lay them both in there to sleep."

"They had to get the mattresses custom made, and Mom made the sheets and bumper pads to fit."

"Let's see how Daniel likes it."

"Mom, that's Benjamin," Noel corrected.

"How can you tell?"

"Because it's the same baby you had downstairs when I told you the last time."

Noel's criticism didn't mar Madelaine's smile as she set the baby in the cradle. She spoke in baby talk into Benjamin's face. "You don't mind you's silly grandma, do you? She's so silly, isn't she? Isn't she? Oh, isn't dat so nice to lie in? Yes, it is. Yes, it is." Madelaine glanced up at Nila. "Lil, honey, put Daniel down here with Benjamin, and let's see how they both fit. I did bring the extra bumper pads in case we need to make it a little more cozy."

Nila obediently placed Daniel next to his brother and took the blanket Noel offered her. She tucked it around the boys, and they settled down immediately.

They loved it. Bernie had called it right about them enjoying being together in the small space. Nila laughed when Benjamin stretched and yawned.

"I think they...." She trailed off when she noticed everybody was looking at her with troubled expressions. "What's wrong?"

Bernie recovered first. "Nothing's wrong." He reached over and touched the top of the cradle, shaking it gently. "Oh, yeah. They like it. That's high class right there. Homemade by Bernard Hezekiah Dearing. Finest cradle in the Commonwealth."

Madelaine turned and walked out of the room without a word.

What happened? What did I do?

Nila studied Noel's pained expression. Did they think she didn't like the cradle?

"I'll let you rest...errr...Nila. You and the boys."

Bernie's eyes cut to Noel, and he clapped him on the shoulder before leaving as well.

"I'm sorry, Dearing. I do like the cradle. How could I not? It's gorgeous."

"It's not that, Nila." He closed his eyes briefly, and when he opened them again, the pain was gone.

"What is it?"

"It's nothing for you to worry about. I'm going to get the rest of the stuff out of the car, and I'll come check on you after a while. Call me if you need me, will you?"

He pulled the covers back on the bed, and guided her to sit on its edge.

"Do you think you could take me to the store after I take a nap? I just want to make sure everything's okay, and I'd like to show the boys off."

Noel nodded. "Yeah. If you feel like it, we'll do that."

"You're sure everything's okay?" she lay her head on the pillow and pulled her feet up on the bed.

"Absolutely."

"You're lying to me, Dearing."

"It's just a little white one." He covered her with the comforter and pressed his hand to her cheek. "You'll let me get by with that, won't you?" Careful not to knock the cradle, he backed away from the bed.

"If I hurt her feelings, tell her I'm sorry. All of this is overwhelming, you know?"

"I know. You want something for pain?" When she shook her head, he responded, "Are you sure? Don't try to be tough about this. If you're hurting, you need to take a pain pill."

"I'm okay if you'll quit bugging me about it."

"Sorry. Try to rest, please?"

"All right."

****

Madelaine wiped her eyes on a tissue and dabbed at her nose. Noel sat back and sighed as he watched his mom fall apart in his kitchen while Nila and the boys rested upstairs.

"Noel, I'm sorry. I'm so sorry," she said for the tenth

time. "I'd never do anything to hurt that girl. You have to know that."

"Mom, it's fine. She didn't catch it, so, please, stop worrying."

Thank God, Nila hadn't realized Madelaine had called her *Lil* when they'd shown her the cradle upstairs.

"I'm just so used to…you know…Lil, and they look so much alike. Well, they did, anyway, when Lil was…" Madelaine dissolved into tears. She tucked her face into her hands, and her shoulders shook with the grief overtaking her. "We'd all hoped and prayed that she'd…she'd…."

Yeah.

Noel stood up and fixed his mother with a somber look. "Mom, cry if you need to, but not in front of Nila. Pull yourself together before she wakes up. This is hard enough on her without having to deal with—" He gestured at her with his hand. "I know you didn't mean it, but for the love of God, don't ever let it happen again."

He picked up his keys and was at the door before he realized they'd blocked him in with their car.

"Dad? Can I use your car?"

"Where you going, son?" Bernie asked as he held the keys up.

Noel took the keys with a grateful nod. "Out to clear my head."

When he backed out of the driveway, he really had no idea of his destination. Without thinking, he'd driven to Nila's house and changed into sweats and running shoes. Daisy had already been moved to his house when he'd met Nila to take her to the hospital and his parents had come in that night. But the habit of coming over to check on the house was hard to break.

And he wasn't about to go in the bedroom and disturb Nila anyway.

He walked out of her house then broke into a run. He and Nila had run her neighborhood enough for him to know the route he could take to make five miles without thinking it.

How could his mom be so stupid?

And how had Nila not noticed it?

Oh, God, Lil, you should be here. All of this is what you wanted. The boys, Lil, they're perfect. You're missing all of these wonderful moments, damn you.

Noel sniffed and realized his face was wet—but not with sweat. With tears. Crying like a little girl. Even Nila hadn't cried as he had. When the boys had been born, that incredible woman had laughed. Though she had been strapped down and unable to move, her joyous laughter had rung out in the delivery room.

She'd put up with so much to have these kids. He'd witnessed her drag herself into the house after closing the store, the discomfort of being so big pregnant, the inconvenience of all the doctor appointments, all because of Lil's desire, and Nila had never complained. And when they'd been born, she'd been so happy.

He wanted her to be happy. He wanted her to stay happy, to have the boys—to have him—because they were all the family she had now.

****

That night, Nila took a shower and put on her pajamas while Madelaine held Benjamin. Then Nila had gone into the bedroom to nurse him. He had to be coaxed every time, as if eating were a chore, and he never ate as long as Daniel did. Benjamin's eyes shut, and his tiny lips relaxed against her.

Oh, sweetie, why aren't you hungry?

His eyelashes fanned against his cheek, his little face so perfect. She tickled his face to wake him up hoping he'd nurse again, but he only nuzzled her breast, then gave a shuddering sigh.

Nila placed him on her shoulder and patted his back. He didn't burp for her either.

Noel walked in at that moment with Daniel in his arms. "Okay. I just changed the little guy's diaper. Do you want to feed Daniel, and I'll take Benjamin and change him?"

"He never acts hungry. Do you think something's wrong?"

132

Noel studied the baby. "Is he not eating at all?"

"A little, but not near as much as Daniel."

"Maybe Benjamin's appetite is normal, and Daniel is a little pig." He smiled down at his son. "My mom said I had a voracious appetite when I was a baby." Then to Daniel, he crooned, "You take after your daddy, huh?"

"What if something's wrong? How would we know?" Nila searched Noel's face needing assurance and shared worry at the same time.

Am I crazy? Is it nothing? Is he okay?

Noel shrugged. "Why don't we see what happens tonight, then if you're still concerned, we'll call the doctor tomorrow."

Nila nodded her acknowledgement. *Good plan.*

Noel set Daniel on the bed beside her and took Benjamin. "What's wrong, huh? You're too sleepy to eat? Your mama's all worried 'cause you're not a pig like your brother."

"Don't call Daniel a pig." She picked him up and immediately he started rooting at her shirt. Nila glanced up at Noel to make sure he was on his way out, but he stood and watched. He'd been in the hospital room when she'd fed the boys several times, but when they'd come home, Nila had always gone in a room by herself.

"See? Voracious appetite just like his dad." He made no move to leave.

Didn't he know she didn't want him in here?

"What are you waiting on?" Nila asked him as she tried to reach under her shirt to unhook her bra cup without revealing too much flesh. Daniel yelped his impatience.

"Maybe…" Noel's brows creased in thought. "Maybe you could nurse them at the same time, then Benjamin might be encouraged by the smell and sounds of Daniel eating. Didn't you tell me the nurse showed you how to nurse both of them at the same time?"

"I haven't…really tried it since she was there to…help me."

"I'll help you. Where's the doughnut?"

"It's on the floor over here. Dearing…can I just confess that I'm not comfortable with you seeing my breasts?"

He walked around the bed, tucked the baby in one arm and bent down to retrieve the pillow which he gave her with the other hand. "Do they look different than they did at the hospital?"

"Well, I don't think so…but this is your house, your bedroom. It feels…." She shook her head and placed the cushion around her waist.

"Awkward. I get it. Let's focus on what breasts are for other than selling beer in commercials." He placed Benjamin on the pillow and held him there then placed her arm around him. "I'm glad you wanted to nurse the boys because mother's milk is the best thing for them, but let's face it…" He leaned over her and picked up Daniel and situated him on the other side of the pillow. "You've never nursed before a week ago, and you're trying to nurse two babies. It's a loving and good thing you're doing with your breasts for our boys. That's what this is about—doing the very best thing for them with the colostrum, which you're probably still producing right now. Do you know they call it liquid gold?"

"Who's they?"

"You know, the *they* who know everything. So let's do this. Let me be a dad and help you feed the boys."

He was right. Of course, he was. This was about nursing their babies. She'd get over the embarrassment, and it would be okay.

Nila squared her shoulders and took a sustaining breath. *I can do this.*

****

She'd done it. She'd nursed them both with Noel's help. He'd cheered her on as he had when they'd exercised together or when she'd debated buying the store and running it. His hands had been efficient but gentle, and he'd made suggestions that led her to believe he'd read some of the breastfeeding material at the doctor's office one of the times he'd gone with her for check-ups. It had all been about the babies and what was best for them. After they had been fed and burped, Noel had bundled them up and placed them together in the cradle.

Regretfully, Nila watched him. She didn't want Benjamin and Daniel in the cradle. She wanted them nestled with her and Noel on the other side. She needed—

"Ready for bed?" he asked.

Nila yawned in response. She needed to rest, and she couldn't if they were in the bed next to her. She would worry too much about rolling over and smothering them. They would be better in the cradle, and they'd still be close.

She propped the doughnut next to the bed and fixed her bra. Straightening the covers, she lay back. "Uh-huh."

Noel peeled off his shirt and threw it in the hamper outside of the bathroom. Nila studied his muscled back and shoulders. She'd seen him without a shirt hundreds of times when they'd exercised together or gone swimming. He'd always been so comfortable with his body. Even now, he seemed clueless of how the air crackled with her awareness of him, how she appreciated the smooth lines of his body. Her feelings were a sharp contrast to his ease with their situation. His matter-of-fact manner when she'd bared her breasts eventually had helped her relax and concentrate on feeding Benjamin and Daniel. Now, that task was done and residue of the connection remained.

Was it her hormones that made her yearn for contact with the boys and Noel too?

This was his bedroom. His and Lil's bedroom. But it was also the room where he and Nila had….

He closed the door behind him, and Nila heard the shower start.

It's not as if we've never done this before. In this very room, we slept together. Literally. And nothing had happened. We'd slept.

And nothing would happen tonight. Even if Nila wanted it to, it couldn't. She'd had the C-section, and they had these two little babies who would probably want to eat in about three hours.

Nila shut off the light, and settled on the bed. She listened to be sure the babies were asleep, then sighed as she closed her own eyes.

When his mom and dad leave, she was moving back to the guest bedroom. Being here with him—it wasn't right. Sure, they were the parents, but they weren't involved. They weren't lovers, and they weren't husband and wife.

In a few minutes, the shower shut off, and the light under the bathroom door disappeared. When the door opened, the aroma of Noel's soap accompanied him. Though it was dark, Nila could see well enough to tell he had a towel knotted at his waist. She watched him walk to the dresser, open a drawer, and pull out some clean underwear. He stood for a moment, and his head shifted over his shoulder.

"Nila?" he murmured. "Are you awake?"

She didn't respond. What would he do? Drop the towel and put his underwear on right here? She waited.

He turned and walked back into the bathroom returning quickly without the towel and wearing the boxer briefs he'd pulled out of the drawer. Padding across the floor, he stepped around the cradle and sat on the bed.

In the dark, Nila smiled.

He was next to Daniel and Benjamin. When they woke up, he was going to have to hand them over.

****

A baby's cry awoke Nila from a sound sleep, and she opened bleary eyes. Noel was gone, and whimpering from the cradle told her the boys were still here. Footsteps sounded in the hall, and the door opened.

Madelaine peeked her head in and smiled tentatively. "Good morning." She looked at the cradle and stepped in the room. "Who is that fussing in there?" she crooned to the boys.

"Good morning, Madelaine. Where's Noel?"

She reached into the cradle and picked up one of the babies. "He went for a run."

Disappointment ballooned in Nila's chest. Not because she'd missed Noel, but because she'd missed the run. "He did?"

"He told me to listen for the boys and to help you when they woke up."

Now both babies were crying. Madelaine hurried over to Nila and handed him to her, then went to the cradle to pick up the other one. "Oh, my goodness," she whispered.

"How long has he been gone?"

"Oh, I don't know. A while now. Is it okay if I give them a bath this morning?"

"I suppose so. What time are you guys leaving?"

Madelaine grinned widely down into the baby's face. Nila looked at the bracelet on her baby and saw she had Daniel. She'd tried to study them to pick out any distinguishing marks, but hadn't found any on their faces. Benjamin did have a little stork bite on the back of his neck, and his face was a little thinner. Other than that, it was hard to tell unless they were side by side.

"I thought we'd stay through tomorrow since Noel's going to work today. Just to help you out since this will be your first day alone with them."

Anxiety and relief bubbled up inside Nila. These were Lil's in-laws. Sure Nila knew them well enough, but they'd belonged in Lil's realm.

All of this did. The bedroom. The house. The babies. Noel.

Daniel blinked at her and rubbed his face on her shirt. His downy hair curled in soft wisps.

Oh, my sweet baby.

Lil. He should have been yours.

Not mine.

The infant blurred, and a guttural cry filled the room.

"Oh, darling, darling, what is it?" Madelaine asked as she hurried around the bed, and sat on its edge.

Nila realized she'd made the grief-stricken sound.

Lil, why did you leave us?

She squeezed her eyes shut against the wave of despair trying to block out everything and everyone that belonged to Lil. Both babies cried in earnest and Nila along with them.

"Bernard! Bernard, come here!"

Hands smoothed Nila's hair and patted her back.

Soothing words flowed over her, but she couldn't make sense of them. When the hands wrapped around Daniel, she resisted.

"No!"

"It's all right, Nila. Really. Let me have him so I can help you. Bernie? Here."

Madelaine examined the baby. "He seems okay. I don't see—"

"He's okay. It's me. I just…I wish Lil could be here. She should be here. This is…"—Nila gestured around her. "And you." She shook head. "I can't do this," she whispered brokenly. She hugged Daniel to her and juggled him. "I'm sorry. I'm so sorry."

"Bernard? Take the baby in the other room."

"No. I want them both with me."

"He'll bring him back in a little while, won't you, Bernie?"

"Yeah, sure. I'll bring back…errrr…the baby in a little while." He walked toward the door with Benjamin in his arms.

After he left, Madeline smiled kindly at Nila.

"You miss Lil."

Unable to speak, Nila nodded.

"She'd be so proud of what a good mother you are becoming."

"I was supposed to be the aunt."

Madelaine didn't respond.

"I know you think I've just stepped in taking over Lil's life—her house, her husband, her babies."

The older woman shook her head. "No."

"Yes, I have. You're too nice to say it, but I know. I mean, this was Lil's bed, and here I am sleeping in it with her husband."

"He is no longer Lil's husband."

"But he was. He was my brother-in-law."

"Yes. But more importantly, he is the father of my grandbabies and you are their mother. You do want to be their mother, don't you?"

Nila nodded as another tear fell down her cheek.

Madeline patted her hand then caressed the baby's head.

"I'm not sure I could have…given them up. And she would have never gotten over it."

"Don't torture yourself, Nila. You can't really know how you would have felt if she had lived. But you and she were so close, and she was so excited about the babies. Maybe these feelings are because she is gone and you knew how much she wanted them, wanted you to have them for her."

"I can't imagine letting them go. Now I know I couldn't. I think Noel feels the same way, but we don't know how to work it out. For so long, we've had Lil. She was our connection."

"And now you have Benjamin and Daniel to connect you."

"But how? Noel insists on staying in the same house, but…."

"But?"

"I always imagined I'd get married one day and love someone and…" She broke down again. "And be loved."

Madelaine reached forward and hugged her. "Noel loves you. You two have known each other for so long."

"It's not the same. Not really. I don't mean to sound greedy, but you know? To be in love, to have a man who loves me not as a friend and not because I've given birth to his sons, and not because I'm a convenient look-alike stand-in for his wife."

Madelaine sighed. "I think you're underestimating my son. Being good parents to two beautiful babies is plenty reason for you and Noel to be together." She studied Nila. "You can learn to love Noel if for no other reason than that he is a father to your children. He's a good man."

"I know he's a good man. I've…."

Madelaine waited for her to finish her sentence, but Nila pinched her lips together.

I've loved him for years. I loved him first.

Chapter Thirteen

Noel wiped the sweat off his face as he walked in the house. Nila and his dad sat at the kitchen table while his mom stood at the sink. Bernie had one of the boys on his shoulder, and Nila brought a forkful of food to her mouth and ate.

"I didn't expect everyone to be up so early," he said. He examined Nila's face but read no clues to her feelings. Her hair was wet from a recent shower, and she wore a terry robe. He knew she was tired because either one or the other of the twins had woken them up about every hour and a half.

"I hate for Bernie and me to leave today. Benjamin and Daniel are such early risers, I know you all could use the extra help," Madelaine said without turning around.

"They're late night risers, too. Good golly, the only way I'm going to get any sleep is to go home. How many times were they up last night?"

"They're babies," Madelaine returned to her husband. "Babies wake up often and eat often, especially breast-fed babies."

"It might be reason enough to give 'em formula."

"No, Dad. Formula is too heavy in their stomachs. It takes them longer to digest it."

Nila still hadn't said anything.

"Nila? You okay?"

"Yeah. Your mom made me French toast."

Really?

Noel looked at his mom's back. She glanced over her shoulder and smiled.

"Okay. Benjamin is a clean boy. I'm ready for Daniel now."

****

"See? The building is still standing," Noel said as they drove into the parking lot at *Play It! Sports.*

Nila let the comment slide. She hadn't been to the store

in three weeks, and she was itching to check on things. Though Nila had done a lot of prep work to be gone while she recovered from surgery and taking maternity leave to be with the boys, she knew no one could take care of the store as well as she did. She'd had a big shipment of UK items on back order, which she knew had to be here by now, and she wanted to talk to Ricky about a display she wanted set out for the items. Teeny had agreed to come back to help out for a little while, and Ricky said Jason, the new employee, was doing a great job.

Early afternoon was a good time to visit because the lunch hour shoppers were gone, and the after school shoppers hadn't arrived.

Noel parked the car in front, and simultaneously, they opened the doors and moved to the back seats to get Daniel and Benjamin.

Nila had dressed them in little referee sleepers Teeny had brought to the hospital when she visited. Pressing the release button, Nila freed the carrier from the car seat mount.

"Stop it," Noel growled from the other side of the car. He glared at her. "You're not supposed to lift that."

"Oh. Right." She pressed the carrier back down, then unbuckled the seat belt. Daniel wasn't too heavy to hold, only Daniel in his carrier.

Noel opened the door for her while he held Benjamin in his carrier in the other hand. She smiled her thanks as she passed him, and the familiar sight of her store widened her grin.

Gosh, it was good to be back at work.

An hour later, Noel stood holding both babies wrapped together in a blanket.

"Nila. Nila, let's go."

Nila sat behind her desk with her ear to the phone listening to the coach from the varsity cheer squad complain about wardrobe malfunctions. Nila placed her finger up in a *one more minute* gesture.

He gave her thirty seconds, then stalked out the door.

"...so that's three different uniforms with loose seams

that I know of." The woman continued, "I bet there's more. Some of the girls just have their moms sew them up themselves. How am I—"

"Tanya, I'm sorry. I've got to go, but I'll call the company today and find out what can be done. I've never had shoddy work from them before. But I'll make it right. When's your next practice?"

"Tomorrow afternoon."

"If you'll have the girls bring the uniforms, I'll try to get Geri over there to stitch up the seams and check the rest of them to make sure they won't unravel. She's got a portable sewing machine, and she's done it for me before. While you all are practicing, she can work on them. I'll call her and see. Okay?"

"Okay. Hey, did you hear that Ironton might be going to State?"

"Tanya, somebody just absconded with my kids. I've got to go. I'll call you back later today. I promise."

Without waiting for a reply, Nila pressed the end button and set the phone on the charger. Would Noel really leave her and take the kids with him?

She hurried through the store and spotted Teeny holding a baby. As Nila neared, she saw Noel crouched on the floor with both baby carriers in front of him. He was buckling one baby in, then held his arms to Teeny for the other one. Teeny kissed the tiny head, then gingerly handed him to his dad.

"I'm sorry that took so long."

Teeny's gaze fell to Noel then to her. The younger woman bit her lip like she did when Nila was about to yell at somebody for screwing up.

"All set," Noel declared. He stood and picked a carrier up in each hand. "We're going home. What do you want to do?"

Calm and confident, Noel held the babies in their carriers as if he'd done it every day of his life. His direct gaze challenged her, but his lips held a hint of a smile.

"You'd leave me here?"

"If you want to stay."

Was he serious? Or irritated at her for staying so long at the store? She'd thought he was angry when he'd stalked out of her office, but his continence was different now. This was the Noel she'd known for years. Her buddy was putting the ball in her court, letting her decide.

What do you want to do?

He'd asked her the same question about how many laps to run or whether they played basketball or swam laps in the pool in adjacent lanes.

Except it was different.

He was letting her choose, but on his terms, which included the terms safely belted snug in their carriers going to his house no matter what.

One of the babies squirmed and cried out. Who was it? She couldn't tell from here. She took a step forward, but Noel pivoted toward the door. Her gaze flew to his.

The jerk. He knew she wanted to stay, but he also knew she wanted the babies to stay too.

He nodded to Teeny and Ricky. "Good to see you guys. You're doing a good job taking care of things. Wouldn't you say, Nila?"

Teeny and Ricky both watched her. They were waiting for her answer.

Noel walked to the door. "If you want to stay, call me when you're ready, and I'll come back and pick you up." He set down a carrier and pushed the handle open. "Have you decided?"

"I *am* on maternity leave," Nila commented. "Ricky? I'll call you in a little while. I need to see if Geri will—"

"No." Noel shook his head. "If you go home with us, you'll be on your maternity leave. That means no work. Take care of your business here, then call me." He picked the carrier up and walked outside.

Nila huffed and placed her hands on her hips. "Dearing—"

The door shut and through its glass front, she watched him stride to the car. She sighed in defeat and walked to the door. "Ricky? It looks like you're going to have to handle this. Call Geri and ask her if she will go out to Varity School tomorrow at four with her sewing machine to stitch up the varsity squad's uniforms. Tell her to check all of them for loose seams."

"Okay."

He had one carrier in the backseat, and he was walking around the front of the car with the other one. She figured she had about a minute before he left.

She smiled at Ricky and Teeny. "You guys are doing a good job. I really appreciate it." Nila left her store and walked to the car. She sat down in the passenger seat and shut the door in the moment Noel fitted the second car seat in its base and settled in the driver's seat.

Without a word, Noel started the engine and backed out of the parking space. He shifted the gear and drove out of the lot. Nila wanted to work up an argument for what had happened a moment ago in the store, but already her body was drooping. At the house, she could lie down and rest with the boys, and that would be okay.

She closed her eyes and laid her head on the headrest. "Dearing?"

"Yeah?"

"What was that about?"

"I've always played it straight with you, haven't I?"

"Yes."

"Okay, then. And I always will, but I didn't want to make a scene in front of your employees. You just had two babies and a hysterectomy three weeks ago. I wasn't going to force you to come home, but I thought it was a mistake for you to stay. I figured if the kids went with me, you'd come, too."

"How could you know I'd go?"

"Because you're their mother."

"But I own that store."

"It was a gamble. I guess we both know now where your priorities lie."

Nila smiled. She was their mother, and she'd chosen

them over her store. And Noel had known she would.

****

After Noel left for work one morning, Nila wandered through the house noticing what had changed since Lil's death. Nila opened the closet door in the bedroom and noticed all of Lil's clothes were gone. The shelves which had held boxes of Lil's shoes were empty. Anger bubbled up in Nila's chest.

She walked to the dresser and opened the drawers.

Only items belonging to Noel.

What had he done with her clothes?

Didn't he think Nila should have a say in what happened to Lil's stuff?

Downstairs Nila opened the cabinet next to the entertainment center where Lil kept her basket of knitting, but it was gone. In its place was a stack of books.

Nila thumbed through the titles.

Thrillers.

Lil hated thrillers.

It was as if she'd never even lived here. What had he done with all her stuff? Given it to charity to be used by strangers?

Nila pushed the books back in the cabinet and shut the door. Turning she studied the rest of the room and a framed photograph on the bookcase caught her attention.

It was of Lil and Noel on their wedding day.

Nila remembered the moment well. Noel knelt before Lil's satin-clad form with the garter he'd retrieved from her thigh. He wore a triumphant grin on his face, and Lil's mouth was open as she laughed. Noel had positioned the garter around his fingers like a slingshot then aimed it at the crowd of eligible bachelors grouped together at the reception.

When Lil had called for all the single women to gather to catch the bouquet, Nila had slipped out of the room and driven home.

She had stood with her sister during the wedding. She'd watched Noel's and Lil's faces as they recited their vows to each other. She'd held Lil's bouquet as the couple exchanged rings and held hands. She'd smiled and posed during the pictures. She'd laughed when several people joked about Noel having no brother to pair her up with when she'd really wanted to scream and punch somebody in the face.

No one had known how torturous it had been to watch her sister marry the man she was in love with. Not even their mother had figured it out.

Nila spotted another photo and walked toward it. This one was taken on the ski trip the three of them had gone on when Noel had proposed marriage to Lil.

In the frame, they posed at the edge of the slopes with their skis and poles when they'd first arrived. Later in the day, Noel and Nila had been riding on the lift up the advance slope laughingly called Kamikaze by Noel. Lil wouldn't go down it, but Nila and Noel had raced down it twice. On the third time up, Noel had fidgeted until Nila had shoved him with her shoulder in disgust.

"What's your problem, Dearing? If you knock us out of this chair because you can't keep still, I'm not going to be happy."

"I want to get married," Noel blurted. He unzipped his jacket and pulled out a ring box. Opening it, he held it up for Nila's inspection.

Nila blinked at the ring and at Noel's shaking hands holding it.

This was it.

She'd lost Noel to Lil. In the past month, she'd watched them together and waited, hoping it wouldn't work out. Hated herself for wishing it. Fantasizing she would pick up the pieces when Lil broke up with him like she had every other boyfriend.

But the evidence of it working out winked at her as the sunlight caught the facets of the diamond.

Noel and Lil were going to get married.

"Well, what are you asking me for?" she snapped. "I don't care if you marry Lil. She'd love nothing better than to cook your meals and have your babies. She bleeds domestic."

"What about you?"

"What about me? I'm finishing school, then I'm going to save up every dime until I can open my own sporting goods store. Getting married and having kids is just going to get in the way of my dream."

"I don't believe that. You can still have your store with a husband and kids."

"You're the one who wants the white-picket-fence fantasy. I've watched you when you're helping with the peewee team. I've never seen a guy who loved being around kids as much as you do. It'd be a real shame if you didn't have kids of your own, Noel. Personally, I don't really want kids unless I can play ball with them. Lil is the one who gets into all that happy-home-having-babies mess. Not me."

"Do you know how much I hate it when you pull your tough girl routine?"

"This isn't a routine. I am tough. Lil is the girly-girl sister. I'm the tough, tomboy sister." Nila pushed the ring toward him. "Put that thing away before you drop it. If you're showing me so I can give you advice on how to ask her, all I can tell you is you should take her to dinner tonight and pop the question. She'll make a good wife, Dearing. You couldn't do any better."

"Nila, you don't—"

"Yes, I do. I know my sister. She loves you. You know that, right?"

"Yes."

"Then go for it. I'll make myself scarce, and you ask her."

"Maybe I will. Then I'll take her back to my room and make love to her for the rest of the night. What do you think about that?"

"I don't think anything about it because I do not care."

They were coming to the drop off. Without another word, Nila jumped off the bench and pushed off as hard as she could with her poles.

She zoomed down the slope and at the bottom she'd taken the B lift for the beginners so she wouldn't run into Noel again. She'd stayed on the slopes until nearly midnight when she'd stopped by the sandwich shop, bought a meal to go, and gone to her empty room in the chalet.

The next morning Noel and Lil were engaged, and at the end of the semester Nila had moved to Tennessee.

Nila picked up another framed photo.

She'd first noticed this picture displayed when Lil had approached her about being a surrogate. It had caught her attention because she'd thought it was Lil and Noel at first. But, no, it was Nila and Noel in the dugout of the Little League team they'd coached. He'd suckered her into being head coach a week after her mom died, and she'd grudgingly accepted the position. By the third practice, Nila realized the wisdom of Noel's coaching request. She'd climbed out of the chasm of losing her mom and led the Raging Rockets to the championship. In the picture, they wore matching baseball caps. Nila leaned forward and smiled into the camera, but Noel's back was against the wall, and his attention was on her. His gaze was pensive, watching her as if he were waiting for her to do something.

****

Noel unlocked the back door of Nila's house and saw her lying on her side on a quilt on the floor with the boys beside her.

She'd texted him at noon.

We r @ my house.

He didn't know whether she was inviting him or not, but he'd stopped by Garibaldi's and picked up some take-out, both vegan and carnivorous fare. She'd commented yesterday she wanted to get back to a vegetarian diet though she'd expressed some doubt about the wisdom of it while nursing.

He thought the best plan was to give her options and let her choose. And not bitch at her about lifting the boys or their carriers when she wasn't supposed to carry anything heavy until she'd healed from the surgery.

Noel deposited the food on the table then dropped to the floor next to his boys. They'd grown since he'd left this morning, he'd swear it. The baby closest to him turned his face toward Noel. The color-coded blue outfit told him it was Benjamin. He still couldn't tell them apart though Nila reassured him often enough he'd be able to in time.

Noel scooped Benjamin up and brought him close. He leaned down and inhaled the baby smell then kissed his son.

Oh, I missed you.

Ben's skin was soft beneath Noel's lips. He picked up his little hand and kissed him there too.

"Hey, buddy. Did you have a good day today? Huh?"

Daniel squeaked, and Noel looked over at him. "What's wrong? Nobody's paying attention to you?" Noel crawled over to the middle of the quilt so he was in between the boys. He crouched over Daniel and kissed him as well. He positioned both boys side by side and grinned down at them.

Damn, they were cute. Had anybody else had such good looking kids? He didn't think so. He put his arm underneath both of them, and picked them up then walked on his knees to the couch.

"I don't like you carrying both of them at the same time. You're knocking their heads together," Nila said.

Huh?

She stood with arms crossed at the kitchen corner of the dining room staring at him as if she were contemplating ways to kill him. When had she gotten up from the floor and moved?

"I'm careful with them." With a little difficulty he stood then positioned a baby securely in each arm.

"Not careful enough," she groused.

Grouchy.

"Why don't you go upstairs and take a nap? I'm here now. You can rest."

Her nostrils flared. *Uh-oh.*

"What's wrong?"

"What did you do with Lil's stuff?"

"What stuff?"

"Her clothes. Her shoes. Her knitting. Nothing's left at your house which belonged to her."

So that's what this was about.

"I packed it up and stored it."

She relaxed a bit. "Why didn't you ask me to help you?"

Warmth spread on his shirt. Noel looked down. Daniel had just spit up all over him. He sat on the couch and carefully placed them on the cushion. Nila walked over and wiped the baby's face. Then she picked him up and went to the kitchen, ran some water in the sink, then walked toward Noel with a damp cloth in her hand.

Noel took it from her and wiped his shirt. "I don't know. I didn't want you upset over it. Do you want her stuff?"

"No." Her voice trembled over the word, and she cleared her throat.

"Okay. I'll keep it for a while, then later we can decide what to do with it." The goo wasn't coming off easily.

"I'm staying here tonight. Me and the boys."

What?

Noel stopped what he was doing and focused on Nila. She watched him defiantly even while one of her hands caressed the baby's back. Benjamin yelped from the couch, and he went over to pick him up.

"Fine. We'll stay here tonight."

Benjamin had his fist stuck in his mouth, sucking on it. Noel grinned at the little guy. *Oh, my Lord.* He loved these boys.

"Do whatever you want to, but you're sleeping in the guest room."

Benjamin's fist got away from him, and he screwed up his face like he might cry. "What is wrong with Mommy, huh? She's in a really bad mood, isn't she? Did you and brother keep her awake all night and day?"

When Noel crooned to him, the baby studied his dad.

"I can hear you, Dearing."

Benjamin found his fist again. Noel kissed the little hand. "Didn't Mommy take a nap with you?"

"Stop it."

Noel turned his attention to Nila whose eyes were narrowed in anger. "What? You want us to put the babies down so you can punch me a few times? What's going on? I told you I didn't throw out Lil's stuff. I wouldn't do that without talking to you about it."

"Why didn't you wake me up to go running with you? That's two days you've gone without me."

"You can't run yet. You need to heal up from surgery. Why don't you wait until your doctor visit at least?"

She growled with frustration. "Because he's just going to say it's too soon, and it's not. I am sick of being treated like an invalid. I'm perfectly fine to run, but you didn't even give me the chance. You just go out, do whatever you want, and to hell with me. I'll just stay home and be the human milk bottle."

"You don't want to nurse the kids?"

"No. I mean, yes. Dearing, that's not it." She sighed. "I don't know what *it* is except…" She grunted in frustration. "I think I'm losing my mind or something. I think if I could…do something physical, it would help."

"Physical?"

She shrugged.

Noel grinned at Benjamin. "She wants to do something physical. Got any ideas, son?"

Chapter Fourteen

The doorbell pealed.

"Dearing, get that, will you? I'm not quite ready yet," Nila called from the bathroom.

Noel held Benjamin to his shoulder and jiggled him as he walked to the front of the house. He stepped around the two jogging strollers he'd brought to the house after Nila had her bout of cabin fever. They hadn't been able to use them for another month much to Nila's dismay. Finally, the doctor had given reluctant permission with a stern lecture to take it slow, so they'd tried the strollers out this morning. Nila had done great, though Noel only let them jog a few hundred feet.

Noel opened the door and stood back to let Michael Summers in.

Mike wore a golf shirt and neatly pressed khaki pants and tennis shoes.

"I know you have nicer shoes than that," Noel commented as his friend walked past.

"You want me to go home and change?"

From the other room Daniel let out a wail. Noel followed the sound and laid Ben next to his brother then stuck a pacifier in Daniel's mouth. Grasping the blanket underneath both babies, Noel bundled them and picked them both up.

"Now, that's impressive."

Noel grinned as he settled the boys against his front. "We've learned a lot of two-for-one tricks in the past few months."

"Getting any sleep?"

"More than Nila. She's nursing so...." Noel didn't finish his sentence. Michael was taking Nila out on a date. He probably didn't want to hear about Nila's milk production. Although if Michael wanted to really be impressed, he should watch Nila nurse both kids at once, except Noel wasn't so sure he wanted the man looking at Nila's breasts.

Being in the same house with her and the babies had afforded Noel with plenty of viewing opportunities. Her breasts were lush, the nipples large and dark. Noel knew it was the lactating hormones responsible for the change. He'd tried hard to focus on the nursing part of it, but *wow*!

The day after he'd helped her nurse both babies, Benjamin wouldn't latch on again. The lactation expert had suggested putting sugar water on Nila's nipples to encourage the baby to eat. In desperation, Nila had thrust the infant at him, stripped off her shirt and bra, and doused herself with the mixture. Taking the baby from Noel, she placed Ben's face against her.

The kid wasn't buying.

Naked from the waist up with sugar water glistening on her nipples and holding his son, Nila looked at Noel.

Tears threatened to spill. It tore him up. Nila almost never cried.

"Keep trying, Nila. He'll figure it out," he urged.

"It's not him. It's me. I'm doing something wrong."

"It's not you."

"Yes, it is. My breasts aren't—"

"They're luscious. I can barely concentrate here because they look so good. The little guy must be nuts not to want to suck on them."

Shock registered on her face, then she burst out laughing. "Dearing." She shook her head.

In his desperation, Noel had changed tactics. At first, he thought stressing the health benefits of nursing would help her, but maybe the comments had put too much pressure on her to make it work. This time he'd confessed how attractive her lactating breasts were. The moment was enough to get her to relax and let the milk come down. Without any more encouragement, the baby latched on and sucked noisily.

"Now, see? His dad just had to fill him in on what your breasts are for, other than looking so hot."

"Hot, right. Every part of me jiggles."

"Yeah." Noel grinned lecherously.

"I never took you for a breast man." Nile held the baby to her and looked around. She tried to reach her shirt on the floor.

Noel picked up a blanket and handed it to her knowing his comment had embarrassed her. "How could I not be? What are you—a D cup now?"

"Oh, shut up." She settled the blanket around herself, attempting to cover up the issue. "These boobs are for Benjamin and Daniel."

Noel took a corner and draped it more securely around her shoulders. "Yeah. That's what I keep telling myself."

Nila's eyebrows creased with a quizzical expression as though she wasn't sure if he was serious.

"Do you think your breasts would be as big if you were feeding just one baby?"

"I don't know."

As if on cue, Daniel stirred from the crib and began working himself up to a full howl. Noel picked the baby up and held him in his hands and gazed down at him. He grinned down at the tiny face. "Guess Mama will have to lose that blanket she just covered herself up with, won't she?"

"Don't act so happy about it, or I'll make you go in the other room."

Nothing else had been said about it, but Nila seemed more relaxed, and both boys were eating well.

Nila walked in the room at that moment wearing a dress that showed a goodly portion of those lactating breasts. Noel's mouth dropped open. She was going to wear that out in public? With Michael? Had she forgotten he was a minister?

Noel glanced at Michael to see his reaction. He returned Noel's stare and shrugged.

"Hi," she greeted Michael, her troubled eyes sliding to Noel before she tugged her neckline up to no avail. "Noel, let me just show you something in the kitchen. Give me the babies."

"Better not," Noel advised. If she took them, they'd

start rooting around and she'd want to stay and feed them.

Understanding dawned on her face. Without another word she led the way to the kitchen, and Noel followed, mulling over in his mind a tactful way to tell her to get back to her room and put on something which didn't show her tits.

When the door closed behind him, Nila pivoted and pulled at her dress.

"Does this look as bad as I think it does?"

"No."

"Nothing fits me. All my pants are still too tight. I've got nothing but maternity clothes and this dress that makes me look like a slut."

"You don't want to wear maternity clothes?"

"I'm not pregnant anymore," she snapped.

"Yeah. As of two months. Big deal if you're still wearing maternity clothes. You'll get back into your old clothes. Give yourself a little time."

"I don't understand. Why would Reverend Summers want to go out with me?'

"Call him Michael. This is a date, not a pastoral visit." Noel had called Michael and asked him to take Nila out to give her a break from diapers, feeding, and spit up. Michael had been reluctant, but Noel had insisted. Michael was his only single friend he trusted to go out with her.

Nila pulled her neckline up, then reached her hand down the front of her dress attempting to push down her breasts. "I look like a cow."

"Oh, stop fishing for compliments. Some women pay a lot of money to have knockers like that, so enjoy it. I'm sure Michael will appreciate the view tonight. He's not allowed to touch though, as I believe you've told me Benjamin and Daniel have exclusive rights."

"Let me just hold them one quick minute before I leave," Nila snaked her hand in the blanket for a baby. She preferred holding them one at a time.

Noel turned aside to block her. "No. They'll catch your scent, and Michael will be stuck here another hour while you nurse."

Nila wrinkled her nose. "Maybe I shouldn't go. Did you put him up to asking me out?"

"Now why would I do that? Yes, you should go and have a good time. You've been cooped up in this house for months. I want the kiddos all to myself for a few hours. No girls allowed."

She studied him for a moment, chewing on her bottom lip.

"All right." She walked over to the fridge, opened the door and pulled out a container. "Here's the milk. If you use all of it, there are two extra bags in the freezer. You want me to go ahead and put it in the bottles for you?"

"No. I want you to leave." He shifted the boys thinking they were both asleep. He walked over to the playpen in the corner and carefully laid them in it. One stirred, Daniel he thought, but neither awoke. "See? They're fine."

"I've never left them before," she confessed, standing next to him and peering down at them. "I don't want to go."

"It will be okay. You'll have a good time. Michael's a great guy."

"Dearing—"

"Nila, please let me show you what a good dad I can be."

"I already know what a good dad you are." She cupped his shoulder, and he thought she was about to say something else. When he glanced at her, she had leaned over to kiss him on the cheek, but when he moved, her lips caught him on the mouth. Fire burned him where her lips touched his. Quickly, he wrapped his arms around her and deepened the kiss, tasting her, reveling in the softness of her. Her hands kneaded his back, and her tongue met his. *Dammit!* Noel grasped her shoulders and pushed her away from him a few inches.

"You took me by surprise there. I didn't mean to do that."

"You didn't?" She blinked at him, her expression unreadable.

Was she angry he had kissed her? Upset?

What an idiot he was. She had the chance to be with a decent guy, and he'd screwed it up by kissing her before their date. "No. It was stupid. I shouldn't have. I'm sorry."

Her lips still glistened from their kiss.

Again! His neglected libido screamed. His fingers itched to pull her to him, but he tamped down the urge.

No.

This was Nila. She deserved a nice night out with an uncomplicated man.

Noel took her by the elbow and pulled her into the living room. Michael had sat down on the couch, but when they entered, he stood. "Sorry to keep you waiting. You guys have a good time," Noel said before giving what he hoped was a friendly wave and escaping back into the kitchen.

****

Why did Noel kiss me?

Nila picked up her water glass and sipped. The question ran through her head for the thousandth time since she and Michael had left the house. He'd taken her to a swanky restaurant, and they'd sat at a candlelit table. Nila had done her best to smile and keep up her end of the conversation while she ate the mushroom risotto with red pepper sauce. She held the dessert menu in front of her face though the pretty script was lost to her.

Why did Noel kiss me?

"Do you want to call and check on them?"

Nila lowered the menu. "What?"

Michael smiled knowingly. "You're thinking about Daniel and Benjamin. Do you want to call Noel and see how they're doing?"

Oh.

Yes. Any good mother would be thinking about her kids and not....

Nila shivered as she relived those few moments in the kitchen.

That kiss. That incredible kiss. He'd kissed her. Nila. Fully knowing who she was, he'd taken her in his arms and....

"I think Noel can handle things just fine," she said with more vehemence than she meant to. Michael raised his eyebrows.

Like how he handled me in the kitchen then pushed me out the door on a date.

"Are you all...living at your house?"

"We aren't..." Nila sighed. "We float from my house to his house." She studied the man across from her.

He was a minister. He was also Noel's friend.

"Did Noel tell you about...how I got pregnant?"

"Yes. You were to be a surrogate mother for him and Lil."

So, Noel hadn't told him.

Nila looked morosely in her glass. "Lil and I...we tricked him. I pretended to be Lil one night." She cut her eyes to him expecting to see shock, disgust, judgment. Instead his expression was calm, and he nodded in encouragement. "He and I...well...he figured it out but not before I conceived, and shortly after that Lil found out she had cancer."

"Why did you do it?"

"Because Lil wanted a baby. It consumed her, like she couldn't think of anything else. It's the worst thing I've ever done, and now it's the best thing I've ever done. The twins are only a few months old, and I can't imagine not having them. But..." She shook her head. "Noel and I, we've got this big problem between us because we want to be the parents, but we've always been the sister and brother-in-law."

"It makes sense for you to step into the role of their mother since Lil is gone."

Nila shook her head. "Even before they were born, I wanted them as my own. And there's no question Noel wants them." Nila's heart thumped in her chest when a vision of Noel cooing to Benjamin and Daniel entered her head. "You ought to see him when he sees the boys. His whole face lights up. It's like nothing else exists but them."

"Not even you?"

"I…sort of get the residue of his love for them. It spills over to me, warming me. And I feel that way about him because if it weren't for him, for that terrible thing I did to him that night, we wouldn't have Benjamin and Daniel. We've fallen into this family mode, but we're not a family. Not really."

"Why do you say that?"

"Because he was my sister's husband." Nila sighed. "I want to tell you something. Something that happened a long time ago."

"All right."

"I knew Noel before Lil did. He and I have always been good friends. But when I first met him…" Nila looked at Michael, still unsure whether telling him was a good idea. "You won't tell him this, will you?"

Michael smiled. "Not if you don't want me to."

"I liked him. Well, I was in love with him, actually. I invited him to my house for Thanksgiving to meet my family, and he and Lil hooked up, and that was it."

Michael's eyes widened. "I find it hard to believe Noel would do that to you or your sister."

"Well, he didn't know how I felt about him, and I had invited another guy friend, too, just in case Lil's boyfriend wasn't there so I could even things out, and it wouldn't be so awkward. I hadn't really met anyone like Noel who was just so…" Nila laughed. "He's just incredible, but we always related to each other like buddies, and I was too scared to make a pass at him if he didn't feel the same way because I didn't want to mess up the friendship. I didn't know Lil had broken up with her boyfriend. If I'd known, I probably would have told her ahead of time. 'You can have Aaron, but Noel's mine.'"

"Did Lil often take your boyfriends?"

"Not on purpose. She is just so feminine and sweet. I mean, she was so feminine and sweet. Guys always gravitated to her. The weekend I caught her and Noel kissing, I confronted Lil. How could you do that? I like Noel, I said to her. And she apologized. She really thought I liked Aaron because she said I treated Noel more like a brother than a boyfriend. She said she'd back off, but that night she had a really bad asthma attack. Noel went with Mom and me to take her to the hospital. On the way, Noel helped calm her down by talking to her and getting her to relax. He was so good with Lil, so tender and compassionate, and I knew he was perfect for her. He seemed to really like her, and he treated her differently, like a man should be with a woman."

"Like you'd like to be treated?"

Nila rolled her eyes. "In theory, I guess. But when a guy opens the door for me, it bugs me. I can open my own door, you know? But when I saw Noel opening the door for Lil, it made my heart hurt because I could tell that's what he wanted in a woman, and I could never be like that."

"Maybe he was just being nice and treating her like she wanted to be treated."

"Which made him a good mate for Lil. But more importantly, I knew he'd take care of her, so I backed off. I let her have him, and he and I stayed friends. Well, actually, he became my best friend. He has been like a brother to me."

But now what was he to Nila?

The kiss they'd shared in the kitchen was not brotherly, and it wasn't friendly either. It was a let's-get-it-on kind of kiss.

"How come you don't want Noel to know any of this?"

"Because we've always been friends, and I don't want it to be more awkward than it already is between us."

"But you said that all of that happened a long time ago. What would it matter now if he knew…unless you're still in love with him."

She shook her head. "He was in love with my sister. He was a perfect husband to her. I love him for that, but that's it. We're friends."

The kiss in the kitchen was just a fluke. Lack of sleep. Hormones. A misplaced kiss on the cheek. She and Noel were just friends.

Just friends.

When Michael didn't reply, Nila looked at him. He watched her steadily, and Nila wondered what he was thinking. He was a good looking guy—dark hair and a cute dimple in his chin. She judged him to be in his late thirties.

"How come you're not married?"

He smiled, and the dimple deepened. "Interested in the position?"

Nila laughed. "Wow. You move fast. We're not even to the check yet."

"We're close though. Want to go see a movie or go home?"

Nila considered his question. Did they have time to be gone two more hours? Her breasts felt heavy, and with one hand she touched the side of her right breast for firmness. When she saw Michael's gaze follow her gesture, she grimaced.

"I'm sorry. That was automatic. I'm so used to…" *breastfeeding.*

Nila didn't finish her sentence thankfully. She'd nursed long enough that she could just about tell when it was time to feed the boys by how full her breasts got.

"Umm…a movie would be nice. Maybe I could just call really quick to be sure everything is okay."

Michael nodded. "Why don't you do that, and I'll get the check. Okay?"

Nila excused herself and walked to the lounge outside of the women's restroom. She called Noel's cell, and he picked up on the first ring.

"Hello." *Abrupt. Tense?* A picture of his lips entered Nila's mind. He'd kissed her.

Why had he done that?

"Noel? Is…everything okay?"

"Fine. We're fine."

Nila listened for any crying in the background but heard nothing.

"Michael asked me to a movie, but I can come home now. If you need me."

"We're okay. You go see a movie. Have a good time."

Why did you kiss me?

"Are you sure?"

"Yes, I'm sure."

Nila waited for him to say more, but he didn't.

"Okay. You'll call me, won't you, if you need me? I'll put my phone on vibrate."

"Yes."

"Are you sure?"

There was a pause. "Trust me, Nila. I can take care of the boys." His voice had changed, all smooth and confident. "We're okay. We're watching wrestling, drinking beer, and smoking cigars, okay? So quit bugging us."

"Fine. No Cinemax, though."

"Boys club. No girls allowed, and we aren't admitting anything."

****

With a bag of popcorn in her lap and a bottle of water in the holder next to her, Nila should have been immersed in the movie. It was an action flick—her favorite kind, but about half way through she lost interest. She kept thinking about being home with the boys.

Were they okay? Did they notice she was gone? Was Noel doing okay by himself with both of them?

She nudged one of her boobs with her arm. Not that she really needed to. She could tell they were full. She might as well have had two cement blocks strapped to her chest. Her skin was tight and almost achy.

Had any lactating woman ever exploded from not nursing?

She held her phone low at her leg and texted Noel, but he didn't text her back. After twenty minutes, she walked out of the theater and called him as she stood in the hallway.

No answer.

Why wasn't he answering? Was something wrong?

She dialed his number again, but it went immediately to voice mail.

"Noel? It's Nila. I'm checking to make sure everything is okay," she said before hanging up.

The door opened, and Michael walked into the corridor.

He spotted her immediately and strode over to her.

"Is everything okay?"

"I can't get a hold of Noel. He's not answering his phone."

"Want me to take you home?"

Nila looked at him apologetically. "I'm sorry. It's stupid, but I'm worried something's wrong."

"No problem." He placed his hand at her back and nudged her forward. They walked toward the exit. "This is a big thing being away from them for the first time. It's perfectly natural to be a little anxious."

With a grateful smile up at Michael, she pushed the exit door open, and they walked into the nighttime air. Nila hurried across the parking lot to Michael's jeep.

This was dumb. Of course, everything was okay.

Right?

In twenty minutes they pulled up to her house. Michael walked her to the door but even before she had it open, she heard the wailing from inside.

In stereo.

My babies.

She tried the knob, but it was locked.

Retrieving her keys, she jammed the correct one in the lock and barged inside. Through the foyer and into the living room, Nila stopped short at the sight of Noel holding both crying babies to his shoulders.

"Why didn't you call me?" she snapped as she went forward to take them.

"Because I can handle this." He released Benjamin to her.

Nila could tell it was Ben because of the mark on the back of his neck. Otherwise, both boys were dressed identically. When she took the baby, she noticed Noel had on her *Fight Like a Girl* shirt.

Immediately, Benjamin started rooting around on her.

"Is this how you handle things? Wearing my clothes and starving the kids?"

She picked up the doughnut which had been tossed to

the floor and laid the baby on the couch. She considered for a second the dress she was wearing and her babies. Nothing else to do but lower the dress and feed them.

Now.

She untied the sash and shrugged out of it. Noel had been on his way to her, when she began to disrobe.

"Nila! What the hell are you doing?"

With the dress hanging from her waist she took Daniel. She unhooked her bra even as she sat down and held his head to her. He latched on immediately. With a little trouble, she placed the doughnut around her waist.

"You don't strip in front of Michael!"

"Hand me Benjamin, Dearing."

Noel did so, but not without a commentary. "What? You go out on one date, and you have no problem taking your clothes off in front of the guy?"

Benjamin rubbed his face against her chest still crying. Poor thing. He was so worked up that he couldn't settle down to eat.

"Here. Hold Daniel for a minute," she said to Noel. He placed his hand against the baby to secure him. Nila positioned Benjamin's mouth over her nipple which was already leaking milk. He whimpered and finally began to suck.

"Some date this must have been."

Nila sighed and relief, then she turned her attention to Noel. "Why didn't you call me?"

"Because I was handling it. I can take care of the boys."

"Oh, really? It sure didn't look like it to me."

Noel stalked over to a baby blanket lying on the recliner and covered her and the babies with it.

"Would you stop?" Nila shrugged her shoulders and pulled the blanket away from the boys. They were hot enough already after all their crying. "I'm sure Michael understands that I need to nurse. Michael, you aren't offended by a nursing mother, are you?"

Noel huffed from his stance in front of her. "Well, what do you expect him to say? Man, you strip down to your panties like he's not even here."

"He's a minister. I'm sure he doesn't have a hang-up with my breasts like you seem to."

"He's also a guy, and I do not have a hang-up with your tits."

"I hate that word. Would you please not use it?"

"Fine. Knockers."

"No."

"Rack."

"Dearing, get out of my house. Now."

"I'm not leaving!"

Daniel kneaded her skin, and she petted his head. *The poor things.* Oh, she'd missed them in these last couple of hours. How could Noel have not called when they obviously needed her?

Nila settled back against the couch with an arm around each baby. Benjamin made little gasping noises even as he ate which told her he'd been crying for a while.

"It's all right, buddy. Mommy's here," she whispered and she rubbed his little back.

What was wrong with Noel? Why didn't he just call me?

Chapter Fifteen

Noel watched Nila nurse the kids, her soft voice comforting them in a way he couldn't. They'd settled down almost immediately when she took them. Why wouldn't they take the bottle from him if they were so damn hungry?

"Noel?" Michael said.

Noel turned his attention to the man who still stood just inside the living room when he'd entered.

Why didn't he leave already?

The *date* was over.

Michael gestured to the front door with his head.

Good. He was leaving.

Noel raised his hand and waved goodbye, but Michael shook his head and pointed to Noel.

What the hell? Mike wants me to leave?

Noel walked toward the man with every intention of escorting him out and locking the door behind him.

When they reached the front of the house, Michael didn't step over the threshold. He stared at Noel and waited.

"If you think you're staying here without me to finish up your date, you got another think coming," Noel growled.

Michael smiled and shook his head. "Come on, Noel. You're the one who insisted I take her out. Take a walk with me. Let's leave her and the boys alone for a bit, and you and I will have a talk." He nudged Noel as he began to go through the door.

Noel didn't move. "You're not coming back in the house tonight. The date's over."

"Fine. The date's over. Walk with me so you can tell me why I can't take her out on another date." His tone was placating as if Noel was being unreasonable.

Was he being unreasonable just because he didn't want Michael in the house with Nila when she was nearly naked?

Noel stepped forward, and Michael came along with

him. They stepped out into the lit porch, and Noel realized he didn't have on any shoes.

"I can't walk far." He gestured to his feet.

"Want to sit in my car? That way you can keep watch on the house."

"Okay."

They walked to Michael's Jeep Cherokee and settled inside. Michael didn't say anything, only sat in the driver's seat. When Noel looked at the man, he was watching him.

"What?" Noel asked.

"You don't have to be jealous of me, Noel. I'm your friend. You asked me to take her out because you trusted me. Remember?"

"I didn't think she'd be wearing that knock-out dress or end up stripping in front of you."

"She took it off so she could nurse."

"She could have waited until you left."

"She reacted as a mother who saw her babies needed her. She probably acted on instinct."

"I tried to feed them with the bottles. They wouldn't take it. I even put on her shirt hoping they could smell her scent and drink. But they wouldn't."

"Have you ever bottle fed them before?"

"A couple of times. They've done okay before. I don't know why they wouldn't take it. Neither one of them would. It's like they…." Noel sighed.

"It's like they what?"

"They don't need me. They only want her."

"They grew under her heart for nine months. That's a powerful connection between them."

"Did you see how she told me to get out of her house?" Noel ran his hands over his face.

"You were being a jerk. Why would you talk to her like that when all she was doing was taking care of your kids?"

Noel laid his head back on the seat. He stared at the ceiling of Michael's car. "I tried to be nice about her breastfeeding, being supportive, telling her how good it is for the boys, but…" He shook his head. "It seemed to put too much pressure on her, and she had trouble. One day I told her how sexy her breasts were, and it distracted her enough to let the milk come down so they could nurse."

"So, you did it so she could nurse them?"

"Well…" Noel shook his head. "The first time, yes, but she doesn't leave the room anymore. It seems every waking moment there she is, and there they are."

"Daniel and Benjamin?"

"No. Her tits. You saw what she did. The last several weeks if either one of the babies makes a peep, off comes her shirt. It's like I'm not even here. And I try to focus on the mothering aspect of it, but this is Nila, and she's showing me her breasts. Well, I mean, she's not showing them to me, but she's not hiding either. And I feel like a pervert for…."

"For?" Michael prompted.

"For wanting her. Wanting to touch her. That's sick, right?"

"It's more than lust. Isn't it, Noel?"

"She's so loving with the babies, so tender. It fills me up, you know? I've never seen this side of her before. Lil was the one who always talked about kids, wanting a baby. I really couldn't imagine Nila as somebody's mother, but she's a natural at it. And I feel like the outsider. They don't need me. Not really. Tonight just proved it."

"She needs you. The boys need you, too. As they get a little older, their bond with you will get stronger. They'll need a dad to play basketball with and buddy around with."

Noel snorted. "Nila is a better ball player than I am. She kicks my ass on the court just about every time."

"They need you. All three of them."

Noel didn't reply. He wanted to think they did, but he'd screwed it up tonight.

"You know what your mistake was?" Michael asked.

Noel turned his head toward his friend and waited for his answer.

"Your mistake was you sent her out on a date with me instead of going on a date with her yourself."

Noel shook his head even as the memory of kissing her

entered his head and bounced around in his brain. He closed his eyes as if that would exorcise the thought. "We're way past the date stage. She's never thought of me as anything but her BFF."

"Really?" Michael's skeptical tone surprised Noel.

"What?"

"You guys need to give one another permission to love each other and be the family you already are."

"What do you mean?"

"Think about it for a while. Now go back inside and apologize to her."

"Is this Pastor Mike talking or my friend Mike?"

"Whichever you need, buddy."

Noel smiled and opened the door. "Thanks, Mike. I'll see you." He exited the vehicle and jogged over to the house. Letting himself inside, he heard the television going. The Reds were playing.

Nila, with her dress back on, was standing in front of the television with one of the boys at her shoulder.

"Hey," he greeted.

She glanced behind her and gestured him forward.

When he approached she handed him the baby and picked up the other one who was lying on the couch. "Burp him," she said.

She placed the baby on her shoulder and began to pat his back. Noel did the same.

Nila turned back to the TV. "Why are they dressed alike?"

"They spit up all over themselves, and in the excitement which followed, I…" *Man, this is hard to admit.* "I couldn't figure out who was who. I should know by now, but I don't. I'm an idiot. They have an idiot for a father."

Nila didn't disagree.

Garcia was up at bat. He struck out and walked back to the dugout.

"And I was a jerk to their mother. I'm sorry. I was frustrated and mad at myself, and I shouldn't have taken it out on you."

Turning, Nila walked toward him and stood. Still patting the infant's back, she pointed with her index finger. "See this birthmark on his neck? This is Benjamin. He has this, but Daniel doesn't. That's the easiest way to tell them apart."

Daniel burped, and Noel felt liquid on his shoulder. He grimaced as he and Nila stood facing each other.

Nila grinned. "Guess you're going to be the one taking off your clothes now."

"This is your shirt."

"I noticed. Want to see if my dress fits?"

Noel snickered. "It's tight enough on you. I know I couldn't wear it."

Nila's expression turned serious. "I hope I didn't offend Michael. Did he say anything to you?"

"Not about your dress."

"Do you think he'll ask me out again?" Benjamin belched, and Nila held him up to her face. "Good boy. Feel better now?" Then to Noel. "He's really sweet, but the date could have ended better. I guess you and I need to get the boys used to you before we try this again."

Shit!

Noel gazed at the ballgame so he wouldn't give away his disappointment. "Do you want to go out with Mike again?"

"Yeah. Sure. If he'd like to go out with me. Did he say anything?"

"Umm. Well...."

What should he say? That he informed Mike this date was over? That he told him Noel wanted Nila for himself? That Michael ended up advising him to go out with her?

"Oh, crud. He doesn't want to, does he? I shouldn't have nursed in front of him. That's a real turn-off to a guy, isn't it?"

In light of Noel's own feelings, her comment struck him as funny, and he chuckled.

"What's so funny?" she demanded.

Noel studied her wondering how much he should disclose. He chose his words carefully. "Actually, we talked about how much your breastfeeding is a turn-on."

Not that Mike had said it, but he hadn't disagreed. "Seriously?"

"The nursing could be why…I kissed you earlier."

Her gaze flew to his.

"That and you look so damn good in that dress."

Her eyes widened then narrowed. She turned to the television and shifted Benjamin so that he lay across her forearm. *What is she thinking? Why doesn't she say anything?*

"Nila?"

She didn't take her eyes off the TV screen. "What?"

What? What do I say? What do I do? He decided to move to a safer topic.

"Want to see if we can lay the boys down?"

"All right." They walked down the hall, and Nila lay Benjamin down on her bed to change his diaper. Her actions brought a wail of protest from the baby, and she picked him up again and rocked him in her arms to quiet him.

Daniel's diaper was dry so Noel laid him in the cradle his mom and dad had brought over a few days ago on their last visit. In a moment, Nila placed Benjamin next to his brother and tucked the blanket around them.

She still hadn't made eye contact with him. "Want to finish watching the game?" he asked.

"Yeah. Sure." She crossed her arms over her middle. "I think I'll change into some sweats." A quick glance at him, then her gaze dropped to the boys.

Noel took it as an invitation to leave the room.

He'd done it. He'd screwed up. He shouldn't have said anything about the kiss. Hell, he shouldn't have kissed her in the first place.

When she walked into the room a few minutes later, he purposely kept his eyes on the ballgame as he sat on his end of the couch. They'd done this hundreds of times, and her spot was on the opposite end, but she bypassed it for the recliner.

"Why don't you sit over here?" he asked.

She pulled the lever back on the chair, and the foot rest popped up. "Because I don't want to."

"You always wanted to before."

"Quit being such a girl, Dearing."

"You say that like it's an insult."

"Can we just watch the game, please? The Reds actually have a chance of winning for once."

"You didn't care about missing the game when you were out with Mike."

Nila pushed her feet down and stood. She glared at him as she stomped to the couch and collapsed on it. "Are you happy now, you big baby? Here I am on the couch. Want me to take off my shirt so you can make some more comments about my chest?"

Noel relaxed a bit. "Maybe."

Her annoyed expression relaxed. "If we're going to live together, you need to stop freaking out when I doll up to go out."

"I'll try."

Daisy jumped up on the cushion and climbed to the back of the couch. Noel reached to stroke the cat as he settled in to enjoy the game. During the next couple of innings he got up to get a beer and sat closer to the middle of the couch. By the bottom of the eighth inning, he realized his fingers rested on the back of Nila's head which was leaned on the couch pillow. He glanced over at her and saw her sleeping. Moving closer, he sidled next to her and wrapped his arm around her shoulders. She gave a soft snore and cuddled into him.

Yeah. This was nice.

He smiled and watched Phillips at bat. The player swung hard, and the ball went high.

Home run.

When the Reds took the win, Noel muted the TV and placed his hand back on Nila who lay next to him. She slept so soundly, so well. He knew it was because of the interrupted nights she'd had since the twins were born. She was exhausted. He was tempted to move them to lie side-by-side on the couch until the babies woke up in a few hours. But they might as well sleep in the beds and be as comfortable as they could.

He nudged her. "Nila?"

She sighed and snuggled into him a bit more.

"Hey, sleepyhead. The game's over." He grasped her close to him and squeezed.

She responded. Her eyes opened. "What?" And she was already moving away from him.

She yawned and stretched. "Who won?"

Noel itched to take her back in his arms. "We did."

"Shoot. I hate I missed it." She leaned back against the couch.

"Don't you think you ought to get in bed?"

He didn't think she was going to move, but in a minute she roused. "Are you going home?"

Home was where she and the boys were, though she didn't realize it.

"I'll stay here tonight."

She yawned. "Okay." She sat up, stood, and walked toward the hall. "Good night, Dearing."

He watched her leave, wanting to go with her.

The bathroom door closed. He aimed the remote and hit the power button. The screen went black. He lay back on the couch and waited. In a few minutes, the door opened and she padded down the hall.

Probably to her room where the boys were asleep in their crib.

He yearned to walk down the hall and crawl into the bed with her. What would she do if he did that?

Maybe she was too tired to notice. What if he pulled her to him and kissed her?

Noel sighed.

It was stupid to even think such thoughts. He'd had the chance years ago to love her and convince her to love him back.

It was too late now.

He watched the darkened ceiling and closed his eyes.

****

Both boys cried in the portable playpen set up in Nila's

173

office. She held the phone to her ear and pushed her finger in the other ear trying to drown out the sound.

"You said you need a size fourteen shoe?" Nila asked the customer on the other end of the line.

"Yes. Fourteen wide."

She gave up trying to plug up her other ear, picked up a pad and pen from her desk, walked out of her office, and shut the door.

"Can I have your number? I'll check to see if we have that size, and I'll call you right back."

The man rattled off his number, and Nila wrote it down, then hit end on her phone before going back into the office.

She leaned over and tried to bundle the babies up on the blanket as she'd seen Noel do. But she jostled them too much, and their heads knocked together.

"I'm sorry. Sorry. Sorry," she said as they cried harder. She sat on the floor crossing her legs and brought them to her pulling up her shirt as she settled down. Pulling the doughnut on her lap, she set them on it so she could breastfeed them.

She didn't think they were hungry, but she didn't know another way to comfort them. They'd been cranky all day. Nothing suited them, and she'd gotten nothing done here.

Nothing.

She thought bringing them to work with her was the best solution. She wouldn't have to put them in daycare, and she could nurse whenever she needed to. But it wasn't working. They weren't content to lie in the playpen or their bouncy seats or even their car seats.

She'd tried everything she could think of short of taking them home.

How was she supposed to handle newborn twins and run her business? How did other mothers do it? Why couldn't she?

There was a knock on the door. Nila looked up as it opened and Noel appeared. His eyes roved over her and the boys. Daniel had latched on, but he was restless. Benjamin was still crying.

Noel entered the office, shut the door behind him, and knelt before her.

"Talk to me," he said.

Nila shook her head. "I can't do this."

Noel reached forward and took Benjamin. Lifting a blanket from the playpen, he swaddled the infant, then cuddled him. "You can do this. You are doing this." His tone was soft and soothing, and he looked down at Benjamin as he said it.

"Dearing, I'm just not cut out to be a mother. I'm no good at it. This isn't working."

Benjamin's cries quieted with the ministrations of his dad. Noel moved behind Nila and stretched his legs out so he couched her body with his. He moved Benjamin around her side and placed him on the doughnut. The baby rubbed his face across Nila's breast before pulling her nipple in his mouth.

Noel's thighs pressed into hers. "Relax," he murmured. He encircled her and the babies with his arms and gently pulled her to lean against his chest. "I've got your back."

Nila sighed in release. She closed her eyes relishing in the strength of Noel surrounding her.

"You know I'm right," she said as she leaned her head back on his shoulder.

"I know you're wrong. This is your first day back. You should expect it is going to be hard until you and the boys establish a routine."

The boys settled in. They were getting milk now. "I can't have another day like today."

"We'll put them in daycare."

"No. They're eleven weeks old. That's not an option."

"Other people put their newborns in daycare."

"I will not put my babies in a daycare when they are this young. They deserve better."

"We'll get a sitter."

"It'll take months to find a good sitter, and besides I'm nursing. I want them with me."

Noel didn't respond. Nila lifted her face and opened an

eye to glance at him.

"I could close the store or sell it."

"This is not Nila Miller talking," Noel declared. "You love this store. You're not going to sell or close. You're going to suck it up, and we'll figure it out." He rubbed his chin on her head to soften the blow of his words.

Nila yawned and relaxed against him. "I'm so tired."

"Let's just go home."

"I can't. I'm closing tonight."

"Then I'll take off early from work and stay with you. I was going to get the boys at five anyway."

"Okay."

Chapter Sixteen

Nila had been back to work a week. She'd gotten Teeny to come in every day and help out with the twins until Noel got off at five to take the boys home. It seemed to be working pretty well.

One evening he was sitting in front of the TV with the boys when his phone rang. He picked it up.

"Hey, Noel. This is Ricky from *Play It! Sports.*"

That was odd. Caller ID was saying it was a cell number calling him.

"Oh, hi, Ricky. Is everything okay?"

"I'm sorry to bother you, and please don't tell Nila I called, but…."

"What's wrong?"

"Well, when I came back from my dinner break, she was slumped on the counter asleep. She didn't even wake up when I walked in, and there was a customer in the store. She'd been there ten minutes and said Nila had been asleep when she walked in too."

Uh-oh. Nila was more tired than he'd realized.

"I'm not sure what to do. I know she's got that big fundraiser coming up that she's been working on, but, well…I mean, she's my boss, but it's kind of a bad idea for her to sleep when she's alone in the store."

"More than kind of, I believe," Noel replied as he rubbed his fingers over his forehead.

"What?"

"I'm saying I agree with you."

"Oh. So, I'm sort of afraid to leave her alone now, but I told my girlfriend I'd take her out. We hadn't had a lot of time together lately because I've been helping out at the store. I'm glad for the extra money, but, you know, I don't know what to do, so I thought I'd better call you."

"You did the right thing, Ricky. I'll go up there."

Noel hung up the phone and walked to where the babies were lying on the floor under an activity set. "Well, boys, looks like we're going up to Mommy's work until closing."

Noel arrived in less than twenty minutes with the babies in their double stroller. He figured he could spend at least part of the time strolling them around while they waited on ten o'clock to arrive. When he walked in the door, Nila was ringing up a customer who was buying some tennis balls. Noel examined Nila and noticed the dark circles under her eyes and drawn cheeks.

"Hi," Nila greeted Noel after the customer left. She leaned back on the counter and crossed her arms. "What's up?"

"We thought you might be lonely."

That brought a smile to her lips. She walked around the counter and leaned over the stroller. "Hi, my sweet babies. Did you come to help Mommy at work?"

"I brought supper." Noel produced a Styrofoam container from a local eatery downtown.

"I'm not that hungry." Nevertheless, she walked over to the counter and lifted the lid. With raised eyebrows she looked at Noel. "Is this liver and onions?"

"Yep. And spinach with a baked sweet potato."

"I don't eat meat. Especially not organ meat."

"You're going to eat it."

She pursed her lips. When she'd gone for her check-up, the doctor had advised her that her iron was a little low. Noel had insisted he'd accompany her and for just this reason.

To his surprise, she didn't argue with him—just unwrapped the fork from its plastic sleeve and took a bite of the potato.

He set a quart of whole milk on the counter next to the plate.

"You're kidding," she said.

"Nope. Completely serious."

"It's cow milk. Couldn't you have at least gotten soy or almond?"

"Quit being such a snob." Noel shook it and twisted off

the cap handing it to her.

She accepted it grudgingly and took a sip. "Ugh. It's like drinking cream." She set the bottle down and cut a small piece of liver with the fork. Placing it in her mouth, she made a face as she chewed. "I cannot eat this."

"Five bites. You need it."

She shivered to show her disgust and shook her head.

"Fine. I'll go get some formula for the kids. Because unless you start eating this kind of stuff, you are not going to be able to keep nursing."

She took a bite of the spinach. "The spinach is pretty good."

They had cooked it with bacon, but he wasn't telling her that.

"How about if I eat all of the spinach and half of the potato?"

"And five bites of liver."

"Three," she bargained.

"Six," he amended.

She dug her fork into the potato. "You're supposed to go down, not up."

There was a squeal from the back of the store, then a crash of the soccer ball display. "Teenagers," she groused and went to investigate. He noticed she took the milk with her.

After closing, he insisted she go home to his house since he was bringing the boys there. She put up little argument, further evidence she was tired.

When they walked in the house, he headed down the hall, ran water in the tub, and herded her into the bathroom. She leaned against the counter. "You're smothering me, Dearing."

He ignored her complaint as he tested the water's temperature. Rising to his feet, he walked to the door. "Tonight you're going to sleep uninterrupted. I'll get up with the boys and feed them."

"Is there enough milk here?"

"You can pump before bed. I'll take care of things."

"You taking care of things didn't work out so well last time. You stretched out my shirt and got your testosterone all worked up with Michael."

"If I can't handle it, I'll stick a kid at your...breast. Okay?"

"Whatever." She pulled off her shoes, then her socks. "Guess I'll take a bath since you insist. Get out, why don't you?"

"Call me if you need your back scrubbed."

"Yeah, right." She pushed him into the hall, closed the door, and turned the lock.

By six the next morning, Noel felt as if he'd been hit by a Mac truck. He'd been up twice with the babies but had not slept well in between feedings because he'd worried about not hearing them in the night. He lay back on the bed in his underwear after getting Daniel back to sleep in the crib and wondered if he could sleep for ten good minutes before the alarm sounded.

Muted footsteps padded in the hallway, and the door opened.

Nila.

Her face registered surprise, but whether it was because he was in his boxer briefs or because he was awake, he didn't know. He motioned for her to enter, and she stepped into the room, her attention on the crib he had moved to the far side of the bed.

"How was your night?" she whispered as she began to walk around the bed.

"Uh, uh, uh, uh, uh." he pointed his finger for her to stop. "Let sleeping babies lie." Then he patted the spread next to him.

She hesitated a second before climbing on the bed and began to bring her knees up to her chin, but she grimaced and lowered them again. "So, tough night then?"

"We did okay. How about you?" He folded the pillow behind his head and studied her. She had on a tank top and those little shorts she liked to sleep in. *Hmmm.* Maybe lying here with her while he wore underwear wasn't so wise.

"I slept like a log."

Her smooth legs shifted, and she crossed one ankle over another. Her gaze traveled up his body to his face. Her tongue appeared and licked her lips as her eyes met his then skirted away.

She's getting turned on.

I think.

Play it cool. Watch for an opening, and take it—gently.

"Have they eaten recently?"

"Daniel about half an hour ago and Benjamin about four."

"Oh." She moved toward the edge of the bed. "I probably should go pump. I'm feeling...."

"Full?"

"Yeah."

Noel turned on his side to face her and pillowed his head on his arm. How could he get her to stay? Just ask?

"Nila, why don't you...."

A whimper from the crib behind him and movement. Nila turned on her knees, intent to reach whichever baby had awoken. She approached Noel, then moved a leg over his, but Noel snaked his arm out to stop her.

"Just wait," he spoke in a low tone.

Nila resisted, and Noel rolled on his back and held her waist to keep her from going further. He shook his head. "Wait. I don't think he's awake."

"Dearing," she breathed as she struggled to get over his body, her hands anchoring on his arms.

He pulled her closer to him. "Let him settle back down if he will. This is good for them to...." She was on top of him now, straddling him as she'd done all those months ago when they'd lain in this very spot.

She was remembering it too. He could tell by the fire that had ignited in her eyes.

Noel's grip loosened, and he felt her resistance ebb. He wanted there to be no doubt he hadn't forced this. He dropped his hands to her thighs, running his fingers along her skin to her knees, then back up and cupped her hips. She watched him not moving away from him.

With one hand he found hers and lifted it to his lips, kissing her knuckles one at a time.

"You're sleep deprived," she stated.

"Probably." He opened her hand and kissed her palm, then opened his mouth and traced a trail with his tongue.

Her mouth opened, and she took a shuddering breath.

With his other hand, he moved up her outer thigh again, but this time under her shorts loving her smooth skin, the muscles firm from running and swimming.

She bit her lip. "We shouldn't—"

"Wake them up, I agree. We'll be very quiet, and if they do wake up, we'll be right here."

Nila closed her eyes, and when she opened them again, she focused on his chest. She sat on his upper thighs, her legs encasing his crotch. His body began to respond.

How could he not?

Nila placed her hands on his stomach, then weighting herself on her knees, she leaned forward running her hands over his chest, then shoulders, then back to chest. Her attention was on her hands.

What was she thinking?

Straightening, she inhaled deeply then finally made eye contact with him. He'd known her ten years, had looked into her face thousands of times, yet he had no clue what was going on inside her. Did she want him, or was she trying to think of a graceful way out of it? On her knees, she was perched above him, and his groin throbbed in anticipation.

He wanted this so badly. Wanted her, but he waited.

She turned her head to the crib and looked at the boys sleeping.

She sighed again.

"Nila Rachel Miller, I really wish you'd kiss me."

She crooked her head at him, then moved her legs out and settled down on him. He bit back a groan of pleasure as the warmth of her body met with his, only the thin layers of clothing separating them. Leaning forward, she lay on top of him, but waited a second before she settled her lips on his, then—boom, it was like a cannon fired, the incendiary contact with her.

Nila. This was Nila.

Her mouth moved across his, tasting him as if she was dying of thirst and he was a pitcher of water. He grasped the bedspread so he wouldn't be tempted to press her to him, restrain her.

It had to be her choice. All her. He'd waited so long, and there was no way he was going to screw it up.

"Hold me, Dearing," she directed against his lips.

He growled in pleasure and wrapped his arms around her moving one hand down to knead the flesh at her bottom and press her into him. She gasped, and he delved his tongue past her lips and explored the inner recesses of her mouth. He wanted to know her as a woman, as the sexual being he'd never had the chance before to appreciate physically. Rolling her on her back, he crouched over her, skimming his hands from her neck and along the sides of her chest careful to avoid her breasts. He wanted to respect her wishes that her breasts were off-limits unless she specifically gave him the go ahead. Down past her ribs to her stomach, he lifted her shirt and studied her. The skin was riddled with stretch marks, but already her flesh was nearly flat.

Nila tried to pull her shirt down. "What are you doing?"

He held her hand and kissed it. "Looking at how beautiful you are."

"You're full of it."

Noel didn't reply. Instead, he kept her gaze as he leaned forward and licked her incision then kissed her just below her navel. He inched down her boxers and panties. "What did the doctor say about sexual intimacy?"

"He said." She squeezed her eyes shut. "He said I can do what I want, but if there's any pain or blood, I should come in immediately."

"We'll be very careful."

Her eyes were still closed.

"Nila? Open your eyes. Please."

She did so, and he saw fear there.

"It's okay. This is going to be good for both of us. I want to taste you. Is that all right?"

Nila shook her head. "I don't think it's a good idea. I don't think I can…."

"Can what?"

"Come."

Noel gave a burst of laughter. "Now there's a challenge if I've ever heard one."

She smiled in response, but it didn't reach her eyes. "They took out all my female parts. I'm just not sure that it's possible anymore to…you know. I mean, I know sex is possible, but whether I can…." She shut her eyes tightly and began to turn away from him.

Noel pressed down on her and kept her on her back. "Nila." He came back up to her and lay with her. "Sweetheart."

"Don't." She turned her face away. "I don't want your pity."

Noel rubbed his crotch against hers. "Does that feel like pity?"

She tensed. "No, it feels like your dick."

Noel kissed her neck and trailed his tongue to her ear where he sucked it into his mouth. His hand grazed her thigh, working his way in between her legs then maneuvered under her shorts and panties. His fingers slipped inside of her and found her wet. "I don't think you coming is going to be a problem."

"Just don't get your hopes up."

He stroked, and he felt her body relax a bit, then her breathing hitched. She turned her face to his and kissed him again. She reached down and pulled off her shorts, and Noel took her action as an invitation. He knelt before her bringing his mouth in contact with her.

In a moment, she shuddered around him, and he smiled. *Success.*

He crawled up next to her and spooned her. She sighed as he pulled her flush against him and reveled in the feel of her body—sated—beside him.

His alarm beeped, and he reached to the shelf on the headboard of the bed and turned it off. He settled back down and pulled her to him.

"What about you?" she asked.

"What about me?"

She tilted her pelvis toward him as she glanced over her shoulder to toss him a flirty grin. "It's your turn, isn't it?"

He cupped her hip and leaned over her to capture her lips. "You want to make sure the first time wasn't a fluke?"

"Maybe. What do you want to do?"

Noel rolled onto his back. He grinned at her. "Whatever you want to do to me. Knock yourself out."

Nila who had also moved on her back to watch him, sat up. She reached for his boxer briefs, her hand grazing his erection, but then she stopped. Her face blanched, and she shook her head.

"What's wrong?"

Nila grabbed her shorts and scooted to the edge of the bed. "This feels…." She stood. "I'm sorry." She leaned over and put on her shorts.

Noel sat up and followed her. "What the hell is wrong?"

She walked out the bedroom door. He slipped off the bed and trailed her into the hall.

"Would you please tell me what's wrong?" he asked her as she headed into the guest bedroom.

"I'm sorry, Dearing." She turned around to face him. "I just had a flashback. That night, going down on you." She shook her head. "I can't help thinking about it—her, your bedroom, her bedroom. I shouldn't have—"

"It's okay. We'll take it slow if we need to or make love somewhere else. Anywhere else. Your house, your store, the car, the street."

"I wish you wouldn't make jokes."

"Who's joking? I got a hard on here that's about to kill me."

Nila's face relaxed. She looked down at his crotch and smirked. Strolling to him, she took him in her hand, then lifted her face pressing her lips to his. "Against the wall?"

Noel lifted her up and held her tightly against his body. "Pick a wall, darlin'."

He felt her lips curve upward. "That one next to the door."

He backed up and turned her around leaning her next to the wall without breaking contact with her lips. She pulled first her shorts down, then his boxers, and he stepped out of them.

This was happening. This was really going to happen.

She nestled him bringing her legs up to ensconce his hips.

"Are you ready?" he whispered.

She nodded, her gaze searing him. "Promise me something."

"Anything."

"When you come, I want you to say my name. That way I'll know you know it's me."

Noel's heart thumped hard in his chest. Did she really think he'd mistake her for Lil? At a time like this?

"Sweetheart—"

She shook her head, her eyes darkening. "No, Noel. Not sweetheart or darling or any other name. Nila. Only Nila. Will you do that for me?"

He held her by the hips and lifted her body a fraction. Positioning himself, he watched her face. "Nila," he murmured. "Nila." He pushed into her, and she trembled but didn't break eye contact. Her legs tightened around him, and he thrust once.

"Nila."

Then again.

"Nila."

This was amazing. She's amazing. I'm making love to...

"Nila."

She grasped his shoulders and mewed in pleasure. Finding his mouth, she covered his lips with her own, and everything else flew out of Noel's mind except her body surrounding him, the sound of her pleasure, and his voice calling her name.

"Nila. Nila. Nila."

Chapter Seventeen

Nila sat at her desk with Daniel on her shoulder while she worked on payroll. Movement from her office door caught her attention, and she looked up from the computer monitor.

Teeny with Benjamin in his sling on her front stood at the door grinning like the Cheshire cat.

"What?" Nila asked.

Teeny stepped aside, and a delivery guy carrying a dozen red roses in a crystal vase walked in.

"Hi. Are you Nila Miller?"

"Yes."

"Here you go." He set the vase on the desk and began to walk out of the office.

"Wait." Nila plucked the small envelope from its holder, held it in her teeth and pulled out the card. Holding the card, she read Noel's name.

She shook her head. Have sex with the guy, and this is what she gets—girly romance. Yuck.

She took the envelope out of her teeth and laid it and the card on her desk. "I think this is a mistake."

The man's face creased in confusion. "Huh?"

"These flowers aren't for me."

"You're Nila Miller, aren't you? You don't know the name on the card?"

"What *is* the name on the card?" Teeny interjected.

"Noel." He turned to her. "Does she know a Noel?"

"Oh, yes. She *knows* him." Teeny nodded then chuckled.

Nila didn't like the direction this conversation was going. Teeny had had enough boyfriends to know red roses meant one of two things. Either someone got screwed or someone screwed up. From Teeny's reaction, she'd rightly concluded the former.

"I'm not accepting these flowers." Holding Daniel

securely to her with her hand, she picked up a pen with the other hand and crossed out her name on the envelope, then wrote Noel's secretary's name and the address of his office. "Here. Take them to this woman at this address."

She had to put up with Noel all day. She'd appreciate these a hell of a lot more than Nila did.

"I don't think I'm allowed to do that."

"Sure you are." Nila said as she put the card in the envelope and thrust it at the man then handed him the flowers. Opening her desk drawer, she reached into her purse and pulled out a twenty-dollar bill, which she stuffed into the delivery man's breast pocket. "If you have any questions, you can talk to Noel yourself. He works at that address. Teeny? Give this guy a ten-dollar gift certificate from the store for his trouble, will you?"

"Nila!" Teeny's face was distraught now. She'd now decided the dozen roses was about Noel screwing up. Boy, she had that right. "Don't send his flowers back. Enjoy them."

"I don't like flowers."

"We'll put them in the front of the store."

"No. I don't like that kind of stuff. Why in the world Noel did this, I have no idea."

The delivery guy left with the flowers, but Teeny stayed. "Did you guys have a fight?"

Nila ignored the question. She laid Daniel in the playpen then went back to her desk.

"Well? Did you?"

"Teeny, I'm not getting into this right now. I need to get payroll done, so if you want to get paid, you'll leave me alone and let me get to my work."

"I'm beginning to understand why you've never had a boyfriend," she shot back as she walked back to the front of the store.

"Who wants one if they spend money on stupid flowers?" she called. Then to herself, she muttered. "Want to impress me? Get me something practical."

She knew the moment the flowers arrived at Noel's

office, because her cell phone rang. She went to her office door, shut it, and hit the screen to answer the call ready to do battle.

"What?"

"Hi, Nila," he purred, and her heart flip-flopped. He said her name as he had a few hours ago when they had….

She cleared her throat trying to exorcise the image from her mind or the picture of him kissing her so sweetly before he left for work, then coming back a second time to kiss her again. "What do you want?"

"I want to make love to you again. I want to feel you against me. I want to taste your lips and be—"

Nila squirmed in her chair. "Stop it, Dearing. This is not what I need from you right now."

"What do you need?" His tone changed. The purr was gone.

"I need you not to pull any more stunts like the roses."

"Let's go out to lunch."

"Where?"

"I'll come pick you up."

Nila huffed. "No, you are not coming here to pick me up. Just tell me where we can meet you."

"Can Teeny keep the boys for an hour?"

Nila chewed her lip. What was he up to? "I suppose so. Where do you want to meet?"

"The Plaza Hotel."

"I'm not in the mood for their food. They only have iceberg lettuce in their salad."

"Who said we were eating at the restaurant?"

Nila blinked. *Oh, my gosh.* He wanted a nooner. Her stomach fluttered.

"I'll meet you in the lobby."

"We have two houses between us. If you want to…." Nila shook her head. "Let's just go to my house."

"We both work downtown, and we both can be at the Plaza in a few minutes. Do you really want to spend most of the lunch hour on the commute to your house?"

No. No, I don't.

"What time can you get away?" she asked.

"Twelve-thirty?"

"Okay."

Nila walked into the Plaza lobby with two minutes to spare. She wiped her sweaty palms on her pants.

Stop it. This is Noel.

She glanced around and saw him standing at the front desk talking to the clerk. He wore the light blue, Oxford shirt with thin red stripes and dress pants he'd had on that morning when he left the house. Her gaze traveled over his body—the breadth of his shoulders too wide for an accountant, the trim waist, the cute butt. He turned then and spotted her. Smiling, he walked toward her.

Was he going to kiss her?

He stopped in front of her. "Hi."

No lecherous grin or suggestive gleam in his gaze. Had she misunderstood this lunch date? Were they going to eat lunch after all?

Noel gestured toward the elevator. They walked to it, and he pushed the button to go up. When the doors opened, they stepped inside and turned around.

"Does this lunch include food?" Nila asked more to cover the silence than to satisfy her curiosity.

Noel didn't respond immediately. When Nila glanced at him, he was watching the numbers light up above the doors. Ding. Ding. Ding. "Why? Are you hungry?"

"This seems rather trashy."

"A business luncheon at the Plaza Hotel? I don't think so."

"This is a business luncheon?"

They arrived at the fifth floor, and the doors opened. Nila didn't move so Noel stepped around her and entered the carpeted hallway. "Yes. I am the accountant for *Play It! Sports*. You are one of the main sponsors for the park fundraiser you've been working on. I thought we could discuss any…details which might have come up recently."

Nila followed him. "In a hotel room?"

"What else would we do?" He glanced at her and

winked.

"You're going to charge me for…for a nooner?" she asked in disbelief.

He stopped at a door and slid in the card key then pushed the knob down and opened the door. The corner of his mouth curved upward. "A what?"

Nila walked into the room. A king sized bed occupied half the room. The other half held a table in front of the sliding glass door leading to the balcony overlooking the river. The table was covered with a white linen cloth and set with a meal for two. In the middle of the table was the vase of red roses.

"I thought I sent those flowers to Kim."

"You did."

Nila shook her head. She turned around to face him and saw him shut the door and stroll to her, loosening his tie as he did so. "Do you know me at all? When have I ever said I liked flowers or wanted this." She gestured to the table with her hand.

Noel walked to the roses and touched one. "What do you mean *this*?"

"A pretty table with a silver service, a white table cloth. I don't need this. I don't want it. Just because we had sex this morning doesn't mean I need you to change on me and start acting all weird. You know me. You know what I like. This isn't it."

Noel reached down into the arrangement and withdrew a small white envelope.

"Your mistake was you thought the flowers were the gift and not the wrapping." He held the envelope out to her.

Nila stepped toward him and took it. Opening the envelope, four tickets dropped into her hand.

Cincinnati Reds Baseball.

"These were not in the roses this morning," she declared.

"Oh, yes, they were, you jerk. And I've a good mind not to let you have them after all. I had to do some fast talking to get them away from Kim, but as it is, she and her husband will be going with us if she agrees to hold the babies, when necessary. I thought we could use the two extra seats for the carriers for the boys, but now it looks like they'll be on our laps."

Nila laid the tickets on the table and wrapped her arms around Noel. "We'd be holding them anyway."

Noel smiled in response.

"Thanks for the tickets. Are we going to eat lunch now?"

"If you want."

"Are we going to use the bed?"

"It depends on how long it takes us to eat. We only have forty-seven minutes left of the lunch hour."

Nila lowered her hand and squeezed a handful of Noel's butt. "I'm not that hungry. Maybe we can work up an appetite and then take the food to go."

****

Nila walked into her house where they'd been staying since the morning she and Noel had started sleeping together. That day Noel had taken the boys to her house after he got off work, and she and Noel had fallen into a routine.

So comfortable.

As if they'd been together forever.

Noel looked over the back of the couch at her as she set her purse down on a chair. He held a baby in each arm.

"Hey. How was work?"

She leaned down and kissed him. "Hey, yourself." Bending further, she kissed the top of each baby's head. Both began squirming for her. "They must be hungry. Good." Her breasts were painfully full. She knew she either needed to pump or nurse. Kicking off her shoes, she sat down beside Noel on the couch, took the doughnut onto her lap, and pulled at her shirt. In a moment, the twins were eating contentedly. Noel scooted close to her and caressed her neck.

Nila leaned into his touch enjoying the closeness of the babies and Noel.

After she nursed, they bathed Benjamin and Daniel, put them in the jogging stroller, and jogged around the neighborhood. The boys were asleep by the time they came back to the house, and she and Noel placed them in the crib.

Noel linked his fingers with hers and led her down the hall. "Come here. I want to show you something."

"What?"

"It's on the computer." He guided her to the kitchen table where his laptop was open. They each sat on a chair, and he rolled his finger over the keypad. A realty site popped up. He clicked on an icon, and a ranch-style house filled the screen. "What do you think of this house?" he asked.

Nila shrugged. "I don't know. It's a house."

Noel nodded. "Yeah. It's got four bedrooms and a double garage, and it's within walking distance of the ballpark and your store."

"So what? Are you wanting to move?"

"Yes. Both of us." His face was alight with excitement.

Nila wrinkled her nose. Was he insane? "What?"

"We'll sell both of our houses and buy a house together. This is a really nice one."

"I'm not buying a house with you, Dearing. I like my house."

"Yeah, but it's yours. If we bought a house we both liked, it could be—"

Nila scooted her chair back and stood. "No."

Noel stood too. He raised his eyebrows as he looked at her. "Why not?"

"Because…I don't know. That's a big thing. Where did this come from?"

"It just seems like neither one of us is really settled, and it would be good for—"

"No, it wouldn't be good. Look. I know we're getting along well with this…" She gestured between the two of them. "The sex and all, but I don't think we need to make any hasty decisions about our future."

"Hasty decisions?" Noel thundered. "Are you kidding me?"

"No, I'm not kidding you. We need to make sure this is all going to work out—"

"Give me a freaking break here. We've got two kids to think about. This isn't some kind of flash-in-the-pan affair." He ran his hands through his hair and began to pace the room.

"Well, it's all well and good for you. Just fall in love with Lil and marry her, then when she dies, well, hey, here's Nila. I think I'll hook up with her. She's got no better prospects, and we've got these two kids to think about anyway."

"That's not fair. You were the one who didn't want me in the first place."

"*You* never wanted me until now. I've always been the second choice where Lil was concerned."

"You were never my second choice. How can you say that?"

"Because it's true."

"I followed you around like a puppy for months, and you pawned me off on your sister."

"I? I brought you home to meet my family and caught you with your tongue down Lil's throat before the weekend was out."

"I thought it was you."

"You're a liar!" Nila screamed. She balled up her fist and punched him square in the face.

Noel touched his finger to his lip, bloody now. He studied its tip grimly.

"Don't you act like choosing my sister was a case of mistaken identity. You married her!"

"I asked you first."

Shock froze Nila. She couldn't have possibly heard him right. "What?"

"The ski trip. On the lift. I told you I wanted to get married, and you shoved my ring back at me and proceeded to tell me how to propose to Lil."

Nila shook her head.

"All you did after that weekend at your parents was push Lil at me. You never even gave me a chance to be with you except for being your damn exercise buddy. I was so hurt when you turned me down on the lift that I went to Lil, and she started talking about how much she loved me, how she wanted to get married and have a family. I wanted that too, but I wanted it with you first."

Tears welled up in her eyes. "You loved Lil. Don't act like you didn't."

"Of course, I loved her. I still love her, but I was *in love* with you."

"You idiot! What's the difference?"

"What's the difference?" Noel stalked over to Nila and clasped her upper arms. He dipped his head and touched his lips to hers, quickly deepening the kiss. Lightning shot through Nila at the first instant of contact, and she wrapped her arms around him, pressing herself to him. After several moments, he ended the kiss, but kept his lips touching hers. "That's the difference. That's how I knew the night we conceived because it was never like that with Lil. Not ever."

Nila heaved a sigh. "Why did you settle for her then?"

"Because you didn't want me."

"I did want you, but she was my sister."

"You were her sister too. But I guess I wasn't worth it." He dropped his hands and stepped back.

"For God's sake, Noel. You...you idiot. How could you...how could you go to her that night and ask her to *marry* you? You're so stupid!"

Noel glowered at her.

"Why did I ever think you should pass on your idiot genes to another generation? What was Lil thinking when she talked me into—"

"That's been your problem all along," Noel stated. "Letting Lil run your life. Always letting her manipulate you into whatever she wanted."

"She did not!"

"Tell me one time. Just one that she gave in to you about something?"

Nila stared at Noel. Different confrontations with Lil raced through her mind, but there had always been the same result. Lil got her way.

"Well, Lil's gone now. She's not around for you to live vicariously through her. You're stuck with me."

"I'm not stuck with you. I want you out of my house." Nila snatched the power cord out of the wall and shoved his laptop at him. "Take your stupid, two-car garage house with you."

"I love you."

"Maybe you think you do now, but nine years ago you made love to my sister on the ski slopes after you supposedly proposed to me. You chose her."

"I did propose to you. I chose you, but you didn't want me."

"Please get out. You can come back in two hours when I've had enough time not to want to punch you again."

"Well, gee. Thanks for that, but I might as well stay in my own house tonight so I don't tempt you to hit me or have to look at my stupid face."

"Come back for the sex, then you can go home again."

"Are you serious?"

"Yes, I'm serious. I'm not going to give up sex just because you're an idiot."

Noel slammed his laptop on the table. He began to unbuckle his belt. "Want me to service you now, since I don't have to use my inferior brain to do it?"

"Fine. It'll save you a trip back."

His eyes snapped fire at her as he finished with the belt, then unsnapped and unzipped his pants. She knew he was calling her bluff.

Fine. Let him. She wasn't backing down. As a matter of fact....

Nila pulled off her shirt and tossed it on the floor. She reached for the front eye-hooks of her maternity bra. In the times they'd made love, she'd never taken off her bra because her breasts had no erogenous feel in them. She figured it had something to do with nursing, but she knew Noel was attracted to them. She'd watched his face and seen the desire.

His chin dropped, and his eyes flew wide open.

Nila shrugged out of the bra and pulled back her shoulders.

With a finger she traced an imaginary line from her neck to one nipple, then the other.

"Want to go up to the bedroom, or do it right here on the table?"

"You would really make love to me, then kick me out?" Noel asked.

"No. I would really have sex with you, then kick you out," Nila corrected.

Noel shook his head. He zipped up his pants and picked up his laptop. "Nila, this was never sex, and I'm sorry you misinterpreted it as such."

He walked to the back door with his laptop under his arm. When the door snicked closed behind him, Nila sighed heavily and put on her bra, then picked up her shirt from the floor.

So, he had been the one bluffing, and she had called him on it and won.

But it didn't feel like a victory. Yes, she had gotten him out of the house, and she'd needed him gone after that bomb he'd dropped on her tonight.

He had to be lying.

He'd actually proposed to her on the slopes? To her— Nila—even though he'd been dating her sister?

Or had they?

For that month, Noel and Lil had always been together.

But if what Noel said was true, maybe it was that Lil had always been with Noel when he had been hanging out with Nila.

After the kiss Nila had witnessed and the emergency room visit on that fateful Thanksgiving, Nila thought Noel had fallen in love with Lil at first sight. Nila thought he had wanted her sister. Nila had gone to Lil and told her she had changed her mind about Noel.

"Are you sure?" Lil had asked. "He's so wonderful."

"I know," Nila had responded. "Yes, I'm sure."

That had decided it. Noel belonged to Lil, even though

he hadn't realized it yet.

If Nila had any idea, any clue, that the ring he flashed at her was *hers*. She wouldn't have had to stand there in agony with her heart breaking when he'd pledged to love Lil for the rest of their lives.

A sob escaped her, and Nila pressed her face in her hands.

What would Lil have done?

Nila raised her head, staring at the far wall.

Lil would have been so upset. She was already so in love with Noel by that time, even though until that night *the three of them had done everything together.*

Nila had thought she was the third wheel.

Maybe Lil had been the third wheel, but Nila hadn't realized it.

When Nila sent Noel off to propose to Lil, it was the first time she'd removed herself from the two of them and Noel had acquiesced.

He'd done as she told him.

He'd proposed marriage to Lil, and he had loved, honored, and cherished her for the rest of her life.

He'd been faithful to his wife, and he had been a faithful friend to Nila because that had been the terms Nila had given him.

Nila folded her arms on the table, laid her head down, and wept.

Chapter Eighteen

Noel paced Mike's living room while he poured out the story of his fight with Nila. "And then she tells me that she wants me to come back and have sex with her since she doesn't think she should have to give up the sex just because I'm an idiot. So, then I tell her I'd just make love to her right then. And she starts taking off her clothes, but she corrects me. She says it's only sex."

"Wow. So, what'd you do?"

"I told her what has been between us was never sex, and I left."

Mike smiled. "I admire your scruples. It took a lot to walk away from what she was offering."

"I'm an idiot. Because I thought we were working up to love and marriage. Mike, I've loved her as long as I've known her, and now I find out she just wants to be friends with benefits."

"Noel." Michael shook his head. "You and Nila have been friends a long time. In the past year, a lot of things have changed. You've lost your wife; she's lost her sister. You have two children together whom you both love. You've got to expect there's going to be some tension as you two negotiate new terms in your relationship. There's a reason why you ended up married to Lil and not Nila to begin with."

"Yeah, because she threw my ring back at me and refused to even consider I could be her husband. But Lil was always about setting up a home. Looking for a house was some of our best times together. And, man! Lil would have never had sex with me when she was mad. Sex always seemed like a chore to her. I can't believe how Nila acted tonight like I'm some sort of...of a piece of meat."

"She's not settled like Lil was. She's never struck me as the type. You've got to give her some room to get used to you as a partner to her. You don't begin a sexual relationship with her then a week later buy a house together. Didn't you think about taking her out on a date like I told you?"

Noel raised his hands in surrender. "It happened before I could get around to the date. I mean, she's kneeling over me in the bed, and—"

"That's okay. I think I've heard enough of the details."

Michael's cell phone rang. Noel glanced at it on the table, and the cell number on caller ID jumped out at him.

Sonofabitch. That was Nila's cell number.

It rang twice, but Michael didn't move.

"Why don't you answer it?"

"Because I'm talking to you. Whoever it is will leave me a message if they need me."

Noel picked up the phone and handed it to him. "Answer it. It's Nila."

Surprise registered on Mike's face. He really hadn't recognized the number. Pressing the screen, he held it to his ear and spoke. She must have greeted him.

"Oh, hi, Nila. How are you?…No, that's okay. I was awake. Is everything all right?"

Noel scowled, and Mike looked at him and shrugged.

"Oh…Sure…Eleven forty-five? See you then…Goodbye."

Michael hung up the phone. "She wants to have lunch with me tomorrow."

"What?" Noel huffed. "And you agreed?"

"Yes, of course, I did. She said something about the Day in the Park."

Noel pounded the table. "She's just using that as an excuse. She likes you. She told me she wanted to go out with you again."

"She likes me, I suppose, but I'm pretty sure she loves you."

Noel threw up his hands in frustration. "Did you hear anything I told you in the last half hour?"

"Did you hear anything I told you? Give her some room to figure this out. You've been unavailable to her for a long time. Let her get used to the idea that it's okay to love you, that Lil doesn't hold a claim anymore."

"Maybe she'll never decide that. Maybe she'll always consider me off limits."

"She made love to you, didn't she?"

"She said it was sex."

"You've told her it's not. Let her think about it. Tomorrow I'll see what she wants. But it's not me, so stop worrying."

****

"Hi, Michael. Thanks for coming over." Nila shook his hand in greeting.

"Sure thing. What can I do for you?"

"Is it okay if we eat here?" Nila led him through the store to the team room she reserved for meetings and parties. "I'm working on The Day at the Park fundraiser, and we have an opening ceremony which we'd like to begin with a prayer. I think it would set a good tone for the day. Can I count on you to do that?"

"The Day at the Park is what? Next week?"

"Yes. A week from Saturday."

"I should be able to help you out," Michael confirmed.

"Great." Nila smiled her thanks.

"You could have just asked me on the phone."

Nila hesitated. "Yes, I could have done that, but I wanted to go over the order of the ceremony with you, maybe let you decide if you'd like a bigger role on our planning committee. I'm hoping to make this an annual event. Our committee is meeting in a few minutes. You can stay, if you like, and see what we're about."

"Is Noel going to be here?"

"Umm… No. He's not on the committee."

"Too bad, as close as he lives to the park. I would have thought you'd ask him first."

"Well." Nila covered her disappointment. Noel hadn't come back last night nor had he called this morning to check on her or the boys. "I actually meant to ask him last night, but…" Nila shook her head. "It's probably better if he doesn't serve on the committee since he can be with the kids while I'm working on the Day at the Park project."

Michael nodded. "That makes sense."

They entered the room, and Nila gestured for Michael to have a seat at the conference table. She sat next to him and shuffled some papers in front of her. She handed him a stapled packet. "Here's what our vision is for the event, including the minutes of our previous meeting and the agenda for this meeting. If you like, you can look this over before everybody else gets here."

Michael took the papers from her and gave them a brief glance then set them on the table. "Are you and Noel doing okay?"

Nila sighed and stared at him. "Are you asking me because we haven't been out again? You never called me to say you wanted to go out."

"Do you want to go out with me?" His gaze was direct, but kind.

Nila dropped her eyes and stared at the papers on the table. "Something happened between Noel and me. I think…."

She wished she knew what to think. Noel had asked her to marry him nine years ago then married Lil. Last night he declared his love and said he wanted to buy a house together.

"You think what?" Michael probed.

"I think I'm not in a position to go out with you again. Things have gotten…complicated." Finally, she looked at the man sitting silently next to her. "You probably picked up on that the night we went out."

"Noel was jealous," Michael concluded.

The idiot.

"Nila?" Teeny said as she walked into the room with Daniel and Benjamin in her arms. "I'm sorry to bother you, but do you think you could take one of these guys before your meeting starts?"

Nila stood. She took Daniel who began rooting at her shirt. The kid was always hungry. He pressed into her chest, and a pain shot through her body.

Ouch. What was that about?

"Excuse me, Michael. If you want to read over those papers. I'll be back in a few minutes."

"No problem, Nila. See you later."

Nila followed Teeny into her office and shut the door. She sat down on the nursing rocker she'd moved into the room, slid up her shirt and unclasped her bra, holding Daniel to the breast which hadn't hurt when he knocked it. He latched on and began to eat.

"Do you want to nurse Benjamin too?"

"Just a minute."

She undid the other cup and looked down at her breast. She probed it and found it sore to the touch. The skin around the nipple appeared red.

"What's wrong?" Teeny asked.

"My boob hurts."

Teeny crouched down and examined it. "It doesn't look cracked or anything. My sister's nipples used to bleed sometimes they'd get so irritated."

"What did she do?"

"She used a guard and some udder balm." Teeny shrugged. "I guess if it works on cows, then it works on people too."

"Maybe if he nurses, it will help," Nila decided. She moved her arm and Teeny placed the baby on the low flat arm of the rocker. When he put his mouth on her and began to suck, the pain startled Nila.

She bit her lip attempting to endure it.

She took a deep breath and tried to relax. Squeezing her eyes shut, she thought of how good the milk was for them. The pain was increasing. Her whole breast hurt now. Opening her eyes, she watched Benjamin. He seemed to be getting the milk.

"Still hurt?"

Nila nodded.

"Can you stand it?"

"Yeah." Just barely, but maybe it would stop after a few minutes.

The pain didn't stop. As soon as Daniel seemed

satisfied, she switched Benjamin to the other breast. Then she went to the meeting. The next feeding was just as painful so she fed the boys from the other breast hoping if she gave the sore boob a rest, it would be better the next time. She'd found the card Susan, the lactation expert, had given her at the hospital, but there was no answer. Though she left a message, Susan hadn't called her back by that afternoon when Noel showed up at his regular time to pick up the boys. Even though she was distracted by the pain, she noticed he didn't say much to her or even make eye contact.

When she left work, she stopped by his house first thinking he'd take them there and continue their house hopping, but no lights shone from the windows so she drove on to her house.

When she pulled into the carport, Noel's SUV was parked on the grass next to the driveway. Had he parked there so he could leave after she arrived home? Nila sighed.

Sleeping together had been a mistake. Now she spent so much mental energy trying to figure out why he did this, why he said that, if they could work things out, and what she'd do if they couldn't.

Even now Noel's admission to her that he'd been in love with her for years made her stomach churn. The years of missed opportunity at first had enraged her. She hated Noel for not making his feelings more clear. She hated Lil for loving Noel and going after him, for marrying him without once asking Nila if she had feelings for him first.

But most of all she hated herself because she had loved him before Lil had even met him. Yet Nila hadn't acted on her feelings. She hadn't been sure Noel felt the same way about her. She had been working up to it, but she'd taken too long. In the meantime, Lil had kissed him, and Nila had given up, given in, given him over to her twin.

Nila leaned her head on the steering wheel feeling bone tired.

Her breast throbbed.

She'd meant to call the doctor but hadn't gotten around to it. Now the office was closed until tomorrow morning.

She pushed open the car door and stepped onto the paved drive. Trudging to the house, she entered and found Noel holding one of the babies to his shoulder. The TV was playing, and a ball game was on. Looking around she spotted the other one on a blanket on the floor. Walking over to him, she leaned down and peered at him. Benjamin. Picking him up carefully so she didn't knock her breast, she settled onto the couch.

"How was work?" Noel asked.

He was speaking to her at least. The familiar question relaxed her a bit.

"Fine. How did you and the kids do?" Benjamin had on different clothes and smelled like baby soap. She lifted him to her and kissed his little cheek then held him on her shoulder and nuzzled him.

Oh, my sweet baby.

"I took them for a walk, fed, and bathed them."

"I get off at six tomorrow, so maybe I won't miss the walk and baths." She wanted to get back on comfortable turf with Noel. No more head and heart games. They did best as friends.

Even if the sex had been so good.

Her stomach fluttered at the memory.

It's not worth it. Not worth it.

Nila toed off her shoes and brought her legs up on the couch. She settled on her side with Benjamin tucked beside her. "Who's playing? Braves against the Astros? They're so going to get their tails kicked."

Noel walked around the couch and stood where Nila could see him from her vantage point. He'd changed from his work clothes and wore basketball shorts and a T-shirt. His feet were bare.

"Who, the Astros? They beat the Pirates last week. I think they've got a chance."

"You're dreaming," Nila scoffed. "I don't know why you hate Atlanta so much. You root for whoever plays against them." Benjamin kicked his foot and flung off his sock.

Nila stroked Benjamin's tummy, then tucked her finger inside his fist. She leaned down and kissed his hand.

They were so beautiful. So perfect.

Noel walked over and knelt before the couch. He set Daniel on the edge of the cushion, and Nila held him against Benjamin. She flinched as her arm brushed her breast.

She really needed to call the doctor in the morning.

"Hey, buddy," she said to Daniel as Noel put Ben's sock back on. Daniel let out a cry. "Has he eaten recently?"

"They both have."

Nila glanced up at Noel so close to her, but his eyes were on the boys.

"Why don't you take Benjamin, and I'll nurse Daniel for a few minutes?"

"Sounds like a good plan." He picked up the baby, and straightened before going over to the recliner and sitting down. "Then I can watch Houston whup up on those Atlanta boys 'til they go crying to their mamas."

Nila smiled. This was the Noel she knew and loved. She raised up and adjusted her shirt and guided her baby to her. He sucked noisily. Petting his head so close to her, emotion filled Nila's heart.

Both boys had light-colored hair with wavy wisps. Nila felt sure as they grew more hair, it'd be curly like their dad's.

She sighed in contentment and lay her head down on the couch pillow. The Braves were up to bat. She hoped they stomped the Astros into the ground. She yawned and blinked.

If I close my eyes, I can still hear the game….

"Nila? Wake up."

She woke up and found Daniel gone. She jerked awake grabbing for him in case he had tumbled over the edge of the couch.

"It's all right. I burped him and put him to bed. You should go on to bed too."

With some difficulty, Nila sat up and pulled down her shirt. The television was off. "Who won?"

"Who won what?"

"The Braves did, didn't they?"

Noel didn't answer—just reached up and scratched his head.

"Loser." Nila stood and stretched. "I should have bet you."

He walked across the room and hit the light switch. The room darkened, and they both headed to the hallway. "I wouldn't have taken it."

"Yeah, 'cause you know the Braves have a good team. You better hope the Reds get their act together before the game comes up."

The tickets he'd bought were for the Reds versus the Braves.

"We're still going then?"

Disappointment ballooned in Nila's throat. "You don't want to go?"

Noel shrugged. "Sure, I do."

"I do too."

"Okay."

Nila stopped at the bathroom. She stepped inside and shut the door softly behind her. When she came out a few minutes later, the guest bedroom door was shut, and her own bedroom only had the boys sleeping in their crib.

So much for make-up sex.

I'm too tired for it anyway. Nila stripped down to her bra and panties and climbed onto her bed, too exhausted to put on anything else.

"So, are we going running or not?" Noel asked accompanied by somebody crying.

Two somebodies.

Nila opened gritty eyes.

Have I been to sleep yet?

"At least a couple of times. It's a little after six now," Noel said unapologetically, leading Nila to conclude she'd spoken her question aloud. "If we're going to run, let's do it. I have to be in the office by eight."

Noel had both boys on the bed changing their diapers. They were expressing their displeasure at being disturbed.

With some difficulty, she sat up and the room started spinning. She closed her eyes and grabbed her head. "I thought you said let sleeping babies lie."

"I didn't say it this...you okay?"

"Just a little dizzy." Nila took a couple of deep breaths.

"Dizzy?" The bed shook briefly, and Noel's hand pressed against her forehead. "You're burning up."

"I'm fine."

"I don't think so. Where's your thermometer?"

"Come on, Dearing. Give me a break here."

"Where is it?"

Nila crawled over to where the boys were lying next to each other wailing. "Don't let them cry like this." When she attempted to pick them up, Benjamin's body pressed against her sore breast, and she herself cried out.

"Nila! What is it?"

"It's my boob. It hurts." Nila tried to shift him away, but he kicked her causing Nila to grunt in pain.

Noel's hands appeared, and he took the boys away from her. She gripped her breast and carefully lay back down on her right side.

"Shh. Shh, boys. It's all right. All right." He rocked his body trying to get the babies to settle down, but his eyes were on her.

"I know there's a problem. I'll call Dr. Garber this morning."

Noel studied her then shook his head. "I don't think you should wait. Let's go to the emergency room now."

Nila grimaced. "No. Not the emergency room." She didn't have time to be sick.

He walked to her dresser, somehow held both infants in one arm, opened a drawer, and pulled out some workout clothes. Laying them on the bed next to her, he said, "Can you get dressed, or do you need help?"

"I don't want to go to the emergency room, Noel."

He paused at the doorway. The kindness in his dark gaze caused her throat to close up. "Duly noted. I'm going to change and get the boys in their carriers, and I'll be right back."

Within half an hour, they sat in the ER waiting room. Nila noted only two other people were there, and they appeared to be together. Apparently early morning was a good time to have an emergency.

"Nila Miller?" a woman in scrubs called from the entrance of the hospital sanctum.

Nila stood up, but Noel made no move.

"Come on," she said.

Noel's eyebrows shot up. "You want me to come back with you?"

She nodded and walked to the nurse who consulted her clipboard.

"Who's the patient?"

"I am," Nila answered.

"They should stay out here." She indicated the double stroller with the boys in it.

"I want them in the room with me. All of them. Please."

The nurse tapped her pen on the clipboard a few times. "The rooms are pretty small, but we're not very busy right now, and I can probably put you in a double. But if we get busy, your husband and kids will have to come back out to the waiting room."

"He's not my husband. He's my brother-in-law." Nila didn't look at Noel as she corrected the woman.

Without comment, the nurse led them through automatic doors and down a hall with glass enclosed rooms on either side, some with curtains closed. Nearly to the end, she pointed them inside and slid open the paned barrier which separated their room from the next one.

Nila sat on the bed, and Noel pushed the stroller into the room and parked it next to the wall.

"The doctor will be here in a few minutes. Want a blanket or anything?" The nurse asked as she pulled down a keyboard from a monitor and typed on it.

"A blanket would be great," Nila said as she tried unsuccessfully to quell a shiver.

The woman nodded in acknowledgement. Her fingers

flew across the keyboard, then she walked out the door and returned with a folded blanket. Placing it on Nila's lap, she smiled at her. "Better?"

The warmth spread from the blanket as a balm. "Oh, wow. This feels good. Can I crawl into the warmer?"

Back in front of the monitor, the nurse shook her head. "Honey, your temperature is nearly a hundred and two. You are the warmer."

A hundred and two?

"I'm going to take it again in a few minutes." She opened a cabinet and pulled out a hospital gown. She placed it on the bed next to Nila. "Go ahead and take off your shirt and bra and put this on."

With help from Noel, Nila did as the nurse asked. When he unhooked her bra and Nila slid it down her arms, she noticed even her arm pit hurt. She examined her breast and saw the flesh had red streaks and splotches on it. She cast a glance at Noel as he held the gown in front of her, but he was studying her breast. His pinched lips and tense gaze told her he was worried.

"I'm going to call Susan, the lactation consultant at the hospital. Can you hand me my purse?"

Noel did so.

Nila pulled out her cell phone and called Susan again. Maybe she knew why Nila's breast looked like a strawberry. Dialing the number, Nila waited and Susan picked up on the third ring. Nila identified herself and explained the situation.

"I didn't get your message until nearly midnight," Susan explained. "You were on my list to call this morning. I'm so sorry, Nila."

"It's okay."

"So, you're at the ER now?"

"Yes."

"I'm on my way in. Would you like me to stop by? I'm not sure I could be any help."

"It hurts so much when I nurse with that breast."

"But you're still doing it, right?"

Nila bit her lip.

"Hello?" Susan said after a moment.

"Not since yesterday."

"Where are your babies? Are they at the hospital with you?"

"Yes."

"Nurse one of them. Start on the good breast, then switch to the infected one after the milk comes down. See if you can stand the pain. A baby suckling is the best thing you can do for your breast."

Nila inhaled a breath of resignation.

"I'll be there as soon as I can."

Nila hung up the cell phone and threw it in her purse. She shrugged out of the gown. "She says nursing will help it."

"Maybe you ought to wait until the doctor looks at it."

"It won't hurt to try this."

Big lie. The last time she'd nursed with this breast, it'd felt like razor blades slicing through her skin.

Noel picked up Daniel who was awake. Nila held him to her and let him nurse on the normal breast for a few minutes before switching him. When he latched on, the pain ricocheted through her body. She stiffened her arms so she wouldn't be tempted to thrust the baby away from her.

I can do this. I...can...do...this.

Through the haze of discomfort, she realized Noel was speaking to her.

"Please stop." Noel gently pulled the baby out of her grasp. "I can't stand seeing you hurt so much. Let the doctor examine you. If he agrees with the lactation nurse, then you can try again." He pulled her gown over her, then nudged her to lie down. Covering her with the blanket, he patted her hip. "You're going to be okay, Sweetheart."

When the doctor examined her, he found a lump in her breast.

"Is this recent?" he asked

Nila took a breath before she answered. Even though he'd been gentle when he'd touched her, the exam was painful.

"I guess so."

His fingers moved around the flesh. "You said you had a complete hysterectomy a few months ago?"

"Yes."

"Why was that? Were there complications in the delivery?"

He pressed on a particularly tender area, and Nila thought about reaching over and grabbing his testicles to clue him in on what he was doing to her.

"Her twin sister died of ovarian cancer about six months ago, so Dr. Garber thought it best for Nila to have a hysterectomy," Noel supplied.

Dr. Finn's hand stilled. He turned to Noel. "Twin sister? Identical?"

"Yes."

"This could just be an infected milk duct, but…." He shook his head. "It feels too hard for that. Have you ever had a mammogram?"

"I'm twenty-nine years old. I have no reason to have a mammogram," Nila argued. "Would you hurry up? That hurts, you know."

"You have every reason to have a mammogram. Women who have ovarian cancer have a high risk of breast cancer."

"How high?" Noel asked.

"Depending on which study you look at, fifty to seventy percent." He pulled his hand back and replaced her gown and the blanket. "Are you supplementing the breast feeding with formula at all?"

Nila shook her head though she wasn't looking at the doctor. She was watching her babies.

My God. Breast cancer.

"Impressive. That you can sustain twins, and now with one breast. But I don't think you can keep it up the way things are going right now. I'm sure we've got some formula we can send home with you. I'll get one of the nurses to check. Today I want to treat this as mastitis, so I'll give you some hardy antibiotics to knock it out. Since you're lactating, it might be hard to read a mammogram, so I'd like to send you over for a sonogram. Just to be sure we're not looking at something more serious."

The doctor stepped away from the bed and pulled at the rubber gloves he had been wearing. He deposited them in a trashcan then stood near the doorway.

"Okay?" He asked.

No. It wasn't okay. Nothing he said was okay.

For a moment, the room was silent, then Noel spoke. "Thank you."

"You're welcome. Good luck."

The nurse who had been present in the room during the exam, began to type on the mobile keyboard. The curtain moved where the doctor had gone, and Susan appeared.

"Hi," she greeted them. "Sorry it has taken me so long. Has the doctor been here yet?"

"Boy, howdy, has he," the nurse replied. "I'm just entering in the order for a sonogram."

"A sonogram?" Susan walked to the computer and peered at the screen. "Huh." Approaching the bed, she looked at Nila. "Let me see that breast," she said as she gently rolled Nila to her back and revealed her breast. "Ouch," she muttered when she saw it. "Did you nurse like I told you?"

"I tried, but—"

"It was so painful," Noel interrupted. "I told her to wait until after the doctor saw her."

Susan placed her arm behind Nila's back and sat her up. "Well, he's seen you. Now, let's get one of those babies over her to drink some milk."

"He says I might have cancer. He says there's a lump."

"Well, of course, there's a lump. It's a plugged-up gland." Susan marched over to the stroller and looked at Benjamin and Daniel. "Which one of these babies is more hungry, do you think?"

"Benjamin, probably. The one on the left."

Susan picked up the baby. "It's going to hurt like the dickens, but it's the only way."

"Susan," the nurse warned. Some unspoken message

passed between the two women.

"It's the *best* way," Susan amended as she took the baby over to the sink, turned on the water, pulled off his sock, and stuck his foot under the faucet. This elicited a cry of protest from the baby. "And if I'm wrong, you can go fill your prescription and have a sonogram."

"What are you doing to him?" Noel snapped.

"I'm getting him good and awake so he can suck that infection right out of his mama."

"Maybe the infected milk isn't good for him," Nila suggested as Susan placed the baby next to her good breast, and he latched on.

"What do I know about it? I've only been doing this for twenty-two years." She positioned Nila's arm so she held the baby to her, then Susan went to a drawer and opened it. Picking up a specimen cup, she crossed her arms and watched Ben nurse for a few minutes. "Prepare yourself. This is going to hurt." She rubbed her fingers against her thumb, then handled Nila's injured breast. She manipulated it until a few drops of milk came out of the nipple. She scraped the edge of the cup on the nipple, then squeezed again until a small stream sprayed into the dish. "Now switch him to this side," she said as she held the cup up to the light. "I see no blood at all." Lowering it, she stuck her finger in it and rubbed it with her thumb. "The consistency is right for breast milk. Not pus. I really think you just need to nurse him. Nurse him as long as you can stand it. Then nurse him some more until he's done. Then put the other baby to the breast."

Another nurse walked in with two cans of formula in her hands.

"What is this?" Susan ranted.

"Dr. Finn said—"

"Oh, did he?" Susan took the offending items. "Thank you. I know exactly what to do with those."

"Susan!" The nurse at the computer spoke sharply. "Can I see you out in the hall a minute?"

The three women walked out of the room.

Shortly thereafter, Susan walked in again. She set the cans of formula on the counter. "If you need this, take it. They're also giving you a prescription and an order for a sonogram. In my opinion—but certainly not that of this hospital or Doctor Finn—they are not necessary, unless you don't improve. What is necessary in my opinion is rest, rest, rest. And lots and lots of water and good healthy food. Eat, drink, rest. Okay?"

"Okay," Nila responded.

"Okay," Noel echoed.

"Come in and see Dr. Garber in the next day or two, and call me when you do so I can check on you. Dr. Garber and I are married, if you didn't know it, and he doesn't mind me being in on his consultations. All right?"

"Thank you, Susan."

"No problem. How's the pain?"

"Not quite as bad."

"You can take something for it. An analgesic. It'll make you feel better and help with the fever too. See you later." And with those parting words, she disappeared into the hallway.

Cold fear blanketed Nila.

Fifty to seventy percent.

****

Nila watched the houses and streets through the side window of the car as Noel drove back to her house. It was a little after nine. She could still make it to work on time, but Noel had already missed his early morning meeting.

And he'd probably fuss if she mentioned going to the store.

She didn't really feel like it anyway, but she'd need to call Ricky.

Fifty to seventy percent.

How many more pieces of her would they have to cut away because of cancer?

At the house, she carried Daniel upstairs to the bedroom and Noel followed with Benjamin. She sat on the edge of the bed and held the baby to her shoulder.

Fifty to seventy percent. At best she had a one in two chance of not getting breast cancer. Sucky odds no matter how you looked at it.

Noel entered the bedroom and stood inside the door. He hadn't spoken since they left the hospital. Had he heard what Dr. Finn had said? Nila studied his face and saw the steel flint expression.

Yep.

What would it mean for them if she did get breast cancer? Of course, she'd fight it. She had Benjamin and Daniel to take care of.

"You're not going to work today," Noel barked.

"Don't get your panties in a wad. I wasn't planning on it anyway. I feel awful."

"You need to stop working twelve-hour days and get some rest. It's ridiculous working seventy-hour work weeks."

"I am a business owner. I have to run my business. And you need to quit ordering me around like you get to decide." Nila scooted back on the bed careful to keep Daniel to her right side. She lay down and yawned. "Give me Benjamin. All three of us are going to take a little nap."

He placed his knee on the bed and leaned forward to set Ben next to his brother. "I think you ought to go ahead and have the sonogram." He straightened and stood.

"Why? Afraid I'm going to lose my enormous tits, Noel? You had your chance nine years ago to play with them, and you chose Lil."

His nostrils flared, but otherwise he didn't react. "I say you have a double mastectomy as soon as possible. That way you remove the risk."

"You don't have a say in what I do. Not now."

"You don't want me? Fine. I've lived for a long time keeping my hands to myself. I'm used to it. And I don't regret for a second marrying Lil. She gave me the last seven years of her life, and they were seven good years for all of us. But I'll tell you this, Nila Rachel Miller. You are the mother of my boys. And I'll be damned if I will let you die and deprive them of having you in their lives."

He shot her a meaningful look and walked out of the room shutting the door quietly behind him.

Nila let the air whoosh out of her lungs.

Oh, my gosh.

She looked down at the boys. Benjamin had managed to get his fist in his mouth and was contentedly sucking on it. Daniel was falling asleep. Nila tucked the blanket around them.

What am I going to do with your daddy?

Chapter Nineteen

The morning of the *A Day in the Park* event dawned bright and sunny, a relief to Nila since the weather guy had predicted rain earlier in the week. She knocked on Noel's door before she left for the day.

"Yeah?"

Nila opened the door and walked into the guest bedroom he'd been sleeping in since their big fight. He lay on his side with the sheet up to his waist.

No shirt.

Nila's eyes meandered over his chest, shoulders, arms—*oh, boy.*

"Big day today," Noel greeted her as he turned and sat up pulling the cover over his bent knees as he did so.

"Yeah. I'm about to leave. I packed a bag for the boys and laid out their clothes on my bed. Can you bring them out around ten?"

"Sure."

"And wear your swimsuit under your clothes. If we don't have enough people for the dunking booth, I want some extras just in case."

"Do I haveta?"

"Oh, it won't kill you to get wet, will it?"

"I'd pay good money to get you in there. Where's your swimsuit?"

Nila grinned and lifted her shirt to show her one piece.

"Oh, come on. Not that old lady one. Where's your bikini?"

"I don't do bikinis anymore."

"*What* a shame." The gleam in his eyes she recognized as naked lust. She hadn't had one of those looks from him since....

Stop it.

"So ten o'clock? That's opening ceremonies. I've got the

high school coming to play *Fanfare for the Common Man.* Won't that be cool?"

"Awesomely cool. Leave me alone so I can go back to sleep until Thing One and Thing Two wake up."

"I'm going to leave the door open so you can hear them."

"Fine with me. See you after a while."

Nila walked out of the room and down the hall. They'd gotten back on even footing since she'd gone to the ER the week before. After that visit, Nila had gone to see Dr. Garber, and she'd invited Noel to accompany her.

At the office both Dr. Garber and Susan had been there. Susan had told Dr. Garber about the day at the ER. Husband and wife had examined Nila's breast, which had lost most of the evidence of the infection.

"The incidence of breast cancer is higher in women who have had ovarian cancer. That is true," Dr. Garber said.

"Still. She didn't actually have ovarian cancer," Susan pointed out.

"No, but she would have since her twin had it."

"Perhaps, though, the breast cancer doesn't present itself in higher rates until after the ovarian cancer has occurred. Maybe Nila having her ovaries taken out before there was any sign of cancer would be the same as not having ovarian cancer at all."

Dr. Garber shook his head. "It's a rare situation, Nila, you're in. Because we could predict one cancer, doesn't mean we can predict another kind. We can only say there is a higher incidence and probably not causal."

"So, what then? Doesn't it make sense to have a double mastectomy just in case?" Noel asked.

"Just in case! I'd like to—" Susan began before Dr. Garber shushed her.

"Certainly, that is something you have to decide for yourself, but if you will do the self-exams and have periodic mammograms, there is no reason why you should take such a radical approach on a chance you might develop breast cancer."

"But a fifty to seventy percent chance. That's pretty high," Nila argued.

"The lower end of that being fifty. That means you have a one in two chance of *not* having it."

Noel spoke then. "If it was Susan who was in this situation, what would you tell her to do?"

"It wouldn't matter what he told me, I would not have a mastectomy if it was even seventy percent chance that I would get the cancer. I'd live in the thirty percent chance."

Dr. Garber shrugged. "She always likes to beat the odds. Glass half full, right, Susan?"

"Even if it isn't half full, it's got enough in it for a drink. That's what you focus on."

After they left the office, Noel had asked, "Well?"

"Well, what? I'll have the mammograms as often as he suggests and do the self-exams. I want to keep my breasts, but I also want to live, Noel."

"You'll tell me if you change your mind, right?"

"I'm not Lil."

"I know that."

"And I'll keep you informed. For whatever her reasons, Lil meant for us to stick together."

"We got Benjamin and Daniel out of her crazy legacy. That's a sweet deal."

It *was* a sweet deal.

Most of the work had been done for *A Day in the Park*, but tying up the loose ends and making sure everyone had shown up to work kept Nila busy until the Opening Ceremony. At the Bandstand, she looked out over the crowd and saw Noel and the double stroller. He was carrying one of the boys in his arms, and he turned him toward her, picked up his hand, and waved it to her.

She laughed at the sweet gesture.

Afterward, she threaded her way through the throngs of people toward them.

"This is incredible, Nila. The park is packed," Noel exclaimed. Daniel, who he held in his arms, made a sound of affirmation.

Nila grinned and reached for her baby. She took him and cuddled him to her. "You think so, sweetie?" she crooned to him.

Nila had ordered T-shirts with *A Day in the Park* design on them in sizes for the boys. Noel had put their sun hats on too. They looked adorable.

Nila kissed his covered head and gazed up at Noel. He also had his Park shirt on she'd brought to him. Leaning to him, she hugged him briefly. "I couldn't have done this without you, you know."

His hand slid across her back, and he cupped her shoulder before stepping away. "Anything you want me to do?"

"Just talk up the vendors. They're donating most of their profit to the park, so the more people buy, the more we make." Daniel rubbed his face against her shirt and squawked.

Noel glanced down at his son, then watched her expression. They both knew she should nurse the boys. She hadn't expressed any milk since six that morning, and Susan had cautioned her about going too long in between emptying her breasts.

"Where can you go?"

"We've got a staff tent behind the Bandstand. Do you want to walk around for a bit, and I'll call you later?"

Noel shrugged. "I can come with you."

"You better look around while you can." She laid Daniel back in the stroller and secured him. "I'm not sure how long they're going to behave themselves, and Teeny's working our store booth so she's not going to be much help."

"I'll go with you until you get settled. How's that?"

They took the boys to the tent, and Noel stood inside the entrance as he watched Nila sit on a folding chair and prepare to feed Daniel

"Are you sure you don't want me to stay?"

"We're fine. Go on. Have a good time," Nila said as she snuggled her baby close to her. They were such *good* babies.

After feeding and changing Daniel, she fed Benjamin

while Louise, one of the park day organizers, held Daniel and talked sweetly to him.

"I'm going to be a grandmother in April," she confided as she patted the baby on his back.

"Get out. What are you—forty?"

"Forty-three. I had Kimmy when I was nineteen. She's been married all of two months. She swears they were trying to get pregnant and that this is a honeymoon baby, but I'm a little suspicious."

"You're happy about it, though, aren't you?"

"Oh, yes. There's nothing like holding a baby. I bet you didn't plan on two."

"I guess I should have realized it was a possibility since my sister and I were twins."

"I didn't know you had a sister."

"Yes. She died before the boys were born."

"What a shame she never got to see them. How did she die?"

"She had ovarian cancer. It was advanced by the time we knew. She…talked me into getting pregnant. Probably if she hadn't done that, I would have never had the opportunity to have children because the doctor recommended I have a hysterectomy as soon as possible so I wouldn't get cancer."

"What about the babies' father? He seems so attentive. Did he have to talk you into getting pregnant too?"

"Not exactly. He'd been wanting kids for years. He's a wonderful daddy."

"What a nice gift your sister gave you—the idea to have children with a man who is a caring father. I'm glad it's worked out."

Nila tilted her head in thought.

It really was a gift.

Nila had two beautiful boys and so did Noel. She'd always have Noel in her life because he was as much in love with the babies as she was.

Gratitude filled Nila because of what Lil had done to manipulate a situation so those babies could be created. They'd always be connected because of the babies.

****

Nila pushed the stroller on the paved path through the park looking for Noel. When she'd called him on his phone, it had begun to ring from where he'd left it in the diaper bag. In the distance, she saw him talking to a woman Nila didn't recognize. He listened attentively to her then nodded.

Nila studied the woman who wore a flowery top with a low neckline, shorts, and stupidly high-heeled shoes. Who wore shoes like that in a park? Obviously, she was on the hunt. With her hair falling in long blond waves down past her shoulders, she looked as if she'd stepped out of a beauty salon. She laughed at something Noel said, then reached forward and touched him, her hand stroked down the front of his T-shirt.

Nila felt a hot flush of jealousy spike through her. *You bitch. Get away from him.*

Nila turned her attention to Noel. Even from this far away, she saw charm pouring off him like heat from Georgia asphalt.

Nila should have no animosity toward the tart. She had no idea Noel was a recent widower with two small children unless he'd told her. Noel was the one at fault here. He had no business flirting with women.

Nila marched forward pushing the boys in front of her and trying to decide if she could get away with ramming the stroller into Noel.

"Hi," Nila greeted the pair, as she looked from Noel to the woman. Stepping around the stroller, she extended her hand. "How are you enjoying *A Day in the Park*?"

The woman's smile fell a bit, but she took Nila's hand and shook it. "Hi. Fantastic. What a beautiful day for it."

French-tipped nails. Of course.

"I'm Nila Miller, one of the organizers."

The organizer and chairperson.

"Samantha Williamson. So nice to meet you. Don't you work at *Play It! Sports*?"

"Yes, I do."

Owner, actually.

"I was on Blazer's tennis team my senior year in high school. You guys sponsored us and threw us a party when we won at regionals."

"Oh, sure. Two years ago."

Which would make her twenty. He's going after a twenty-year-old?

Nila cast a brief withering glance in Noel's direction and smiled amiably up at Samantha Williamson, who was a good two inches taller than she, thanks to the heels.

"You left your cell phone," she informed Noel as she took her place behind the stroller and pulled his phone out of the diaper bag. She threw it at him, and he caught it. "Nice to meet you, Samantha. Come by the *Play It! Sports* booth. I'll leave a twenty-dollar gift certificate there for you." She turned the stroller around making sure she ran over Noel's foot with one of the wheels.

On her way back to the organizer's tent, one of the workers stopped her because the noon concert singer hadn't shown up yet. While she was talking, Noel came by, pulled the diaper bag off her shoulder and took the stroller.

She let him without even a nod, thinking maybe having the boys would keep him out of trouble with Samantha, who still accompanied him.

Or maybe knowing he had two sweet babies would make him more attractive to Samantha? Who could resist Benjamin and Daniel? *Dammit.* Why had she let him take them?

Pulling out her phone, she called Teeny. "There should be a tall blonde coming by any moment to pick up a gift certificate. Give it to her, and if Noel is with her, take the boys from him and keep them with you until I can get over there. Noel's scheduled to work the dunking booth. They're waiting on him. Let me know what happens."

Her next call was to Maurice, who was working the dunking booth. "Maurice? This is Nila. If you see Noel, I want you to stick him in the dunking tank immediately."

She went to the drinks stand to check to be sure they weren't running short of anything and ended up having to make a store run for ice. Teeny called her as she was stacking the bags of ice in the cooler back at the park. Wiping her hands on her shorts, she touched the answer icon.

"Hello."

"He's in the dunk tank, and so far nobody's been able to knock him down."

Nila shut the cooler lid and looked in the direction of the dunking booth, but it was on the other side of the food vendors. "If you're at the dunk tank, who's manning the *Play it! Sports* table?"

"Ricky."

"Who's watching the store?"

"He put a sign up and told people to come to *A Day in the Park*."

Nila pursed her lips. Saturday was their busy day. She didn't like being closed even if it was for *A Day at the Park,* but she'd worry about it later. Right now, she wanted to go throw some baseballs.

She heard his big fat mouth as she approached.

"Hey, I'm over here. Why are you throwing the ball way over there?"

A chuckle arose from several people watching.

The unsuccessful thrower was Michael Summers. He threw another ball, and it went far left.

"Come on, Rev. This is getting embarrassing. Didn't you ever play ball when you were growing up?"

"I was more into contact sports, actually." Michael said as he picked up another baseball. He drew his arm back and threw it.

Nila shook her head as this one went high. She marched up to the table and laid a twenty in front of Maurice. "I'm next," she said.

She reached down and grabbed a ball from the basket. Tossing it up in the air and catching it in her hand, she glared at Noel.

"Well, well, well," Noel drawled. "Lookee here. It's Madame Chairperson of *A Day in the Park*. Let's hope she can throw a ball better than she can take a day off to rest."

Nila studied the round metal target, threw the ball, and nailed it.

The bench Noel sat on collapsed, and he dropped into the water.

Nila smiled in glee, and a man appeared from behind the protective tarp and reset the machine. Noel hoisted himself up and before he could sit on the bench, she threw another ball, and he fell again. Water sploshed over the side of the large cylinder.

"How about letting me get back on the seat before you drench me again?" Noel complained once he regained his footing.

Nila didn't respond—just held a ball in her hands and waited. Noel climbed on the bench. He raised his hand and wiped water off his face.

She watched his eyes follow the ball as she threw it straight up in the air and caught it.

How could you go after her as if you had any right? As if you were available? As if your wife hadn't died seven months ago? As if you hadn't made love to me thirteen days ago?

She threw it and felt the good pull of her right arm as she did so.

Bull's eye.

The jerk hit the water below.

He stood and climbed up. "How many times are you going to dunk me?" he called to her.

"As many as it takes," Nila replied.

He barely sat before she threw it, and he went down again.

"As many times as it takes for what?" He came up and leaned his elbows over the side as he waited for her answer.

"Get your butt back up there."

From the corner of her eye she saw Teeny maneuvering the stroller so it sat next to the low rail which kept people a safe distance from the balls being thrown. One of the twins whimpered, and the other one answered similarly. Nila glanced over and saw Teeny kneeling in front of the stroller tending to them. She turned her attention back to Noel.

"Can I ask you a question?" he said.

"What?"

He perched his elbows on the edge of the water tank. "How come in all the time we've been friends the only guy you ever went out with was Mike?"

Heat crawled up her face. "Because I…I was too busy with work."

He shook his head, and water droplets flew. He slicked his hair back, the water running down his chest and arms.

"I think it was because the guy you wanted wasn't available."

Climbing on the perch, he sat staring at her.

She scowled and threw another ball, hitting the bull's eye. Noel went down, but he was ready this time, and he caught hold of the side so that his head wasn't submerged.

He climbed on the seat and leaned forward. "Is this how you treat the man you love?"

Everything inside of her froze at his question—heart, blood, lungs. Then in an instant all systems detonated. Even her skin prickled.

No!

With a guttural cry, she threw the ball. It skimmed the edge of the target, and whumped the tarp behind it.

"Interesting. Did you miss because I'm wrong or because I'm right?"

"Shut it, Dearing!"

"It's okay to love me, you know."

The ball sailed out of her hand and connected this time, pinging the metal plate and sending Noel down. When he emerged, he coughed then climbed up. "I want to marry you and buy a house and raise our boys there."

Another ball hit the tank itself.

"I want to be clear this time so there's no misunderstanding."

"Would you stop this before I come in there and drown you?" She ran up to the target and knocked it hard with her hands.

Without looking back, she stepped over the rail and

marched away from the booth. From behind her, she heard Noel call, "Anybody else want to humiliate me? It's only fifty cents a throw."

"You're doing a good enough job humiliating yourself," someone responded back, eliciting laughter from the gathered spectators.

Nila fled to the staff tent fully expecting Noel to show up for round two of this…whatever it was. But he never materialized. When she stopped by the *Play It! Sports* table to tell Ricky to go back to the store, Teeny handed her a note from Noel. With shaking hands, she opened the folded paper.

Took the boys home. Call me if you need me.

Nila snorted in laughter. *Call him if I need him. Need him for what? To inform the town they are in love? To broadcast the private details of their relationship?*

What an idiot.

She replayed the scene in which Noel announced to the town what he wanted. She lost her breath, and her head spun. Leaning over, she closed her eyes and tried to calm down.

That idiot wanted to marry her.

****

A Day in the Park officially ended at five, though the park still held a large crowd. Talk among the organizers as they shut down the booths and cleaned up was that next year they could go into the evening. The event had been a great success, and the accomplishment carried Nila's spirits as she drove to the house. When she arrived, she sat in her car, bolstering up the courage to walk inside.

Why was she so scared?

He'd told her he loved her before. He'd already said he'd wanted to marry her years ago before he asked Lil. Why was it so hard to walk in and finish the conversation?

Taking a fortifying breath, she left the vehicle and entered the house. Daniel was in a bouncy seat on the floor, but Noel and Ben were not in the room. Approaching the baby, she sat beside him. "Hi there," she said as she unbuckled him and picked him up. "What have you been doing this afternoon, huh?"

She scooted to the couch and leaned her back against it, then pulled up her shirt to nurse him. He settled in quickly, and Nila watched him as he suckled. He gazed up at her and kneaded her breast with one small hand.

Heavy footsteps from the hallway signaled Noel was coming. Nila looked up as he came through the door.

"Hello. You're back." He had Benjamin against his shoulder rubbing his back.

"Yeah."

"Somebody was hungry, huh?"

"Well, I needed to either feed him or pump."

"What about you? Are you hungry? I thought we could have some tortellini."

"Anything but hotdogs and hamburgers. I'm starving."

Noel knelt on the floor and put Benjamin in the bouncy seat Daniel had been occupying. When he had secured the baby, Noel went to the kitchen, and Nila could hear him running water in a pot and setting it on the stove.

So, was he going to wait for her to bring up his proposal of marriage, house-buying, and living together with the boys?

"I thought you might come find me after you finished at the dunking booth," she called.

"I started to, but Mike stopped me. He said my delivery was a little too public and thought you might need some time to cool off."

Wise man.

A cabinet door opened, and dishes rattled.

Benjamin squirmed, and Nila hooked her toes to the metal frame of the bouncy and bent her knee, dragging the seat closer. When it was within arms' reach, she pulled it so she could touch the baby, then leaned over and kissed him.

"What about Samantha?"

The microwave door opened, shut, and several beeps indicated he was pressing buttons on it. When it kicked on, his steps left the kitchen and hit the carpet. He rounded the couch so he was within sight. He had a smirk on his face.

"I think I'll send her flowers."

Nila's mouth dropped. "What?"

He sat down on the floor across from her.

"If it wasn't for her, I wouldn't have seen you jealous and figured out you do love me after all."

Nila stared at Daniel refusing to look at Noel.

Afraid. Afraid of admitting the love she'd felt in her heart for over a decade. Oh, Noel. She'd loved him for so long. Even though he now knew it, she was still afraid to say the words.

"You were married to my sister."

"Were. Past tense. I *was* married to her."

"She's only been gone seven months. People will talk."

"What will they say?"

"They'll say we were having an affair before she died."

"The people who know us and knew Lil will know differently."

Emotion swelled up in Nila's chest. She sighed loudly. "I…" She shook her head. "I made love to you that night. I knew it was you. I tried to make it just be about getting pregnant for Lil's sake, but…she put this idea in my head, that…."

He motioned for her to hand over Daniel. She did so, and he began to pat his back.

Nila picked up Benjamin and held him to her other breast. He latched on, and Nila risked a glance to Noel.

"What idea?"

"She…" Nila's voice caught. "She gave me permission to love you and let you love me."

Noel's hand stilled on the baby's back.

"I knew it was wrong, and I tried to make it be only about conceiving, but I'd loved you for so long, and when you pulled me to you…" Nila heaved a breath past the lump in her throat. "For a minute, I let it be me you were loving."

"Nila." He sidled up next to her and kissed her. His lips were so sweet and gentle on hers that it nearly undid her. "It's okay. It's okay to love me now. Because I love you. I really do as a friend and as a lover and my buddy and the mother of these guys."

Nila drew back. "We shouldn't fall into this relationship

just because it means we don't have to fight over the kids."

Noel patted Daniel's back again, and the baby belched.

"If you had not made love to me that night. If there had been no Daniel and no Benjamin. If Lil had not given you permission to love me and let me love you back, how do you think things would be between us?"

Nila thought about it. She considered Susan's words about her risk of having breast cancer. *It wouldn't matter what he told me, I would not have a mastectomy even if it was a seventy percent chance I would get the cancer. I'd live in the thirty percent chance.*

"We'd be friends."

"And that's all?"

"Is Samantha in this scenario?"

"Pick any woman to be in it."

"I'd like to think…that I would live my life in the thirty percent chance. I gave you up once, but I don't want to do that ever again. I'd like to think you and I—we would have come around to loving each other, letting ourselves love each other, and eventually getting married then buying a house."

Noel's shoulders slumped in relief. "Marriage then house buying. Good to know." He leaned over and kissed her again.

"So, what happens now?"

"I put the tortellini on to boil, and we plan a wedding."

THE END

AUTHOR'S NOTE

"…and he loved Rachel more than Leah."
Genesis 29:30

The inspiration for this book began with one scene—a husband tricked into sleeping with the wrong sister, which happens in the Bible, Genesis 29: 14-30. After seven years working for her hand, Jacob thinks he is marrying his true love, Rachel, but "when morning came, there was Leah!" (Genesis 29:24), Rachel's less desirable, older sister. Jacob works seven more years and gets to marry Rachel as well.

So begins a very tragic family story in which two sisters compete with each other for their husband's affection. In that culture, having a son meant everything, so the women play out their drama by trying to get pregnant in a heartbreaking series of births.

Leah obviously loves Jacob desperately, and with each son, she displays her hope that since she has given Jacob sons maybe his feelings for her will change. She names her first son, "Reuben, for she said, 'It is because the Lord has seen my misery. Surely my husband will love me now'" (Genesis 29:32). When her second son is born, she said, "Because the Lord heard that I am not loved, he gave me this one too" (Genesis 29: 33).

And so each son's name signifies the competition between the two sisters (find the series of births of all twelve sons and the significance of their names in Genesis 29). As if this isn't bad enough, both sisters bring in slave women to become surrogate mothers when they have trouble conceiving. Four women. One man. And a whole lot of jealousy and bad feelings. Is it any wonder the hard feelings spill over into the next generation when the brothers end up selling Joseph, Rachel's firstborn son, into slavery (find this in Genesis 37), not to mention a whole slew of other family dramas Jacob alludes to on his deathbed in Genesis 49? I'm telling you, this family needed some serious therapy.

This story is a good case study in several things—why polygamy is a bad idea, the cons of limiting the role of women in society, and the terrible practice of slavery we see here that forced women to have sex to produce children for their masters.

I have always felt sorry for poor Leah, who just wanted to be loved by her husband. I wanted to write a happy ending for her. I wanted to create a world in which her husband loved her, but I wanted to write it as a contemporary romance since that's what I love to read.

There were several nonnegotiable elements—pieces of the story I felt had to be included. These were:

*Jacob (who is Noel in my story) being tricked into having sex with the wrong sister.

*Both sisters loving the same man.

*Barrenness and fertility since it's such an integral part of how the sisters compete with each other for Jacob's affection.

But of course, since it's a contemporary romance, I had to change some of the elements. Noel couldn't have two wives at the same time, nor did I want him to even consider being unfaithful to his wife. I wanted the sisters to love each other and not see each other as competition. I wanted the children to be loved as children and not as tools to win a husband's affection.

So, in my version, both sisters get their happily ever after, and even though one sister dies, she had a sister who was deeply devoted to her…and a sister like that means a lot.

Faithful is the first book in my Family Tangles series. Each book is a stand-alone book. Each is a modern spin on a Biblical tale.

Want to read an excerpt from *Tomorrow's Child*, the second in the series?

AN EXCERPT
FROM
TOMORROW'S CHILD

Tomorrow's Child is my second book in the *Family Tangles* series, based on an interesting story in Genesis of a woman named Tamar.

Here is an excerpt:

Nick stood behind his desk in a suit. Another man stood in front of the desk, but Tamara's attention riveted to Nick. He studied her face for a full minute, then his gaze wandered down to her body, snagging on the orthopedic boot.

Desire exploded in Tamara. Images of two nights ago

played through her brain. She didn't want to think of that right now, of him kissing her, worshipping her body, whispering how beautiful and soft she was.

His expression gave nothing away, but she saw a muscle twitch at his jaw.

Oh, Lord, help me do whatever it takes to save Miranda.

"Ms. Wallace?" a voice said. The other man, though Tamara still watched Nick who hadn't moved.

Tamara tore her gaze away from him and saw the other man standing next to her with his hand outstretched. "I'm John Levine. How do you do?"

"It's Dr. Wallace. I am well, thank you."

"You're a doctor? Of what, may I ask?"

"Medical Doctor. I work in the emergency department at Acorn County Hospital in Arms Fork."

Nick crossed his arms over his chest. "Easy access to medical equipment like air casts. Is that to illicit sympathy?"

"The boot is to ambulate the foot which sustained two fractures two nights ago. I can have the X-rays sent to you, if you like."

"Very convenient, the fall. It engendered an escort to your hotel room," Nick snapped.

"Have you two met?" John asked. "Nick, I thought you said—"

"Oh, we've met. We are *very* well acquainted, even though I was not aware of it until now. Would you concur, Tamara?"

Tamara glanced behind her. The administrative assistant was gone and the door shut, thankfully.

Tamara approached his desk. "Nick, can we talk alone?"

"I'm afraid not," John said.

Nick's perfect mouth turned up in an evil smile. "You do your best talking alone with me, is that it?"

She probably deserved that, so she didn't try to defend herself, just waited for the next jab.

His predatory gaze moved over her once again. "Yes. I would like to talk to you alone."

"No, Nick. Bad idea. As your lawyer, I'm advising you

against it."

"Two minutes," Nick said between gritted teeth.

John shook his head. "No."

"Get out, John, dammit."

John sighed. "I will step outside for two minutes." He walked over to the door, opened it, and walked out, leaving the door ajar. Nick strode over to the door and slammed it shut.

He glared at Tamara. "So, you're going to blackmail me. If I don't give your daughter what she needs, you'll go to the media, is that it?"

"No, Nick. I swear, I'd never do anything like that. I don't want anyone to know what happened between us the other night. I have a daughter to think about."

He stalked toward her until they were almost touching. Tamara stood her ground and tilted her face to keep eye contact.

"I hope you don't expect me to believe the other night was a coincidence."

"No, I don't expect you to believe that."

"How long have you been stalking me?"

"I found out you were at the conference and flew down there hoping I could—"

"Entrapment."

"I just wanted to talk to you, to try to convince you—"

He barked out a laugh of derision and stepped away from her, turning his back. "Convince me? Dammit, I didn't know how gullible I could be. Here I thought all of the sharks were the lawyers at the conference. And I escort the most bloodthirsty one to her room and order wine!"

Tomorrow's Child is available in print and digitally. Also available is *Steadfast*, the third book in the Family Tangles series.

I hope you will look for them.

About Jennifer Johnson

Who am I?

I am a writer.

I write contemporary romantic fiction.

I aspire to be Wonder Woman with the awesome leotard and the criminal-fighting boots on some days.

On other days I am Wonder Woman with my lasso of Truth and my no-nonsense-pursuit of justice.

I live in the South across the river from the Midwest.

I'm married to Super Man with a Tony Stark mind.

We have Wonder/Super children and a bionic dog.

All in all, it's a comic book kind of life.

You can find out more about me at my website **www.booksbyjenniferjohnson.com** and connect with me on Facebook at **https://www.facebook.com/booksbyjenniferjohnson** and through Twitter at **https://twitter.com/BooksbyJennifer**